There was nowhere to go

Paula flattened herself against the wall. She wouldn't just stand there and do nothing. She dragged off a shoe and held it aloft.

She couldn't see him. Suddenly he leaped up before her, grabbing her wrists, wrenching away the shoe. She opened her mouth, but no sound would come.

"Be still," the man hissed. His head was close, and she saw his pale eyes glint through slits in a ski mask. His threat was accompanied by cold sharp pressure on the front of her neck. Paula struggled not to faint.

"Listen carefully, Paula Renfrew. If you want to live, get out of Amsterdam."

Paula's eyes grew wide with fear. This wasn't an accidental encounter. He *knew* her....

ABOUT THE AUTHOR

It's not just the diamonds that glitter in *All That Sparkles*. Stella Cameron has captured the brilliant kaleidoscope of sights and sounds—even smells—of colorful, romantic Amsterdam. The British-born author was fortunate enough to visit the historic Dutch city to research this book, her second for Intrigue. Her first was a collaboration under the pseudonym Alicia Brandon. This busy mother of three is also a successful writer with the Harlequin American and Superromance lines. It's no mystery that Ms Cameron, with her fluid style and versatility, is in such demand!

Books by Stella Cameron

HARLEQUIN AMERICAN ROMANCE
153–SHADOWS

HARLEQUIN SUPERROMANCE
185–MOONTIDE

ALL THAT SPARKLES
STELLA CAMERON

Harlequin Books

TORONTO • NEW YORK • LONDON
AMSTERDAM • PARIS • SYDNEY • HAMBURG
STOCKHOLM • ATHENS • TOKYO • MILAN

Marmie Charndoff—
this one's for you

Harlequin Intrigue edition published September 1986

ISBN 0-373-22050-2

Chapter One

Friday of the First Week:

"Why did you lie to us?"

"Lie? What do you mean, lie? Did your father send you to Holland to call me a liar? I knew you when you were a boy, Christophe St-Giles, a boy in short pants."

Christophe swore under his breath and turned back to the window. "The past has no part in our business now. Nor does emotion. This is a fine old diamond house with a great reputation. Or it was—"

Benno Kohl's fist slammed into his desk. "Enough!" His vehemence jarred Christophe. "When you were a boy you also had some respect for your elders. I won't tolerate this insult. Kohl's is still great, the best. We've had some problems. The diamond industry always has problems from time to time. Natural recessions—or deliberately engineered ones—are a part of life with us. We need a loan to get us through a bad time. Is that so much to ask of the bank my family has done business with for generations?"

"Normally, no." Christophe narrowed his eyes to peer morosely from the third-floor window onto Rokin, the street that housed the cream of Amsterdam's diamond dealerships. "And I hold you in the deepest respect, sir.

But we aren't talking about a normal situation here, are we?" He heard Benno's chair creak, and the sound of the older man breathing heavily. The ball was in Benno's court now. Christophe rubbed a knuckle over cool, rain-splattered glass and waited. The weather, and the row of stone buildings facing him, matched his mood—gray.

Benno came to stand beside Christophe. "Why did your father send you? Couldn't any questions you had have been cleared up on the phone?"

"This can't go on," Christophe said, suddenly weary. He turned to face Benno. Odd how the years changed men. Not so long ago, Benno had towered over him; now he, Christophe, was the taller.

"What can't go on?" Benno prompted.

"I've already spent a week digging through mountains of confusing records," Christophe said as tonelessly as possible. Anger wouldn't help. "You could have saved me the effort—by being honest. I'm sorry dealing with me is proving uncomfortable for you. My father believed it would be otherwise. We could have sent someone else to look into this. I came as head of our bank's special loan investigations department because you and your family mean so much to us. We at St-Giles wanted to give you special consideration."

"Oh, thank you." Benno's mouth turned down at the corners. His thin features were set inscrutably as his pale blue eyes shifted from Christophe's face to the scene outside. "Such kindness. And now, have you finished your digging, as you put it? If so, I'd appreciate receiving the money I've asked for as soon as it can be released. I hope your return flight to Zurich will be uneventful." Benno straightened his tall, reedy frame. The man had lost weight in the four years since Christophe had last seen him, and his once iron-gray hair had turned totally white.

Christophe clamped his hands on his hips. As soon as he'd arrived in Amsterdam, he'd figured out this would be a tough assignment, and he'd been right. "There will be no loan, Benno."

Benno grasped Christophe's elbow, the expressionless mask slipping from his face. "Yes," he rasped. "Yes, there will be a loan. There has to be a loan. Without that money, we will fail. Kohl's House of Diamonds will die. Do you understand? Your father has worked to keep St-Giles a successful banking institution—for you, just as his father did for him. You're being groomed to take his place one day. It's the same with Lukas and me. You and your family cannot watch another old family business fail and do nothing because . . . because . . . "

"Because someone is stealing from you?"

Seconds of silence slipped away. Christophe stared hard into the other man's eyes, eyes so much older than his own, paler and strangely defeated. He felt the strength and vitality of his own thirty-five years, the advantage of his prime over the other's failing vigor. The sensation gave him little pleasure.

Finally Benno shook his head and dropped his hand. "That's madness. You don't know what you're talking about."

"I know exactly what I'm talking about." Fumbling for a cigarette, Christophe was adamant. He felt vaguely sick. "I know because everything I've learned so far makes theft the only possible reason for your difficulties. Cigarette?" He offered the pack of Gitanes to Benno who waved dismissively.

"Suppose you tell me what you've learned." He ran a hand over his thinning hair and returned to slump in his chair.

"I'd be glad to," Christophe said simply, rounding the desk to sit opposite Benno. He lit up and inhaled deeply, hunching his powerful body forward. "At first everything seemed to coincide with your report to the bank. But—"

Benno interrupted quickly, "Why didn't St-Giles simply give me the advance? Why did your people question me?"

"Because," Christophe said patiently, "Kohl's has been through a dozen of the recessions you just talked about and never needed a loan of any kind. This time, you not only need a loan, you need a very large sum. You've also poured other personal sources of capital into the business in a brief period of time. Yet you're still in trouble. We have to know why—what's so different on this occasion. No bank can risk the kind of money you ask for simply in the name of friendship." What he said was fact, but he hated every cold statement he'd had to make.

"Go on." The bone in Benno's hawklike nose whitened when he pinched his bridge. He was fighting for composure. "My young friend," he said softly, "will you please say what you have to say—quickly."

Christophe shoved his own straight brown hair back from his brow. Hurting this distinguished old merchant wasn't what he wanted. "It didn't take long to sniff something out of line, something sinister. Benno, two months ago, a few weeks before you asked for the loan, you made refunds on a number of valuable stones—thirteen, I believe the number was."

Benno's head came up. "Our policy has always been total satisfaction to the customer. Any buyer may change his mind if not completely happy with a purchase."

Christophe caught and held the other man's eyes. "I understand that. But where are the stones you took back?

Why weren't they reentered in your inventory lists to be sold again?''

"I—I—" Benno made a steeple with his fingers. His hands trembled. "I can explain."

"Yes," Christophe said softly. "I'm sure you can, if you want to. Someone stole those stones before they could be replaced in stock, didn't they? And our job is to find out who, how, and to stop it from happening again. You think an infusion of money will buy the time you need to recover. It won't if we don't stop the thefts. And your reputation in the industry is already sinking. We heard rumors as far away as Zurich—another reason I'm here. Rumors are a luxury you can't afford in your business. Distrust is death to the diamond merchant."

Silence settled in around them, broken by the tick of an antique clock on one wall and the muted whirring of grinding wheels in the workroom outside the office.

"You have it almost right," Benno said at last, shaking his head slowly. He leaned heavily into his chair. "Only we know the diamonds disappear before they ever get to the buyer's hands."

Christophe rested his elbows on the desk and sent another plume of pungent smoke into the air. "I don't understand. You mean they never arrive?"

"Yes and no. Stones arrive. They are of almost duplicate weight and cut to those purchased. And they are diamonds. But they are of vastly inferior quality." He tilted his chin, stretching hollows and rigid tendons in his neck. "Somewhere between this building and the point of delivery our flawless gems disappear. Clever, so very clever."

"My, God," Christophe muttered. "You know what this means, don't you? Since no one on staff has reported the switch, the answer has to be here, right here in your own operation."

"No!" Benno made fists on the desk. "That cannot be. The switches must have occurred when the stones were being...when they were..."

"Being delivered?" Christophe raised one brow. "In which case your people would still be implicated. Our first step must be to start taking Kohl's employees apart."

Benno leaped to his feet, drawing up to his full height. "Over my dead body. I know how it looks. It was meant to look like this. Sabotage, Christophe. We are being sabotaged. And I suggest you look at Metter Brothers, not here. Philip Metter hates me, just as his father hated my father. For four generations that firm has competed with Kohl's, tried to find ways to overtake us in the trade and never managed it. This time they're close, but they won't make it by tearing apart the trust I've built, both with my customers and with my employees. Nothing, you hear me, Christophe, nothing will be done or said to undermine my people. They are above reproach. If you have to play detective, do it with Philip Metter's staff."

"Sit down," Christophe begged quietly. Benno's face was mottled, and a faint blue tinge darkened his lips. "You look ill. Please, Benno. I'm here to help you. Believe that. We'll work together and I won't do anything to undermine Kohl's."

Benno sank to his chair once more, his chest rising and falling rapidly. "The thefts have stopped. There's been nothing for three weeks, and I don't believe it will happen anymore."

"I do." Christophe stubbed out the half-smoked Gitane and immediately reached for another. "I don't know for certain why they're laying off for a while, but I have a pretty good idea, and unless we find out who's behind the scam, it'll start again. Remember, Benno, my arrival has been anticipated for about three weeks, which fits in with the possibility that I may be what's holding them up, and as soon as I leave, they'll hit again." He flipped his lighter, changed his mind and stuffed it back into the pocket of his suit jacket. "I talked to Lukas—"

"That's another thing," Benno broke in, agitated. "One of Metter's boys, Herbert, I think, smiled at Lukas the other day. He *smiled* at my son. Enemies who haven't spoken for a hundred and fifty years don't suddenly smile at each other. They are involved. I know it. And they've done what they intended to do—tainted our reputation. Now we must recoup as quickly as possible. The way to do that is to make no more fuss. Carry on as usual and re-build our reputation."

"You don't think an official investigation—"

"No!" Benno shook his head vigorously. "No, no. That would finish us for sure."

"Very well." Christophe squared his broad shoulders. "You need me to okay the loan and you won't consider an official investigation, therefore you must play by my rules and trust me to do the best, for everyone."

"Which is?" Benno asked flatly.

"An investigation of my own—my way. Anyone who had anything to do with those missing diamonds, or could have, no matter how insignificantly, is a suspect. Why didn't you tell me about this Renfrew woman?"

"Paula?" Benno's throat moved convulsively. "Why should I tell you about Paula? What would I say? She's only been with us nine months."

"Exactly." Christophe settled against his chair and propped an ankle on the other knee. "She's the newest Kohl employee. And she also has an interesting history. You might have considered telling me about that, too."

Benno massaged his temples. "This is too much. Who has been talking to you? And you—" he glared at Chris-

tophe ''—what made you think you had the right to ask
questions behind my back? If you wanted to know something, *I* was the one to ask.'' He collected himself, avert-
ing his face. ''Anyway, there's nothing to know about
Paula. She is the daughter of an old American friend who
is now dead and she's studying to become a polisher. She
will make an excellent craftswoman.''

''And?''

''And?'' Benno flexed his fingers. ''And her parents
apparently divorced some years ago. Her mother remar-.
ried. There is a brother in the American Air Force. Paula
is, of course, single—twenty-six years old. A delightful
young woman. What more can I say? That's all there is.''

''Not quite all,'' Christophe said. He twisted the ring on
the small finger of his left hand, weighing what he would
say next. ''My old friend, Lukas, is cool to say the least,
but he does understand the necessity to supply the information I need if we are to get you out of this mess. Your
son resents me as much as you do; however, he answered
my questions about your personnel. Too bad he didn't also
explain the stones were switched. That gives another interesting dimension to our little puzzle. Perhaps now you
will both work with me, rather than against me.''

Benno bristled. ''Lukas should have cleared anything he
intended to say to you with me first. But I understand his
reasoning. What did he tell you?''

''That Paula Renfrew's father worked for your father
many years ago. Michael Renfrew was also an apprentice
diamond finisher, just as his daughter is now.''

''That's correct.'' Benno relaxed visibly. ''Michael and
I were the same age. We became friends and I was sorry
when he decided to return to America. He died a year ago
and his daughter asked to come here and work. Naturally,
I was delighted. Anna is delighted. Since Lukas married,

our home has become empty. Now we have Paula living in our guest house and she is like the daughter we never had.''

''But Michael Renfrew didn't simply *decide* to return to America, did he?''

''Lukas...'' Benno closed his eyes for an instant. ''Lukas has obviously said too much. I'm tired, Christophe. I'm getting old. Stop this game of hide-and-seek and tell me exactly what you know—or think you know.''

Christophe leaned to grip one of Benno's thin wrists. ''There was another theft—a long time ago. That, too, was hushed up, and Kohl's was lucky because only one stone disappeared. But a man disappeared, too, didn't he Benno? Michael Renfrew skipped Holland and returned to the States. There was never absolute proof he was the thief, but why else would he run away at just that time? And now, after his death, his daughter shows up, pretending to be nothing more than an aspiring craftswoman. Can you believe she knows nothing of the other crime? Can you honestly convince yourself she's oblivious to this one—that her presence is purely coincidence? What about vengeance, Benno? Don't you think Renfrew probably told his daughter what happened here, insisted on his own innocence—suggested he was framed, perhaps? And now she's collecting on the debt you owe her father.''

''That will do.'' Finality colored Benno's words. ''That is all I will listen to about Paula. Her father was innocent. I've always known it. Lukas should never have told you about the incident. If you insist on checking the records of my employees, so be it. Do so with discretion. But I never want to hear another suggestion like this about Paula.''

He would back off for a while, Christophe decided. At least, Benno knew where they stood. ''Trust me, Benno. I'll do nothing you wouldn't approve of.'' *Please, God, let that be possible.* ''I admit I'm puzzled by Lukas's hostility. He has his reason, of course, but is that enough to totally withdraw from me? We've been friends a long time. I didn't think anything could completely destroy that.''

Benno looked away. ''That year you spent with us when you were—how old?''

''Twenty-two,'' Christophe supplied promptly.

''A special time. For all of us. For Lukas you became a brother. Give him time to understand that you must put your own business interests first.''

A rush of gratitude warmed Christophe. ''Thank you for that. For understanding. This is hard on all of us.''

''We would have liked you to stay with us.'' Benno made circles on the desk with a forefinger. ''Anna wanted that.''

''It wouldn't have done. Not this time. When I come to dinner next week, I'll talk to her about it myself.''

Benno nodded. ''Your hotel is comfortable?''

''Ah!'' Christophe exclaimed. ''I forgot to tell you. Peter insisted I use his houseboat. Now he lives in that apartment in Lukas and Sandi's house; he rents the barge, but it was vacant and he thought I'd be more comfortable—and private there.''

''Good, good,'' Benno said with a laugh. ''That old barge should be enough to bring you and Lukas back together. Peter Van Wersch is a good man. The most faithful friend Lukas ever had. I remember the three of you working to convert the houseboat. The Three Musketeers, you called yourselves.'' He smiled broadly. ''Anna and I spent many nights wondering what you did when you weren't hammering loose decking.''

Christophe joined the laughter. ''Nothing you wouldn't have done, sir, I assure you.''

Tension had evaporated from the comfortable office. ''Perhaps that's what worried us, eh?'' Benno asked wryly.

"I wonder," Christophe began tentatively. "Do you think this would be a good time for you to introduce me to some of your people?"

"Now?" The strain returned to Benno's features. "Why? How—I wouldn't know how to explain what you're doing here?"

"You mustn't explain," Christophe said quickly. "Not exactly. But you needn't lie. Just say I'm an old friend and a business associate, and that I'm interested in what goes on. I am interested. I haven't been through your workrooms since I was a boy visiting with my parents."

Benno seemed to consider, then pushed heavily to his feet. "No questions?"

"You have my word." Christophe raised both hands. "Only polite interest."

Benno crossed quickly to the door with the air of a man anxious to dispose of an unpleasant task.

No head lifted as they entered the long, narrow room. Perhaps a dozen men and one woman sat at benches behind curved glass screens. Each worker concentrated intently on a rapidly rotating wheel surrounded by piles of grimy steel equipment. Deft hands repeatedly turned, pressed, turned crystalline lumps against grinding surfaces. These shapeless chunks would emerge as beautiful pieces of cold fire, many of them worth small fortunes. Now they resembled oily clots in their tight metal clamps.

"Come." Benno took Christophe's elbow and resolutely approached an elderly, balding man wearing half glasses. "This is Victor Hodez, my senior polisher. He worked for my father before I took over the firm."

The man looked up, pushing his glasses to the top of his nose. He made no attempt to speak but watched Benno politely, clearly waiting for some sign of what he was supposed to do.

"Victor," Benno said. "This is Christophe St-Giles, a . . . business associate and friend." He smiled nervously at Christophe. "More Lukas's friend than mine, I suppose. He hasn't been through the workrooms since he was a boy."

Victor seemed to consider this before wiping his right hand on his blue overall and half rising to shake Christophe's hand. "Little changes here," he allowed, indicating the bare room with its single window and powerful angle lamps.

"Certainly looks much the same," Christophe responded pleasantly, trying to keep his eyes on the man while he wanted to look at the woman seated to Victor's right. "Don't let me interrupt you. I'll just watch, if you don't mind."

Benno exerted gentle pressure to move him toward the man on Victor Hodez's left. Christophe stood fast. "A woman," he said a little loudly to make himself heard above the equipment. "This, I think, is certainly quite a big change."

Paula Renfrew looked directly into his eyes. "I'm sorry," she said. "What did you say?"

He smiled and felt his mouth go dry. She was lovely in that wholesome, American way. Gorgeous teeth and skin. Like an ad for health food. Masses of shining dark hair. And those eyes—the bluest damned eyes. Dammit all. "I said you're the first woman I've seen working in this room. I didn't think diamond polishing was considered woman's work."

He'd started to cringe until she laughed, dulling his embarrassment at his stupid comment. "I'm Paula Renfrew, Mr.—?"

"Christophe," he said, "Christophe St-Giles. And I'm not a chauvinist. Honest—how do you say it? Honest to Betsy?"

"I don't know if I believe that," she teased, laughing again, "but I'm certainly glad to hear some good old American slang again. I'm not sure I'll ever master your language. Dutch is so complicated."

"I'm not Dutch." Christophe plunged his hands into his pockets. Time to close off the male-female reaction. And with this lady that might not be easy to do. She was looking at him quizzically. "Oh," he muttered, feeling a total fool. "I'm not Dutch, I'm Swiss—from Zurich. Benno and I—" he risked a glance at the older man's face and quickly turned back "—Benno and I joke that we speak four languages between us and can only communicate in one—English."

"There's Lukas," Benno broke in, a trace of desperation in his voice. "I'll show you around some more later."

Christophe backed away, still studying Paula Renfrew. She returned his gaze with equal frankness and no sign of nervousness. But why should she be nervous? She had no idea who he was, or why he was here.

"See you again," he said, uncertain if she could hear him now. "Maybe you'll explain more of what goes on here?"

She smiled and as he turned to follow Benno, his last impression was of a full, soft mouth devoid of lipstick. Lucky St-Giles, they'd called him in school, partly because of his reputation with women students. Lucky was the last thing he hoped to feel in the near future, particularly if Paula Renfrew turned out to be a thief.

Lukas Kohl waited at the open door to his father's office. Christophe was struck once more by his austere good looks. An inch or so shorter than Christophe, about six feet, with blond hair and gray eyes, Lukas had the face and body of a film star. Christophe remembered well the bevy of adoring admirers Lukas had attracted at twenty-one. Then he'd been an attractive boy; now thirty-four, he was a handsome man who wore power and maturity as only men of privilege wore them—naturally. Little wonder he'd married one of Amsterdam's most successful models.

Christophe lengthened his stride, only to feel the smile freeze on his face when Lukas turned his back. With Benno, Christophe went into the office and closed the door.

"Let's get this over with," Lukas said harshly. He swung to face Christophe, his eyes pure slate. "My father and I have suffered enough. We want to get on with our business—and our lives."

Christophe opened his mouth to speak, but Benno cut him off, "Lukas, Lukas, my son. Christophe is our friend, not our enemy. This is hard on him, too. We must work together."

Lukas studied the back of his right hand, then the palm, before fingering his wedding band. "I must do what I must do, Father. And I must also be true to myself and what I believe to be right. Victimizing one's friends isn't right."

"Dammit," Christophe exploded, finally unable to control his temper. "Can't you be man enough to understand this is business?"

"How much of a man I am isn't the question here," Lukas replied coolly. "But perhaps you should think about it yourself."

Christophe exhaled sharply and automatically reached for a cigarette. "This isn't your style, Lukas. And none of us needs a sniping match. Please, both of you, it's time to get started on cleaning up this chaos. Tell me, step by step, what happens to a stone after it's ready for sale."

"Oh, hell—" Lukas began.

Benno cut in sharply. "Do it. Now, Lukas. The sooner we stop fighting each other, the sooner this will all be over."

Lukas shrugged eloquently. "There isn't that much to know, actually. But if you insist . . . the stones are graded, cataloged, placed in paper packets—a blue sheet inside a white sheet—the packet is marked, then filed in a small box with other packets." He stood and paced between the desk and the window. "Always the same, always the same. Satisfied?"

"Lukas," Benno said quietly. "Christophe knows exactly what happened—the thirteen stones, everything. He's only trying to figure out how."

"He knows?" Lukas's eyes widened incredulously. "You told him?"

"I didn't have to tell him. The books did that. All I supplied was the fact that the stones disappeared after they left Kohl's and before they reached our customers." A curtain of defeat lowered over Benno's features. "Now he needs to know how, and make sure there can be no repeat performance, or . . ."

"Or?" Lukas's mouth turned up in a bitter, questioning grimace.

"Or there will be no loan," Benno finished.

Christophe rubbed a hand over his eyes. "After the diamonds are filed, what then?"

"They're put in the strong room," Benno said.

"I'll tell him," Lukas interjected. "The strong room is in the basement. It's the same room the customer enters when he intends to select stones for purchase. My father or I, or sometimes both, conduct the sale, then close the packets and deal with formalities, date for payment and so on. We pass the stones to the page who gives them to the messenger for delivery. It is our policy to secure the packages ourselves. A guard travels with the messenger. Once these things were handled directly, stones of immense value carried in a man's breast pocket. Today that is not possible. Amsterdam is a different city now."

"Do you understand the bottom line here, Christophe?" Benno asked, his eyes strangely bright.

"I think so." He wasn't certain.

"No, no you don't. I'll help you, but sit down. Your job, however you decide to pursue it, will not be simple."

Christophe hesitated, then did as Benno asked, dropping to the edge of a straight-backed chair. "Go on."

"The counterfeit goods arrived in packages that did not appear to have been tampered with. You have not only to find the thief, but to discover where he got his so excellent copies and how he made his switches."

Lukas stopped pacing and stood beside his father.

"Here," Benno said clearly, "here at Kohl's, Lukas and I were the last to see the real merchandise. So you see, my dear Christophe, you had better look elsewhere than Kohl's for your criminals. Unless you want to report to your father that I've been stealing from myself."

"Or that I have," Lukas added softly.

Chapter Two

An elbow in the middle of Paula's back sent her grabbing for Peter Van Wersch's arm. Ice cream went up her nose and she sneezed violently. "Yuck," she groaned, wiping her chin with the back of one hand. "Anyone got an extra napkin?"

Peter hitched his camera strap higher and dug in his pockets until he produced a kleenex. "Strawberry suits you, darling. Wipe it off if you must, but please, let me get a shot of your face first. Hey, Lukas, Sandi, hold up a minute, we're having a significant experience here."

"Clown," Paula sputtered, taking the tissue to finish her mopping job. "If everyone didn't keep telling me how nice you are, Peter Van Wersch, I'd say you were a sadist."

Lukas and Sandi Kohl pushed a path back through the crowd, Lukas's arm protectively around his tall wife's shoulders. "So, Paula, what happened? You don't like our Queen's Day celebrations? They are too wild for you, perhaps?" Lukas took her crushed ice cream cone and tossed it in a trash can.

"Not if I don't get mangled by the crowd." Paula grimaced at her sticky hand. "Every April 30th the city goes wild like this, right?"

"April 30th and any other day we can make an excuse for a bash," Sandi said, lifting a heavy, auburn braid behind her shoulders. "We Amsterdammers love our festivals."

Paula smiled into Sandi's green eyes and wondered, not for the first time that day, why the beautiful woman's expression lacked her usual animation.

Peter put a long arm around Paula's waist and smiled his sunny smile at all of them. "She's loving every minute, too, aren't you Paula?" He bent to search her face briefly, then moved her forward without waiting for a reply. Lukas and Sandi fell in behind.

At least she'd become familiar with Amsterdam's warren of narrow streets and canals, Paula thought with satisfaction. After nine months she was beginning to feel like a native. She took a deep breath of warm late afternoon air and sighed.

"A happy sigh," Peter remarked sagely. "Good. We like our inhabitants to be happy."

Peter was a delight. A big, rangy, blond man with laughing blue eyes, he made Paula feel a comradeship with him, a safety. He was a man a woman could have as a friend—she hoped. There was nothing in Peter that seemed to touch her romantically, but his humor and strength were irresistible. Sandi had explained how Peter and Lukas were the same age, thirty-four, and had met in school. Somehow Peter seemed much younger than the frequently somber Lukas, or even twenty-nine-year-old Sandi.

The closeness Lukas and Sandi shared with Peter was easy to understand. He lived in an apartment on the top floor of their house, yet it was clear he knew how not to intrude in their life at the wrong times. And his schedule as a successful commercial photographer with a big, new studio kept him busy.

Today was a national holiday, and Peter had insisted he would take the day off like everyone else: "To teach Paula to be a true Dutchwoman," he'd announced while lunching with Paula and Sandi the previous week, "and to make sure Lukas takes some time to relax. That man is growing old before his time. He's too serious these days."

Paula had agreed to go without hesitation. Sandi had seemed less enthusiastic, but soon gave in to Peter's persuasive charm.

"Come on, you lot," Peter said, forging ahead, pulling Paula with him. "Leidse Plein and the American Hotel in sight." He hopped to see over the boisterous crowd's massed heads, pointing toward the square at the end of the street, Leidse Straat. "You promised us all drinks, Lukas," he called. "And I'm dying of thirst."

Lukas and Sandi caught up. Sandi was tall, almost as tall as her handsome husband. They made an impressive couple, and heads turned as they passed.

Paula trotted to keep stride with the other three. Even at five foot seven, she felt short between these long, lean people. "You don't make allowances for pygmies," she complained, dodging weaving cyclists every few seconds. "Have pity, please." Her pleading went unheeded, possibly unheard, in the din, and she leaped from the path of yet another bicycle. She'd already learned cyclists ruled the streets here—and the sidewalks. They were a fearless, ferocious bunch. "I'm going to get one of those!" she shouted breathlessly.

Peter stopped, Sandi and Lukas with him. "One of what?" Sandi demanded.

The remark had only been for effect really. "A bicycle," Paula explained. "I'm going to buy a bicycle and finally get some respect around here."

Lukas gave one of his rare and quite delightful smiles. "Can you ride one, Paula?"

She shook her head. "Never learned. But I will. I'm going to pick one out."

The peals of laughter that met her announcement made it impossible to remain serious. "Okay, okay. Glad I'm so entertaining. Why shouldn't I have a bicycle? Everyone else does. Average of three a year per city dweller, I read. I only want one."

"Didn't you wonder why anyone would need to buy three bicycles in a year?" Peter draped an arm over her shoulders and made owl eyes. "You didn't sniff a little foul play in that statement?"

"No—I—"

. "Knock it off, Peter." Lukas punched his friend's shoulder. "Give the girl a break. This has been a long day. We'll tell her all about bicycles and anything else you think her education needs—at the American. I want that drink, too, now."

Peter pretended to be insulted for an instant before whipping his camera from its case and insisting on a candid photo in front of a garishly painted barrel organ. When the shutter clicked, Paula was flinching and covering her ears against a hurdy-gurdy tune, punctuated by the rattle of coins in the organ grinder's brass cup.

Within seconds, they passed from the narrow, cobbled street with its skinny old buildings and colored awnings over shop doors, into the broad expanse of Leidse Plein. The American Hotel dominated the north side of the square, and Sandi, holding Lukas's hand, moved quickly ahead. Paula watched the woman's fawnlike grace, the way she stayed almost shyly close to her husband. How could such a reserved creature become the pouting temptress featured in so many glossy fashion magazines? The stab of envy Paula felt came and went quickly. Even if she had what it took to be a model, her temperament was all wrong. She smiled at the thought of the photo Peter had just taken. There was unlikely to be much market for shots like that.

At that moment, Sandi swung back, smiling. The Kohls had seemed tense all day, and Paula was relieved to sense a lightening of their moods. Her relief was short-lived.

"Lukas!" Sandi stopped, almost tripping Peter who was close behind.

Lukas grabbed her arm. "What is it, my love?" He shook her gently. "What's wrong?"

Sandi looked beyond Paula, frowning, some indefinable emotion darkening her eyes. Paula checked over her shoulder, searching the shifting crowd for a sign of what had troubled Sandi. Only a mass of shouting, singing strangers confronted her.

"Sandi, listen to me." It was Peter, speaking low and earnestly. "I don't know what it is with Lukas and Christophe—and you. But Christophe has a right to be here, too. Couldn't we let it go for now?"

Paula stared at Peter who leaned close to Sandi, reaching behind her to grip Lukas's shoulder. What the hell was wrong here? She made another sweep of the crowd...and saw him—*Christophe St-Giles*. Why would that upset them all?

"Stay out of it, Peter," Lukas muttered. "This is something that doesn't affect you. Let's move."

"Damned if I will," Peter said, suddenly very serious. "And anything that makes my two oldest friends behave like deadly enemies *does* affect me. Anyway, it's too late, unless you want to make a complete ass of yourself by running away. He's seen us.''

Paula watched, fascinated, as Christophe St-Giles approached. Her attention was divided between the striking, powerfully built man who swung his shoulders purposefully through the crowd toward them and Sandi and Lukas Kohl. Sandi appeared to shrink and grow paler by the second. Lukas's patrician features were cast, stonelike, his eyes hard. The jumpiness in Paula's stomach reminded her of the feeling she always got in the dentist's waiting room. Painful confrontation seemed inevitable.

"Small world," Christophe called, waving and swiveling his narrow hips to sidestep a group of children sporting bright paper crowns. "Hoped I might run into someone I knew. Queen's Day in Amsterdam shouldn't be spent alone."

"Hey up, Christophe," Peter whooped, going to meet the newcomer and slapping him on his broad back. "Good to see you. Forgive me, friend, I should have thought to invite you today. Guess I'm not used to having you with us again yet."

Paula glanced at Lukas and read a clear message in his expression: *I don't want to get used to you, buddy. I hate your guts.* She pressed her lips together and her chin quivered. Nausea pooled in the pit of her stomach. Conflict was an element she couldn't handle. She'd run from it, even as a small child.

When she looked at Christophe again, he was studying her, a friendly smile on his wide mouth. His lips had a natural upward tilt.... She forced a weak grin. "Are they treating you well, Paula?" he asked, laughter in his deep voice. "Let me know if they don't and I'll take over. I love to play tour guide, and this city is my second home."

The odd noise Lukas made startled her, and she glanced at him. He immediately bent to tie his tennis shoelace.

"Would we neglect anyone so gorgeous," Peter put in, a trifle too hurriedly. "As you know, Christophe, I'm kind to children, dogs, the aged—how much kinder would I be to such an angel?"

"My God," Christophe moaned. "Your lines haven't changed, Peter. Still sickening. Paula, watch this roué. Three times engaged, three times an escapee—significant, I think."

She couldn't stand much more of this banter, this circling. "Yes" was as brilliant an answer as she could manage.

An awkward silence followed before music burst from a nearby bandstand. A single horn blared a deep note that rose to a piercing height. Paula drew in a sharp breath of protest before she recognized a raucous rendition of "Wish I Could Shimmy Like My Sister Kate." Dixieland, well played or otherwise, was her favorite kind of music.

The group turned together toward the noise, but Paula was most acutely aware of Christophe St-Giles standing behind her shoulder. He was as intriguing as his name. On Friday, in dark suit and tie, he'd exuded elegant professionalism; today jeans and a soft cotton shirt made even better use of a very tall, very athletic body. She glanced from his chest to his face and found him watching her, too—with candid interest. They didn't smile, nor did she blush. No man or woman objected to being admired. Why pretend?

"You're very quiet," he said, too low for anyone else to hear.

Paula tilted her head, openly taking in his straight, well-cut brown hair, graying at the temples and determined to fall over his broad forehead. "I'm always quiet when I concentrate," she replied. Daylight was seeping out of the afternoon, and low sun formed a shadow beneath his cheekbones, emphasizing the creases beside his mouth. Every visible inch of his skin was olive, right down to the open V at his neck where she glimpsed the start of dark hair that must cover his chest. "I'm also quiet when I feel an emotional bomb about to explode and I can't do a thing about it." She met his eyes squarely then—deep, deep brown eyes. Oh, Christophe St-Giles was one sexy man, and she enjoyed the pleasure looking at him brought her.

"There'll be no explosion," he whispered. "Trust me. We are all old friends who just need time to get to know one another again." He put a finger in each ear and shouted, "Peter, where are you off to?"

"We've about had it," Lukas began in a rush. "We thought we'd head—"

"To the America," Peter inserted, cutting him off. "Drinkies time for the Three Musketeers and their ladies." He frowned, first at Sandi, then at Paula. "We're missing a lady, which never happened in the old days. Ah, me. We'll just have to make do. I'll share Paula with you, Christophe."

Christophe met her gaze steadily. "Maybe the lady won't like that."

"The lady will manage, Mr. St-Giles," Paula parried. "The lady is very capable."

For a fleeting moment, Paula thought a hard light entered Christophe's gentle eyes. Immediately she decided she was mistaken. He slid a cool hand beneath her arm. "I'm absolutely sure you are capable. But if you call me Mr. St-Giles, you'll have to be Miss Renfrew, and I like Paula so much better."

Sandi, who had been silent almost since Christophe arrived, whirled away and bent to examine a pile of treasures spread for sale on a blanket. "Look at this, Lukas." She held up a crimson beaded purse. "I used to play with one like this when I was a child. Hans bought it for—" She stopped abruptly and stood, dropping the purse. Tears brimmed in her eyes, and she walked into Lukas's outstretched arm.

Paula leaned toward Peter, "Who's Hans?"

"I don't know. Old boyfriend maybe... Look out!"

His warning was too late. Bodies pushed in on Paula. Somehow, a foot tangled with hers and she started to fall sideways. Christophe tried to grab her and so did Peter, but the throng swept her down until her shin met something hard and she cried out. Sandi's reaching hands only succeeded in landing them both in a crumpled heap on filthy cobblestones.

Facedown on the ground, Paula covered her head instinctively and waited to be crushed. "Get back!" It was Lukas's voice she heard as a small space opened around her. Sandi was pulled up.

Large hands closed about her waist and lifted her with swift ease. "Okay, *chérie*?" Christophe turned her to face him. He wrapped one arm firmly around her and pushed the tousled hair out of her eyes. "Okay?" He peered at her closely.

Paula looked around. "I guess," she said shakily, bending to rub her leg. Lukas was already dusting Sandi off. "I don't know what happened except I hit one of those damned Amsterdammagers."

"Thank God she hasn't lost her sense of humor," Peter said. "That means she's okay. You have to watch out for our little red posts or they'll get you—particularly if you really do decide to become a cyclist."

Ruefully, Paula checked her grit-embedded palms. "They're useless." She glared at the knee-high posts lining the sidewalk that were designed to keep cyclists—and sometimes motorists—from plowing down pedestrians. With sidewalks as crowded as Amsterdam's, she was convinced they were more of a hazard than help.

Paula became aware of Christophe once more. He held one of her hands and carefully flicked away tiny rocks. He took a handkerchief from his pocket and wiped her palm before starting on the other hand. Paula watched the top of his bent head, the movement of muscle in his wide shoulders, and suppressed a smile. One wasn't supposed to be glad when knocked on one's face, but if the consolation prize was the undivided attention of a man like Christophe, she might have to fall more often.

"I hate to break up this touching Florence Nightingale scene," Peter said, shattering the moment all too effectively. "But you're standing on your purse, Paula, dear, and half your possessions are probably smashed."

"Good Lord," Paula exclaimed. "I didn't even notice."

Christophe stopped her in the act of bending. "Allow me," he said, holding her wrist a fraction longer than necessary before dropping to his knees to gather her bag and its spilled contents.

Lukas helped by retrieving a pen and a tiny perfume atomizer, miraculously untouched, and handing them to her. "You women and your bits and pieces." He shook his head, but a smile hovered about his lips. "When will you learn a few guilders in your pocket is all you need?"

"Lukas," Sandi said warningly. "Don't be mean."

"Here you are." Christophe stood, dropping a comb and wallet inside Paula's purse. "I think that's everything and all intact."

Peter swooped to pick something up. "Except this." He held a folded piece of paper aloft. "A secret love note, no doubt."

Paula glanced at the sheet. "Not mine, I'm afraid, Peter. No one writes love letters to me." Immediately she closed her mouth, avoiding Christophe's eyes.

"Then you won't mind if I read it?" Peter flapped the yellow paper in front of her eyes.

Unaccountably, Paula felt irritated. Sometimes Peter went too far. "Be my guest, Peter. This is a day for sharing, right?"

If he felt her asperity, Peter showed no sign. He shook the paper open and read quickly. Silence made Paula turn her full attention to him. The smile had disappeared from his face. Lukas, Sandi and Christophe were staring expectantly at him.

Peter glanced at Paula, his brilliant smile once more in place. "Nothing to do with us, after all." He started to crumple the paper.

"No," Christophe said. "We all get to see this, Peter. You love to make mysteries, my friend."

With a wordless shrug, Peter handed over the note. "I want my drink, darlings. Come on."

No one moved. Christophe scanned the lined sheet and gave it to Lukas, who read it with Sandi looking over his shoulder.

Paula grew edgy. What was the big deal? She hooked a hand through Peter's elbow and leaned against him. Her shin and hands still stung.

"Yes," Lukas said slowly, starting to push the paper into his pocket, "Sustenence for the weary. Onward."

Christophe stayed him with a firm hand. "Soon, Lukas. Soon. But don't you think Paula should read that, too? After all, if she hadn't dropped—fallen, we wouldn't have had this little diversion. Surely she shouldn't be the only one to miss the fun.''

She sighed. These people did love their jokes. Lukas gave her the rumpled sheet and she scanned a single printed line before she began to laugh. Peter immediately joined in.

Paula read aloud, " 'They're getting closer. Watch for slips.' '' She looked up to find Lukas, Sandi and Christophe watching her expectantly while Peter wiped his eyes. "Well." She shoved the paper in her purse. "I don't know where this came from, but it was certainly meant for me. It would have been even better if it read, 'Watch for Amsterdammagers.' '' Paula thought her joke was funny. She was surprised when no one laughed.

Chapter Three

"Mata Hari, Peter?" Paula said with patent disbelief. "The spy?"

Christophe settled deep into his tufted velvet chair, every nerve alert, while Peter nodded seriously and said, "I swear. She was married in this Jugenstil restaurant in 1894. That's what keeps the American Hotel so famous. Must have been your mysterious note that reminded me."

Paula ignored the comment and looked around the packed room with its brilliant blue and yellow stained glass windows and odd contrast of exposed brick and squared dark paneling. Christophe kept a bland smile on his face but didn't take his eyes off Paula. She was becoming more of a disturbing enigma by the minute.

Finally, she folded her arms and frowned. "An architectural monument, you said, Lukas? Because of Mata Hari, I assume. This looks more like a shrine to me."

Everyone laughed. "I take it you don't go for Greek frescos and potted palms," Peter suggested. "Or maybe the Japanese parasol lamps with lighted handles are what throw you?"

She raised her brows as a waiter approached to take orders for Black Forest cake and jenever all around. It hadn't taken her long to learn that everyone drank the strong Dutch national drink with everything—including cake.

As soon as the waiter left, squeezing through a sea of crowded little tables, Paula leaned toward Sandi. "What do they keep announcing?"

The noise level was as Christophe remembered—deafening and punctuated by constant loudspeaker messages.

"Nothing, really." Sandi's cheeks turned slightly pink. "It's all a game. The Jugenstil has always been known as an artists' haunt. A lot of theatrical people hang out here, too—everyone trying to make an impression. Someone wants to look important, so they get someone else to page them. With the right arrangements, a telephone can be brought to your table. It goes on all the time."

"Ridiculous," Christophe put in. "Juvenile."

"And you did it yourself, Christophe," Peter said, pretending to trace stains on the gold tablecloth with a fingernail. "I know because I placed some of the calls."

He had to laugh. That seemed so very long ago. "Only to keep up with you arty types. Even a young man doomed to the life of a banker can dream of fame and recognition." Not quite true, not in a glitzy way. But at twenty-two he had played the games here. "Remember, Lukas?" He met those familiar gray eyes, hoping for some softening, but found none. Muscles tightened in his jaw. Forget old friendships, he instructed himself grimly. Forget the past. This was today and this was business. He might not be an artist in the conventional sense but he was a creator, constantly arranging and testing the intricate patterns spawned in the financial world. He thrived on what others might term his own games.

He turned sideways toward Paula. Her hair fell softly forward to hide her face, and he looked at the pale skin at the back of her neck above a striped T-shirt. Her figure was enticing, slender, gently feminine in the way that had always turned him on. What were her legs like, he wondered? She wore jeans today, and on Friday she'd been sitting. He squinted into the distance. Her legs were about the last thing he should be wasting thought on.

"And you, Paula," he said quietly. "What do you think of silly games—ploys to achieve effect—results even?" Some sign. He needed signs. A subtle change in her expression. Telltale tension in those capable, well-shaped hands.

Blue eyes turned on him slowly. "I've never had time for ploys, Mr.—Christophe. I've always been too busy doing what had to be done."

Had her voice risen—just slightly? "And what always had to be done?" His nerves jumped. He was reading too much into every comment. She wouldn't give direct hints. It was that damned note that had got him going.

She seemed to consider, winding a strand of hair around a forefinger. "Getting through school. Helping my father. Just living, I guess. Nothing important."

He bit back the urge to say he thought she was very important. "Your father. What did he do?" She mustn't find out how much he knew about her.

"Here's the waiter," Lukas interrupted.

Christophe looked at Lukas and quelled a surge of irritation when he saw the satisfaction on his face. The irrational bastard intended to hamper any attempt to question Paula, dammit. Benno had probably given him hell for talking about the woman's past, told him to protect her. Christophe locked his hands behind his neck and inhaled deeply. If the Kohls hoped to sidetrack him from finding out what was going on here, they'd chosen the wrong tactics. Nothing would divert him now.

Huge wedges of cake and shot glasses of jenever, the Dutch gin that seemed a part of every meal, arrived. Paula had ordered the citron, or lemon flavor, rather than the stronger clear variety the rest of them had chosen.

Paula sipped her drink and immediately reached for a water glass.

"Too strong for you, Paula?" Peter asked solicitously. "You'd prefer something else."

She patted his hand on the tabletop. "It's fine, thank you, Peter. Not what I'm used to before dinner, that's all." She laughed and stuck her fork into the cake. "This isn't what I'm used to for dinner, either."

"Queen's Day madness," Peter said, gazing intently at her face. "We'll eat properly later, maybe Indonesian, if you like." He held her fingers and turned her hand to check the palm. "You really went down with a bang. This looks bruised. I hope your fingers don't stiffen up."

"As long as she can work that wheel tomorrow, she'll be too engrossed to notice," Lukas said lightly. "Victor says he never saw anyone more eager than Paula, or with more natural talent."

Christophe watched and listened. Was Paula already talented enough to copy gems? Benno had said the counterfeit efforts were good, but not perfect. Tomorrow he'd make more inquiries, find out just how advanced Paula Renfrew was in the execution of her work.

He switched his attention to Peter. "Three times engaged, three times escaped" had been his own quip. He might have said three times disappointed, had he not known how important pride was to Peter. Now he was giving Paula the kind of attention an infatuated man gave a woman. Christophe drained his own jenever, scarcely noticing its sting in his throat. He couldn't be put off by anything. If she turned out to be a criminal, Peter would be better off saved from her.

The note had been Paula's. Christophe was sure of it. And she'd tried to pretend ignorance. Lukas had been disturbed by the incident—Sandi, too, yet Lukas was still determined to run interference for Paula. So what, Christophe thought, pushing cake crumbs around his plate. The note had served a purpose for him. He'd been almost certain one person couldn't have pulled off the thefts. Now he knew he was right—Paula had an accomplice, or more than one.

Watch for slips. He stopped eating, his fork halfway to his mouth. Could the note have been meant for him? Had someone meant to tip him off to Paula? "They," could be anyone. But who would warn him, and why? Unless the Kohls weren't the only potential losers in this scam.

"You're very thoughtful, Christophe."

At the sound of Paula's voice, he started. "I was thinking about work," he said, smiling, feeling the effort might crack his face. "I have difficulty thinking of anything else for very long."

She regarded him seriously. "You're a banker. Is that really dull?"

"Not so dull," he said, setting down his fork. She was cool—he'd give her that. "I probably get as much of a charge out of solving money puzzles as you do when you make a perfect facet in a diamond."

She looked doubtful. "I can't imagine finding money very interesting—as a job," she finished faintly.

"This is a vacation for you, isn't it, Christophe?" Peter asked. "You said you needed a rest. Take it. That's why I thought the houseboat would be more relaxing than a hotel."

"It is," Christophe said quickly. "But I do have to combine a little business with pleasure. Benno and Lukas and I have a few matters to deal with, don't we, Lukas?"

"Yes." Lukas finished his drink and signaled the waiter. "Another round?" He didn't look at Christophe.

Only Paula declined Lukas's offer, and he placed the order.

"Paula Renfrew. Call in the lobby for Paula Renfrew."

The paging system announced a call for Paula. Christophe gripped his empty glass tightly. His Dutch was rusty, but he had no difficulty understanding the message.

"That was my name?" She looked blank. "What did it say?"

"A call, darling," Peter said, frowning. "In the lobby. I'll come with you."

"Who would call me?"

If she wasn't completely surprised, the woman was quite an actress. "Better find out," Christophe said evenly. "Stay put, Peter. I'll go with her. It'll remind me of old times."

He started to get up. Paula pressed his forearm. "I can manage. Please, all of you, carry on. I'm sure it's a mistake. I'll be right back."

Christophe let out a slow breath. He'd bet she could manage. And she wouldn't want an audience if she was receiving another message from an accomplice. While he watched Paula's retreating figure, he felt Lukas's eyes upon him.

"You're a joker, Peter," Lukas said. "How did you manage to arrange that?"

"What?" Peter looked startled. "Arrange what?"

"You can't pull the wool over my eyes, friend. I remember your tricks from years ago. Who did you get to make the call?"

Christophe studied Lukas. He was smiling for the first time since they'd met in the square. Maybe he'd hit the truth. Unwillingly, Christophe acknowledged how strongly he hoped Lukas was right and that Peter had engineered a ruse.

"I didn't fix anything, Lukas. When would I have been able to? I thought you had," Peter said and leaned back to allow the waiter to put their fresh drinks on the table.

Christophe stopped Lukas from paying by throwing a handful of guilders on the waiter's tray and telling him to keep the change.

"Must have been you then, Sandi," Peter said, sighing deeply. "And I always thought you were such a sensible woman."

"Could there be some emergency?" She spoke directly to Lukas. "Perhaps there's been a call from America to your parents and they're trying to track her down. Did you mention we'd be coming here?"

"Ah—yes, yes. Now I think of it, I did."

Christophe lowered his gaze and took out a pack of cigarettes. Lukas was a liar, but this wasn't the time to say so.

The four of them sat in uncomfortable silence, the room around them a noisy blur. Even Peter said nothing. He made little circles with his glass and checked the door every few seconds until Paula wove her way back.

"Weird." She sounded breathless. Christophe noted the heightened color in her cheeks. "There was no one on the line."

"Really?" He propped his chin on one fist and drew on a cigarette. "Was it a man or a woman?"

She sat beside him. "No one. I said no one was on the line."

"I mean, was it a man or a woman who placed the call and hung up?" He turned to face her. "Would you like a cigarette?"

"I—no, thank you. I don't smoke."

"Do you mind if I do?"

"No."

"Was it a man or a woman?"

Her lips parted. He'd pushed her off balance. "Oh, I see." She threaded her fingers through her hair. "I didn't ask the desk clerk."

"Maybe we only thought it was your name," Lukas said.

Christophe made sure their eyes met and he didn't hide his disgust. "Yes," he said clearly. "We all made a mistake. We must really be in a mood to invent mysteries today. A bad habit we'll have to watch."

"I'm just glad it wasn't an emergency," Sandi said, scooting her chair away from the table. "Excuse me. I see some people from my agency. If I don't go over there, they'll come here and bore all of us instead of just me." She squeezed Lukas's shoulder and walked to another table where an animated group quickly made room for her to sit. Seconds later she was back, urging Peter to his feet. "They want to meet you. Your reputation as a hot photographer precedes you these days, Peter. Lukas, could you bear to come, too, just for a few minutes? Christophe and Paula don't need to suffer."

Peter immediately got to his feet. Lukas hesitated fractionally before standing. "Of course. We'll be right back, you two." No one would have missed the warning in the look he gave Christophe. Christophe raised a brow and his glass in mock salute. He'd use whatever opportunities presented to get what he wanted.

He waited just long enough to be sure Lukas couldn't hear before saying, "What did you say your father did?"

A vaguely disoriented light flickered in Paula's eyes. Tossing her back and forth, forcing her into a mental balancing act, could produce a slip. *Slip.* Not if she was heeding all the warnings she appeared to be getting.

"Your father?" he prompted.

"My father was a jeweler."

He didn't know what he expected. Certainly not that. After his early experiences, Michael Renfrew might have been expected to stay away from anything to do with jewels. Christophe cleared his throat and stubbed out the Gitane. "He had his own business?" That took a lot of capital, didn't it?"

"Yes. In New Jersey. He was a gifted designer. We did quite well." Her voice was markedly tighter.

"You said 'was.' Has he retired?" He saw her swallow and instantly disliked what he was doing. Regardless of present circumstances, he hated hurting another human being.

"My father died a little over a year ago. Fourteen months now."

Dammit, she had tears in her eyes. He steeled himself. Deep love and deep loyalty went hand in hand. Blind faith and a willingness to do anything to preserve a memory belonged to the same group of emotions. "I'm sorry," he said after a while. She'd averted her face. "Is your mother running the shop now?"

"I don't know where my mother is." Paula turned her head and riveted him with a sharp glare. "And I don't care. My brother and I sold the shop. Grant's in the Air Force. We're both doing what we wanted most in life. Dad would like to know that."

"Good."

"How about you?" She took a good swallow of her jenever and flinched. "Are you doing what you want to do?"

He'd touched some raw nerves. "Yes. I already told you I like my work."

"The other day, on Friday, you said you and Benno spoke four languages but only communicated in English. I thought most people in Zurich spoke German, but you speak French, don't you—your name's French, isn't it?"

Laughing, he held up a hand. "Slowly, slowly. So many questions."

"I thought you liked questions. Asking them, anyway." Her eyes were dry now, and appraising.

She had him. "Okay. Yes, I'm an inquisitive devil. And to be fair, you're right, I'm French-Swiss. You're also right in thinking there are far more German-Swiss in Zurich. I also speak fluent German. I have to in my business. And, let me see. I have a father and two uncles and one cousin all actively involved in the bank. My mother is dead. I have no brothers or sisters."

"A wife, perhaps? Children?"

He took in a breath and stared at her. She could give lessons in shock tactics. "No wife. No children. Should have at thirty-five, right?"

She shrugged.

"Well—" Without thinking, he touched her hair. Soft. Good Lord, he must stay on track. "Well, I had a very long and very meaningful relationship with someone I probably loved. Unfortunately things didn't work out. Now she's married and seems happy. And I'm glad for her. Life goes on." He wasn't supposed to be telling his life history to the only feasible suspect in the Kohl case.

"Yours will." The softness in her voice unnerved him. He'd best back away from the personal stuff for a while until he gained some perspective. She was reaching him in a way that he didn't want to be reached—not in this situation.

"What made you do something as . . . as—"

"As off-the-wall as coming halfway around the world from my home to take up a man's profession?" Her eyes challenged him.

"I asked for that when we spoke last Friday, didn't I?" he said wryly. "But yes, that's what I meant. I don't imagine many little American girls grow up wanting to become diamond polishers in Amsterdam."

She was so lovely when she smiled. "This one did. My father made me fall in love with diamonds." The smile was broad now, ingenuous. "Many years ago he worked for Benno's father. That's what made me decide to see if I could get a job here. When Benno agreed to hire me I could hardly believe my luck."

Christophe's heart missed a beat. Just like that. She'd told him the truth, at least the truth that her father had worked at Kohl's before her. "I see," he said lamely. "Following in father's footsteps like so many of us."

"Oh, yes. And he would have been thrilled. You have a couple more questions coming, you know." She had a single dimple—beneath her right cheekbone.

"I seem to have forgotten what they were." And he had, too, dammit.

"I'll just give you the answers, then. I'm twenty-six and I'm not married, either."

"Ah. Congratulations." He'd almost said he was glad. Could a woman who looked like this be crooked? The note could have been a fluke. Lukas or Peter, probably Peter, could have arranged the call as a joke. Her father could have been . . . He raked his hair back. "You're living in Benno and Anna's guest house?"

"Benno must have told you that. Yes, I'm in the back-house, as they all those places. I love it there. Have you seen what they're like—the backhouses?"

"I stayed where you are once myself. And yes, I've seen a lot of backhouses. Clever how the Dutch built high and deep to save taxes on their front footage. I always liked the little courtyard between the backhouse and the main house at Anna and Benno's. Lukas and I used to..." He trailed off, unable to allow the memories to become important again.

Paula appeared not to notice his change of mood. "I like the courtyard, too," she said. "I've planted tubs of bulbs out there. I have my own tulip patches. Appropriate, don't you think?"

"Yes," he said, watching as her enthusiasm animated her features. "Will you be at dinner with Benno and Anna when I come on Saturday?"

She hesitated, glancing up as Peter returned with Lukas and Sandi. They sat, and Paula turned to Christophe once more. "Anna invited me this morning. I'll be there. I can't imagine turning down anything Anna cooks."

"You'll be where?" Lukas interrupted. Without asking, he took a cigarette from the pack Christophe had left on the table and offered one to Peter, who accepted. "What's all this about an invitation for my mother's cooking?"

"Dinner," Christophe said, flipping his lighter, first for Peter, then for Lukas. Sharing used to be so natural between them. "I'm having dinner with your parents on Saturday, and now I discover I'll also have the pleasure of Paula's company."

"How nice," Lukas said, sounding anything but pleased. "Too bad Sandi and I can't join all of you. We've accepted another invitation."

The heavy silence sifted in around them once more, and Christophe remembered the other question he should have asked Paula. The one that might have made a real dent in her composure: why had Michael Renfrew decided to leave Amsterdam so suddenly? He'd have to wait now—maybe for Saturday evening.

Paula found herself unable to keep her gaze from Christophe's face for more than moments at a time. She liked him, truly liked him. And something more, much more. The staggering relief she'd felt when he'd said he wasn't married didn't come from any need for a simple friend. Paula had friends. What she didn't have was a lover. She shivered, almost pressed her thighs where the muscles ached. This was a first. Just as she'd told him, she'd been too busy coping with day-to-day life to play games. He hadn't asked her if she included romance and sex in those games she's had no time for. But the answer would have been yes—most of the time. She had never experienced an attraction this strong or instant.

"Perhaps we should start for the home front," Peter said. "It'll take a while to make our way back. The crowd will only be getting rowdier."

"True," Lukas agreed.

What was it with Lukas, Paula mused? She hadn't forgotten Peter's comments when Christophe approached them outside. Lukas and Christophe were supposed to be old friends. Nothing in Lukas's manner backed up that idea.

She scraped her chair away from the table at the same time as she noticed a familiar face at a table half-hidden by a screen. Frank Lammaker glanced up and saw her, too. Paula waved and smiled.

Lukas looked over his shoulder, then back at Paula. "What the devil's he doing here?"

The reaction puzzled Paula. "It's a holiday for everyone, isn't it, Lukas? Frank included?" Frank also worked for Kohls.

"Of course," Lukas replied formally. "I'm surprised to see him here, that's all." He raised his hands, indicating their surroundings. "Sandi, you know some of that group he's with, don't you? Aren't they a little rich for the average man's blood?"

Sandi followed Lukas's stare and nodded at Frank. "Yes," she muttered. "Mostly writers. Saul Otis paints. They're all fairly well-heeled and on the inside track, if that's what you mean."

"That's what I mean." Lukas's voice dropped. "I didn't think we paid our messenger enough to allow him to move in that kind of company." He glanced around again. "Or to dress like a visiting prince and evidently pay his share of the money and they're probably expecting to drop in a place like this. They look settled in for a long night."

Christophe became restless at Paula's side. She noticed that he stared at Frank and his friends with interest. "Your messenger, Lukas? Is he Kohl's only messenger?" he asked.

"We only need one," Lukas said shortly.

Now Paula was more angry than puzzled. This wasn't fair. Why shouldn't Frank have a life outside work? He was a nice man, open, a breath of fresh air around Kohl's. He was twenty-two and full of energy. She'd found him friendly and helpful since she'd arrived. His mother did Anna Kohl's cleaning. Perhaps that was it. Lukas didn't think Frank should be frequenting the same places he considered suitable for himself. She pushed the idea aside. Lukas was no snob.

Peter tapped the table. "I remember him. His mother used to work for yours, didn't she, Lukas?"

"Yes," Lukas said distantly. "Madeleine. She still does. She's my mother's housekeeper."

"Ah, yes, of course." Peter tipped up his chin. "Frank was the one you thought Benno shouldn't hire for some reason. Unstable as a kid, or something."

"That's history," Lukas said.

"Shall we go," Sandi suggested, obviously edgy. "I'm tired, and we could all use a decent meal."

"In a minute," Lukas snapped. He moved his chair closer to Paula's where he could see Frank without turning around. "The man to Lammaker's right, Paula. Do you know him?"

"Yes." By now everyone at the other table must know they were under scrutiny. Paula shifted uncomfortably. "Lukas, what's wrong. Is there any reason why Frank shouldn't be here? We are."

"Who is that man?" Lukas pressed as if he hadn't heard her. "I'm sure I recognize him."

"You should," she said impatiently. "Willem Bill. He works for Metter Brothers as a page."

Chapter Four

Tuesday of the Second Week:

"How many times must I tell you to spit in it?"

Paula's face bobbed up. "Oh, Victor—" she looked into the pestle and mortar where she was mixing diamond paste to coat her wheel, then back at Victor Hodez's wizened face "—why on earth do you insist I have to spit in it? Why can't I use just olive oil like others do?"

A Gallic shrug lifted permanently hunched shoulders. "I am the expert, Paula—correct?"

"Correct, Victor, but..."

"I am also said to be somewhat superior to most other polishers, yes?"

"Absolutely. I just..."

"The others use only olive oil in their paste. I spit, as well." He bent over his wheel again, and Paula spat into the mixture of diamond dust, abrasive powder and olive oil. The paste created the cutting action between stone and wheel. Only diamond could cut diamond, so no part of the rough material was wasted. Minute chips became the dust that fashioned other gems.

"You are a good girl, Paula."

At first she thought she'd misheard. She stopped pounding and stared at Victor. His head remained bent over the spinning wheel.

Paula cleared her throat. "Thank you, Victor." He'd never shown any real sign of accepting her until now.

"You have the instinct," he muttered, stopping to examine the piece he worked on, "but any child of Michael Renfrew was bound to have the touch. He was good."

Without her prompting, Victor had actually broached the subject of her father. Paula slid from her stool, clenching her fists on the bench. Her father had known this man. Benno told her so, but before this morning Victor had evaded any attempt she'd made at finding out more about Michael Renfrew's time in Amsterdam.

She'd moved a step closer to Victor, deciding what might be safe to ask, what would be unlikely to make the old polisher close up again, when the outer door swept open. Benno entered, closely followed by Lukas and Christophe St-Giles.

Excitement shot into Paula's nerve endings. All her senses were sharpened. She stood very still, scarcely breathing, knowing any moment Christophe would turn her way and smile.

His hands were characteristically sunk into his pockets as he walked into Benno's office and closed the door. He hadn't even glanced in her direction.

Paula flipped her hair behind her ears. Her skin felt clammy. Quickly she checked around the workroom to see if anyone had noticed her reaction. All heads were down. She was a fool. Yesterday, she'd misinterpreted Christophe St-Giles polite attention for the same type of interest she'd felt—darn it, still felt—toward him.

Heat crawled uncomfortably up her neck to her cheeks, and she sat on her stool once more. At least he hadn't seen her staring at him like a smitten sophomore. Dammit all, she'd allowed a dumb emotional reaction, based on a brief interlude, to ruin a perfect opening to talk to Victor about her father.

Paula was deeply sunk in thought when she realized Victor was talking again, this time to Kersten Gouda, Kohl's senior page. Kersten spent time working in the showroom on the ground floor, dealing with retail clients. She also escorted the more important wholesale buyers in and out of the strong room. Kersten, Paula had soon discovered, wore many hats and was very knowledgeable.

Kersten stayed in front of Victor's glass shield. They spoke in Dutch, and Paula could only wait until she caught the older woman's eye and smiled.

"How are you?" Kersten asked politely. "Victor tells us you are a prize student."

Two compliments in one morning, Paula thought. The unexpected praise was almost sufficient to make up for her chagrin over Christophe's cold-shoulder treatment. "Victor is a prize teacher," she said honestly.

"Hmm" was Victor's offhand response. He stopped working and reached for an oily rag to wipe his hands.

"This arrived from Antwerp." Kersten gave Victor a small package. "Mr. Kohl said you'd know what to do with the delivery."

Victor set the parcel beside his scaife. "Yes." He nodded, unsmiling, at Kersten. "I was expecting it, Mrs. Gouda. Thank you."

The formality caught Paula's interest. She'd been at Kohl's only nine months, and although Kersten Gouda was reserved, they'd immediately used each other's first name. Victor must have known the woman for the fourteen years she'd been employed in the same building, yet he behaved like a rusty courtier around her. He even bowed slightly when Kersten turned to leave. Could Victor...? No, Victor couldn't be interested in Kersten Gouda. He'd mentioned his wife and children and grandchildren, with undisguised pride. And slight, blue-eyed, blond Kersten could be no more than forty-five, at least twenty years Victor's junior. And she was married. Still...

Curiosity got the best of Paula. "Kersten is a pretty woman." She moved closer as Victor unwrapped the brown-paper package. "She makes me feel dowdy when she arrives in the morning. Her clothes are so beautiful."

He took a padded plastic bag from a small box. "Mrs. Gouda doesn't like to wear her uniform outside the building."

The response surprised Paula. It was true that Kersten waited until she arrived for work to change into the navy blue suit Kohl's provided for her. That had never seemed unusual to Paula. "The junior salesgirls downstairs wear pretty much the same outfit for work. Don't they all change into uniform when they get here?"

"No." Victor slit the bubble plastic. "Only Mrs. Gouda."

Paula's attention was divided between their conversation and the already cut stone Victor slid from its protective cocoon. "Her own suits must cost a bundle," she commented abstractedly. "Maybe I'll buy something like that when I can afford it."

Victor grunted, peering at the gem through his high-powered loupe. "I wouldn't know about such things. You will look at this, Paula. I want you to tell me what you see."

Before she could pick up her own magnifying glass, Benno's office door opened again and he emerged with Christophe. The two men laughed, exchanged several low-spoken comments while they shook hands, then Christophe turned away. He paused to find a cigarette and cupped his hands to draw against the flame of his lighter. Paula held her breath. He was going to ignore her again, walk out as if she didn't exist. She couldn't look away.

Christophe lifted his chin. The tip of his cigarette glowed briefly and he exhaled. Paula gripped the edge of her bench with both hands. The blood in her body seemed to stop circulating. Dark eyes, narrowed to slits found her face through a thin veil of smoke. She smiled tentatively before the muscles around her mouth quivered and cold slid up her spine. Christophe didn't smile. He stared at her as he might a stranger, or perhaps a dull anatomical specimen in its glass case. She sat with a thump and pushed tools from one side of the wheel to the other. He didn't even remember she was there.

"Goodbye, then." Benno's voice had a penetrating quality.

Cautiously she glanced up. Lukas's animosity toward Christophe hadn't been imagined. But Benno's warm smile suggested he didn't share his son's dislike of this man.

Christophe's parting remark was inaudible over the machinery. He held his lighter between finger and thumb, twisting it in circles before he strode away. Paula returned her gaze to Benno. She mustn't think of that empty stare.

Benno hesitated, one hand braced against the door to his office. Paula watched thoughtfully. Again she'd misread signals. He'd made a tight fist of the hand by his side while he stared into space his smile gone, deep lines of worry etched in its place. The complete transformation turned her stomach. So Lukas wasn't the only Kohl who reacted violently to M. St-Giles, after all. He simply wasn't as adept as Benno at hiding his feelings.

"Paula!"

She swiveled toward a man, another worker, who called her name. "Yes, Jacob?"

"For you." He waved the receiver of the wall telephone. She hadn't even heard its ring.

Hesitantly she took the instrument from him, waiting until he turned curious eyes back to his work. She remembered yesterday's call at the American Hotel. If this was another dead line she'd start looking over her shoulder from now on.

"Hello," she said uncertainly. "This is Paula Renfrew."

"Hello, Paula Renfrew. This is Christophe St-Giles."

Confused, she glanced toward Benno's office. Benno had gone inside again. "I . . ." What did this mean? A few minutes ago he'd been in the same room and ignored her. "Where are you calling from?"

"Downstairs."

"In the showroom?" The showroom where at least a couple of curious employees could listen. Evidently Christophe hadn't forgotten how to play games. "You were just here, Christophe. In this room, where you know I work. Didn't you see me?"

"Of course." There was laughter in his voice.

"I'm afraid I don't understand. Did you think you shouldn't say hi in front of anyone else or something?"

There was a noticeable pause. "Or something, I guess. Forgive me. But I didn't want to leave without reminding you how much I'm looking forward to seeing you at dinner on Saturday evening."

"Good." What else could she say? She didn't know the man well enough to tell him she thought he was rude.

"I've offended you." His voice became deep velvet. "That's the last thing I want to do. But sometimes we have to put our own wants aside. We'll have more time to talk on Saturday.''

The receiver slipped in her hand and she held it tighter. ''Yes,'' she mumbled and listened to his warm goodbye before realizing she'd allowed him to get away with giving her the brush off, while leading him to believe she was looking forward to being with him again. Slowly she hung up the phone and rubbed her damp palms together. She *did* want to be with him again—desperately.

''Are we ready, Paula?'' Victor asked sharply. ''Or do you have better things to do?''

The diamond. She'd forgotten the diamond he'd told her to look at. ''Sorry,'' she mumbled. ''I'm ready. Why are they sending you already finished stones?''

''Look at it,'' he said abruptly.

Paula pressed her glass to her eye and bent over the stone Victor had set in the adhesive wax used during polishing. ''An excellent brilliant cut,'' she murmured, tipping her head to peer through the facets from one side. ''Eight carats?''

''Slightly more. But you have a good eye.''

''I can't . . .'' She twisted her wrist slightly. ''I can't find any flaw. It's perfect—no, almost perfect. There's a small minor natural flaw. That should have been taken care of when the rough stone was cleaved. But by the time you finish and this is mounted it *will* be perfect.''

Victor chuckled. ''Good, Paula. Very good. You learn fast. Mr. Kohl obtained this stone specially for a client. It's already sold. I will attend to that little imperfection you so accurately noted, and this will be on its way.''

Paula remained at his side, soaking up every move he made. One day, she'd be as good as Victor Hodez. The prospect exhilarated her.

Victor checked through his loupe once more and began to lower the arm that held the gem against the wheel. His curse, even in Dutch, wasn't wasted on Paula. She jumped. For the first time, she'd seen Victor make a mistake. His hand had jerked, twisting too far left and bringing the stone down in the groove between the wheel and its surrounding rigid plate. He corrected the error quickly, but Paula saw that his hands trembled slightly.

A masculine voice snapped the tension, "Is everything all right, Victor?"

Startled, Paula looked up into Lukas's intent gray eyes. An inexplicable anger overtook her. He'd obviously seen Victor's slip and chosen to comment. She'd never heard him offer encouragement to Victor or thanks for his excellent work. In fact, she'd never seen him taking any interest in the artists who created the product that kept him rich.

Victor had made no attempt to give Lukas a reply. He continued to work, and Paula noted with satisfaction that his fingers were as steady as usual.

"Good morning, Paula," Lukas said. "Have you recovered from yesterday's revels?"

Why, she wondered, must he always be so formal? "Yes. Thank you for taking me. I'll call Sandi and Peter later. I had a wonderful time." Lukas, she knew, had had a miserable time, not that his smooth expression betrayed other than calm today.

He checked his watch and remarked offhandedly, "Almost twelve." His suit jacket was slung over his left shoulder. "How about lunch?"

Paula almost gaped. Mr. Iceberg wanted to have lunch? With her? This was a first. She set down her loupe. "Sounds marvelous. I think I saw a little sun somewhere outside. Fresh air and food are just what I need." She glanced at Victor who was ignoring the exchange. "I'll finish up here and meet you downstairs in a few minutes, if that's okay."

"Fine. I'll be in the showroom." Shrugging on his jacket, Lukas headed for the door.

Paula began to untie her coverall. "Lunch with the boss. I must be doing something right."

Victor wasn't listening. Paula stood very still, her coverall trailing from one arm. This was turning into a strange day. There was no mistaking the expression on Victor's face: hatred. He stared at Lukas's back until the younger man left the room, then continued to watch the closed door blindly. Slowly Paula finished taking off the coverall. She straightened her tools, giving Victor time to recover. The reason for his obvious loathing for Lukas was something she couldn't begin to guess at. And personality conflicts here were none of her business.

"Right," she said finally. "Guess I'm as ready as I'm going to be. You don't mind if I leave for a while, do you Victor?" Usually, all the finishers brought sandwiches for lunch and ate in the workroom.

Victor looked at her blankly for an instant, then he said, "Why should I mind?" and bent immediately over his wheel.

A few minutes later, walking along Rokin beside Lukas, Paula lifted her face to a warm wind and tried to forget her shabby, oil-stained workclothes. Lukas, as elegant as ever, drew the admiring glances his good looks and panache would always command. They must make an odd pair, Paula decided.

Lukas walked her to a comfortable but nondescript sandwich bar on Spuistraat, half a mile away. They sat at a window table and placed their orders before Lukas fell silent and stared outside, apparently lost in thought.

Paula watched the people in the street, too, then the other patrons inside the café, and the waiters. She might as well be alone. Self-consciousness built until she fidgeted with her silverware. Lukas Kohl was a complex, disturbing man, and Paula wished she were back in the workroom, eating pickled herring on soft rolls and laughing with the others.

"Your work is going well?" Lukas said suddenly at the same moment their food arrived.

"Very well, thank you." Paula sipped water and waited. Lukas returned his attention to the passersby. He crossed his arms tightly.

Now what?

"This was nice of you, Lukas. Unexpected. I always eat at my bench." She would have to prompt him to disclose whatever was apparently tying him in knots. She took a bite of her open-faced liverwurst sandwich. Lukas made no attempt to eat. Paula tried again. "Did Sandi enjoy yesterday? I wish you could both be at dinner with your parents and Christophe on . . ." *Nice going, Renfrew.*

"St-Giles," Lukas almost shouted, then, dropping his voice to an urgent whisper he said, "Has he spoken to you since yesterday?"

His desperation bemused Paula. "We did speak— briefly. Why?"

"When? Did he call you last night? What did he ask you?"

She ignored the first two questions. "Christophe asked me nothing. He merely said he looked forward to seeing me on Saturday. It was an unimportant conversation. He was being polite. Please, Lukas. What is it? What's going on?"

Lukas leaned back in his chair, gripped the arms so tightly that his knuckles turned white. "I knew it." He moistened his lips. "Look—listen, Paula. You shouldn't be involved in any of this. No one should. St-Giles is mixing up a bloody mess purely for his own gratification."

"Lukas. I know something about the man is eating you. But you aren't making much sense. If there's something I should know, tell me. As it is, I can't imagine how I figure in your differences with Christophe, or the way you feel about him. He's nothing to me. Why should I be a factor?"

"Damn." Lukas motioned a waiter and ordered a shot of jenever. Paula said she'd rather stick to coffee. "As I've already said," he went on, "you shouldn't be involved at all. But Christophe's obviously zeroing in on you and he must have a reason." He met her eyes squarely. "You're a beautiful woman, Paula. But Christophe has no shortage of beautiful women. I'm confused. For him to pursue you suggests he has some motive other than the obvious, yet . . . I don't know. I just don't know."

Paula blushed and sipped her coffee. Even when she did get a compliment, it was double-edged.

"I'm going to tell you some things you must promise never to repeat," Lukas said, leaning across the table. "Most particularly, you must not let Christophe know I've spoken to you. Can you agree to that?"

For an instant she considered refusing. But how could she? Her loyalty belonged to the Kohls. They'd given her so much when they owed her nothing. "I can do it," she agreed slowly.

"First . . . Thanks." His drink was delivered, and he swallowed it in one gulp. He immediately signaled for a refill.

Paula looked away. Lukas hadn't eaten, and the middle of the day wasn't the time to start tipping back glasses of neat liquor—not if he valued a clear head.

"Anyway," Lukas continued. "As I was saying. First, I want to warn you that Christophe may hope to find an ally in you—an inside track to tidbits of information on the business."

"That's ridiculous," Paula said before she could stop herself. "I mean, I'm an apprentice who works for you and your father—a nothing, at this stage. I don't know anything about the business."

"But if he starts seeing more of you, he might try to coach you into noticing—or I suppose reporting would be a better word—reporting other people's movements, chance comments, anything he could use against us."

"Lukas," Paula snapped, exasperated. "Why does Christophe want to find out things to use against you? He's your banker, right?"

"That's correct." The jenever refill arrived and promptly disappeared, as rapidly as the first drink.

"Don't bankers want their clients to be successful?" While Lukas seemed to be gaining some relief from his tension, Paula's own nerves had begun a slow burn. "Well, don't they?"

"Usually." Lukas ran a fingertip around the rim of his glass. His sandwich remained untouched. "Unless you've already hit bad times and they're looking for a way out of their obligations."

Paula stiffened. "Kohl's has hit bad times?"

"No...no, not really." He didn't meet her eyes. "The diamond market fluctuates. It's just been a bit worse for us lately. We need a small loan. Nothing unusual—an interim measure to help us through a rough spot. Within a few months we'll be as strong as we ever were. Kohl's has always been a success."

"So what's the problem? Are you suggesting Christophe's resisting the loan or something? I don't know a

thing about any of this. I ran a small store by the seat of
my pants for a few months after my father died. And I did
it with the help of a very good accountant.''

"Waiter!" Lukas shouted and Paula cringed. He jig-
gled his glass back and forth. "Christophe St-Giles isn't a
banker in the ordinary sense. Oh, it's his family's bank and
he's slated to slide into the president's chair eventually, but
he isn't a banker. The man knows the business and he's
smart, too damned smart for his own good, but he doesn't
care to settle down and work at it. He prefers to flit around
the Continent playing sleuth. He's what he terms a financial investigator. That's a polite title for insatiable snoop.
He doesn't give a damn about what happens to our firm.
Tradition, an old establishment with a great reputation…means nothing to him." He paused while the waiter
brought a bottle, poured, then left.

Paula caught curious glances from nearby tables. "Lukas," she said persuasively. "I know you're upset, but
don't you think you should eat something."

"Sure." He laughed shortly and took a bite of bread and
cheese. "There. Satisfied? Good. Christophe St-Giles is a
crusader for truth, justice, and above all, for Christophe
St-Giles. He's determined to make his mark by ensuring his
precious bank only deals with clear winners. He's going to
prove we aren't a good risk. Throw us away if he can. The
guy's a shark out to gobble up extraneous flotsam on his
family's beautiful, swelling ocean of money. Their fortune is so large you wouldn't even be able to imagine it.''

Paula shifted restlessly in her seat. Lukas was downing
more liquor, yet he still seemed in control. She prayed he
wouldn't drink any more.

"Do you believe any of this?" His abrupt question
startled her.

"I...I believe you think this is what he intends," Paula replied quietly. "But, Lukas, isn't he perhaps doing what's always done—making sure everything's okay before they hand over the money you need? Is that kind of approach routine, do you think?" She was speaking too slowly, too much like a patient adult to an obtuse child.

"No, I don't." Lukas's own thoughts absorbed him. He didn't appear to notice how she'd spoken. "I think he's out to make himself into even more of a golden boy with daddy and his uncles by showing them how astute he is. And the process is killing my father."

Paula turned icy. "Benno? Lukas, is Benno ill?"

"Yes, he's ill," Lukas replied bleakly. "Sick of fighting for what's rightfully ours. Every day I watch him get thinner. It was bad enough for him to have to ask for money in the first place. Since then he's been drawing into himself. If St-Giles had agreed without any fuss, he'd have gotten over it. It's only going to take a matter of time before we're firmly in the black. As it is, Christophe's poking around in every corner he can find—some we never knew we had. He's taken over the books and asks Father a hundred questions a day." His disgusted shove sent his plate clattering against Paula's. "That man is ruining my father's and my mother's lives. I want him out of here as quickly as possible . . . after he okays the loan.

"You shouldn't have to listen to all this, but the way he came on to you was transparent. I could be wrong, I suppose, but I had to warn you to be on the watch."

Paula made a doughy ball out of crumbs from her sandwich. Without knowing why, she believed Lukas. A stunning man like Christophe could have his pick of gorgeous women. Why bother to cultivate her, unless he thought she might prove useful?

"I'll be careful," she said simply.

"You must be more than careful." Lukas grasped her wrist painfully. "This Saturday you must watch every word that's said. Take note of questions he asks my father, and the way he responds to answers. And above all, Paula, don't let him get you alone where he can find a way to catch you off guard. Do you understand?"

She wanted no part of this. "I understand. But I don't think you have anything to worry about."

"Paula." The grip on her wrist made her wince. "Christophe was once my friend. We were closer than brothers. I look at him today and I see an executioner, the potential killer of my father. Will you take what I tell you with absolute seriousness?"

Her flesh crawled. "Yes, Lukas," she whispered. "I'll take you absolutely seriously."

"Good girl." He motioned the waiter for more jenever. "You may never meet a more dangerous man than Christophe St-Giles."

Chapter Five

Thursday of the Second Week:

Christophe zipped his windbreaker up to the neck and pushed damp hair away from his brow. He couldn't have chosen a more miserable evening for what he must do. But there really wasn't a choice, was there? Timing was everything in this dangerous game he was playing. Time was running out. In the end there would be winners and losers. He intended to be on the right team.

He spotted his quarry now, on the other side of Rokin, moving quickly. Christophe crossed and fell in behind, shielded from the man by the hurrying mass of workers on their way home.

Dodging, pressing close to the buildings, he kept the other's dark blue blazer in sight. The man carried a briefcase in one hand, a plastic sack in the other, and his step was purposeful. Christophe smiled grimly and risked drawing nearer. The chase sent adrenaline pumping through his veins. He'd spent too many hours behind a desk lately, and in boardrooms and his father's office with its smell of cigar smoke and old leather. This new challenge was what he'd needed...as long as he could guide the course of what would surely follow.

The man in the blazer slipped right, down a narrow street, and Christophe lengthened his stride. They were heading west, but where, where and to meet whom, to do what? He had his own ideas, but little proof as yet.

Awnings almost touched over gray cobbles. Signs swung above Christophe's head as he passed—Heineken, Cinzano, Coca-Cola, and the ever-present Sex Shop. This seething, open city didn't change. But he'd lost some of his familiarity with the labyrinthine streets and canals, and he could not let his man out of sight with any hope of heading him off farther on.

A surge of movement made him pause. Running children, their sport bags flying, careened around him, shouting, urging each other on. They would miss their bus. They'd be late for their game, maybe even have to forfeit.

Christophe hesitated, making room for the children's charge. When he looked ahead again, he was just in time to see the man in the blazer squeezing between vegetable stalls to enter a tiny bar.

Damn, damn. Christophe cast around until he saw a boy selling newspapers. He bought an issue and took up position outside a delicatessen. What if there was a back way out of the bar? He gritted his teeth and immediately reached for a cigarette. He could do nothing but wait, and hope. The bar was too small to allow him to go in without being noticed.

Words passed unread beneath his eyes. Every few seconds, he checked the doorway of the bar. Finally two men emerged. He shifted impatiently and glanced back at the paper. More movement in the doorway brought his attention up once more, but this patron was again the wrong one.

Christophe started. He wasn't the wrong man. Frank Lammaker had changed clothes and now wore casual tan pants and suede jacket. That accounted for the contents of the briefcase or the sack—probably the sack. Christophe ground his cigarette underfoot, feeling the flood of energy once more. Frank's briefcase was what really interested him, that and where the messenger was going. On Tuesday and Wednesday Christophe had watched Frank leave Kohl's after work, each time with the unexpected briefcase, each time alone and hurrying, and had decided to follow today if the pattern was repeated.

Frank left the bar, setting a stiff pace, threading an artful path through the tide of people, still heading west and farther from the city center. He cut along alleys and over narrow canal bridges with the skill of a man who knew his territory unerringly. Christophe was surprised when a turn brought them into Leidse Plein. In the next couple of days he must spend some time walking, and studying a map to reacquaint himself with Amsterdam's lesser-known streets.

Without looking to right or left and, Christophe hoped fervently, oblivious of his pied piper role, Frank passed the American Hotel, reached the next major street and hopped between horn-blasting cars and cursing cyclists. Christophe followed, ducking his head against loud comments and waving fists offered through open vehicle windows.

The chase became trickier now. Once away from dense crowds, Christophe heard his own footsteps like whipcracks on the concrete. He fell back slightly, but dared not stroll for fear Frank would make an unexpected move.

They walked on, past a ruined church, an unlikely sight between rows of already deserted offices. Frank's next turn was sharp. He broke into a trot, rounding the end of the church and heading into a park. Vondel Park, Christophe remembered suddenly. Years ago he'd come here on Sunday afternoons to lie on the grass with crowds of students. He also remembered the place as a maze of serpentine paths, bandstands, little bridges leading no-where in particular...and dense trees. A perfect place to meet someone privately...or to lose an unwelcome fol-lower.

Christophe was almost certain Frank didn't realize he was being tailed. At the bottom of a short flight of steps, after checking his watch, he set off more slowly, tucking the plastic bag beneath his arm, swinging his briefcase. Christophe thought he heard a whistled tune, but couldn't be sure. The mist thickened by the second, blanketing the air with dense moisture, deadening sound. The thud of his own feet on sodden turf echoed back at him.

Frank's sudden halt brought Christophe's heart into his mouth. Swiftly he slipped from the path, walked without looking back for a hundred yards, then veered into a grove of trees parallel to the trail. When he dared look sideways he saw no movement. He tipped up his head and exhaled sharply then crisscrossed between the trees, drawing closer to the path again.

With the trunk of a huge tree as a shield, he looked ahead and saw a gate leading out of the park. Frank must have been heading for this. Spreading his hands on the tree trunk, bracing his weight, Christophe calculated rapidly. If the other man had run, he could be outside by now, gone, and this charade had been for nothing. He slumped against rough bark and drove his fists into his pockets.

A piercing noise reached him. This time he definitely heard whistling. He leaned back and saw Frank come into view, heading for the gate. For the moment there was no alternative but to stay put and watch. Frank moved slowly, strolled, twirling the bag now, nonchalant.

Christophe narrowed his eyes. Maybe this young man was too convenient a suspect, but he certainly was a sus-pect. Managing a few glances at the Kohl employees personal files was taking ingenuity on Christophe's part. What he'd read in Frank's records so far was definitely interesting. Benno was either extremely generous, with a deep understanding of the hidden strengths in human nature, or he was a fool. Frank Lammaker had spent more of his teenage years in correctional institutions than anywhere else. His crimes had been petty: shoplifting, stolen bicycles and hubcaps, stolen... Christophe crossed his arms. Frank had been a small-time thief, but most big-time thiefs started out that way. And Benno knew the man's history, had written his intention to give Frank more and more responsibility to "give him a chance to prove himself. Responsibility," Benno's notation had gone on, "brings out the best in men."

Christophe wasn't so sure Benno was right in this case. The steady drone of an engine punctured the mist and he moved to the other side of the tree. *Dammit!* He started to run.

Too late.

Why hadn't he noticed the small white car at the curb?

Frank broke into a loping stride and slid into the passenger seat. Immediately the car sped away.

Christophe kicked up a muddy divot. He'd been careless. With his eyes closed, he stood, arms outstretched, a hand on each gatepost, breathing deeply of the scent of damp earth and leaf mold. There would be no way out but to repeat this procedure tomorrow. Tomorrow he'd be ready. He only hoped Frank hadn't noticed him, and that the scenario would be reenacted.

The distinctive squeal of tires snapped him to attention and he flattened against one gatepost, edged out as far as he dared. The white car had only gone to a wide spot in the street to make a U-turn. Now it sped back, and as it passed, Christophe had a clear view of the two men in-side.

For an instant, he frowned, groping for the name that went with the other face. Then it came. *Willem Bill.* Once more Kohl's messenger and Metters' page were together, this time deep in conversation . . . and alone.

"DON'T TURN ON THE LIGHTS."

The man stared briefly at the woman, then nodded and moved past her into the gloomy bedroom. "I'm wor-ried," he said quietly. "One piece of bad luck, even a tiny one, and they'll find out."

"There will be no bad luck," the woman replied. She shut the door. "We've done everything exactly as we planned, and our plans were perfect. As long as we keep our nerve, we'll get what we want. Everything we want."

"It's almost dark." The man peered through a slit be-tween the drapes. "We drop one more tonight, then wait. Did he say anything when you spoke to him last?"

"Only that he's getting closer and we should not worry. As long as the supply of stones can be kept up, we are as-sured of achieving our goal."

"The supply cannot be kept up indefinitely. We all knew that from the beginning."

The woman sighed. "We'll have four diamonds left af-ter tonight?"

"Yes. The best four." The response was curt. "He will have received nine exceptional stones, but none like these. Look. Turn on the light. No one will see."

She did as he asked then crossed the room to stand be-side him at a small desk. He reached beneath a ledge, feel-ing, until a slender drawer clicked open. Five diamonds glittered on a bed of black velvet.

"Sparklers," the woman said, her voice silken. "No wonder men die for them. Which one goes tonight?" She touched a long fingernail to the closest stone.

"That one." He picked it up and folded it carefully inside a sheet of paper. "These—" and he covered the rest "—are flawless. We may need them."

"You know so much about these things."

"I've learned my lessons well. I had to."

She smiled tightly. "Soon this will be over and we'll be in the clear. No one knows and no one ever will know.... We'll have it all."

"Right." The man's voice was less sure. "You did remember to tell him we had only nine gems?" He watched her nod, anxiety clouding his eyes. "Good, good. Then these shouldn't have to go anywhere we don't want them to go."

"Yes," she said softly, prying his hand away from the stones. "But we do have these for insurance if we need them, although—" the fingernail outlined a huge, pear-shaped diamond. "—I hope we never have to let this one go."

Without replying, he brushed her hand aside and snapped the drawer shut. "Paula Renfrew should be watched."

"Why?"

"I'm not sure. The company she keeps could mean trouble. I can't figure out exactly where she fits in—if she does—but she might just be behind our secretive friend. If she is . . ."

Rain began a steady tapping at the window. The woman laughed nervously. "Another wet walk," she said. "I hope this will be the last." In the pause that followed, they stared at each other and listened to the rain. "What made you bring up Paula Renfrew?" she asked cautiously.

"I read some things. The lady definitely has her skeletons. If she's trying to bury them, and I think she could be, she may have to be left holding the whole bundle."

"Oh, God." The woman huddled on the edge of the bed. "We've come too far to turn back now. We're winning. I know we are."

"Yes. And one way or another we'll make it all the way without anything touching us."

She drew in a deep breath. "No death, though, my dear friend. Please tell me there won't be need for that."

He looked at the folded paper in his hand. "I hope not. But, as you said, no wonder men have died for these…and women…."

Saturday of the Second Week:

Paula flopped on the bed and spread her arms wide. "I don't want to go to the damned dinner party," she said loudly to the beamed ceiling. "I don't want to worry about every word Benno says, and Anna says, and *I* say. *Damn, damn, damn.*"

She was crushing her dress, too. Hell, she wouldn't go. If she slipped over to the main house quickly, she could plead a headache and escape before Christophe arrived.

Christophe, Christophe. He fascinated her. Even this bed in the little guest house that had become so dear to her reminded her of Christophe St-Giles. He'd said he once stayed there. Now she never climbed into bed without instantly remembering he must have lain in the same spot, looking at the same ceiling. Had he always slept here alone…? She even imagined him descending the spiral stairs leading from the loft bedroom to the living room and kitchen below. Paula saw him everywhere. *Good God.* She was suffering from a sophomoric crush.

Mumbling irritably, she got up and smoothed her skirt. That was another aggravating element about this evening—she hated dressing up. Already she longed to slip back into a comfortable pair of jeans.

The clock on her bedside table read six-thirty. She'd promised to help Anna with last-minute preparations, though Paula wasn't fooled by the request. Anna would have everything under control. The older woman had simply sensed Paula's reticence over attending the dinner and had contrived a reason for her not to back out. At Paula's protest that her presence wouldn't be appropriate, Anna had cajoled, "Christophe's like family—and so are you. Of course you'll come. And it would be so nice to have a little help in the kitchen for a change."

Paula clattered down the metal stairs and let herself out into a central courtyard. The houses along the canals mostly adjoined each other. Benno and Anna's property butted with another house on one side, a wall screening an alley barely wide enough for a man, on the other. Paula's backhouse formed the fourth side of the courtyard, and she came and went through the Kohls' home.

She shivered. The last pallid wisps of gold showed above the high rooftops. The day's timid sun was slinking away, sucking with it any hint of warmth. A jacket would have been a good idea, but if she turned back she might completely lose her nerve.

Delicious smells met her when she entered the main house. Paula went first to the kitchen. The room was empty and, true to her guess, everything appeared perfectly organized for the meal.

She dithered, gathering courage.

"There you are, Paula. Good, good. We're all waiting for you." Anna Kohl breezed into the kitchen and slid a hand through Paula's arm,

"I . . . you said I could do something to help. Give me a job," Paula said hurriedly, too hurriedly. "Can I peel something . . . or . . ."

Anna's blue eyes looked unwaveringly into Paula's. "Why are you so nervous?" She tilted her head and light shone on her still-blond hair drawn back into an elegantly loose chignon. "You've already met Christophe, I understand."

"Yes," Paula said, hoping she'd hit a firm note. "We've met." What, she wondered, would Anna think if she knew how Lukas felt about Christophe?

"So why do you back away this evening? Is he so difficult to be with?"

Paula instantly blushed. "No, Anna. He's, he's . . . he's . . ." He's what, should she say? Charming, intriguing, and Lukas says he could be dangerous and could ruin your life and his? Should she tell Anna that Lukas had accused Christophe of slowly killing Benno and destroying his business, that tonight she, Paula, was supposed to listen to every word spoken and then make a report?

She felt sick.

"Ah, I see." Anna smiled gently. "I understand. Please forgive me, Paula. It must be too long since I was your age. Christophe is very attractive, isn't he, and delightful? Yes, of course. Come on, my dear, I think perhaps the appeal is mutual. He's already asked about you twice."

Smiling wanly, at a loss for words, Paula allowed Anna to lead her into the passageway and up a short flight of stairs to the living room. On the threshold she took several breaths through her mouth. The air seemed thin and this wasn't the time to hyperventilate.

She saw Benno first. He turned from a rosewood trolly where he was mixing drinks. "Paula." His haggard face showed genuine pleasure. "I was afraid you'd forgotten."

A wave of protectiveness freshened her determination and she lifted her chin. "Sorry I'm late." She wasn't, but it didn't matter. "I got too relaxed in my little nest and didn't watch the time closely enough."

"Hello, Paula. How are you?"

At the sound of Christophe's voice, she turned, concentrating on moving naturally. "Hi, Christophe. Nice to see you again. I'm fine—you?" She sounded cool, just right.

"Better now you're here."

Paula felt rather than saw Anna and Benno look at each other. She *would not* blush. "I was warned about Frenchmen," she said lightly. "Silver-tongued devils, I think the description went."

Christophe sketched an airy gesture. "We are blessed with a certain skill when it comes to words. Can I help it if charm comes naturally?"

Benno and Anna laughed. Paula kept her eyes on Christophe and saw little humor in his expression. He might be charming, but there was something else about him, something...? Dangerous would do. That's the word Lukas had used, and it fitted the aura surrounding this almost too-handsome man as well as the dark suit he wore.

Benno coughed, interrupting the heavy silence. "All right, you two. You can discuss each other's charms later. Christophe's having a martini, Paula. What would you like?"

"Nothing for now," she replied, deliberately giving Benno her full attention. "I'm sure Anna has planned wine with dinner, so I'll wait."

"Wise," Anna said. "In fact, why don't you men bring your drinks into the dining room. Dinner's ready and I shall be insufferable if my soufflé collapses."

Christophe came to Paula's side as they crossed the marble entry hall behind the Kohls. He settled a hand at her waist—a firm hand that radiated heat through the thin fabric of her dress. By the time they'd covered the short distance to the dining room table, her nerves felt filleted.

Anna presided over the meal with practiced efficiency, whisking away plates, replacing each dish with the next delicious course. Paula wasn't hungry, but she made herself eat.

"Everything is perfect, Anna," Christophe commented as chocolate mousse was served in delicate stemmed dishes. "But why isn't Madeleine helping you?"

Glass clattered on china. Anna barely missed tipping the dessert she set in front of Christophe. "Madeleine?"

He looked up at her. "Madeleine's still with you, isn't she?"

"I . . . yes, yes. She's in Haarlem for the weekend."

Paula glanced at Benno and found him staring back. She looked at her hands in her lap. It was beginning. The questioning she'd been told to expect. Christophe knew Madeleine still worked here. Lukas had told him. But why would Anna lie about her housekeeper? Surely there could be no harm in Christophe's showing interest in the woman.

"Yes." Benno's voice was too loud. "Madeleine's visiting her sister's son, I think. She left yesterday."

Madeleine had been in the courtyard at three that afternoon. She'd admired Paula's tulips and talked about the new television Frank had bought her and that she looked forward to watching this evening.

"She's been with you a long time," Christophe said between mouthfuls of mousse. "Her son works for you now I see, Benno." He half rose from his chair while Anna sat again.

Paula lifted her own spoon at the same time as she noticed Benno's expression change and an unnatural pallor replace the color in his cheeks. He swallowed uncomfortably. It suddenly occurred to Paula that Benno and Anna had lied about Madeleine to spare her the questions that Christophe was probably about to subject them to.

"Frank, isn't it?" Christophe persisted.

"Frank, yes," Anna put in. "A good boy. He's been the man of the family since he was fourteen. Very responsible, isn't he, Benno?"

"I trust him implicitly," Benno said tonelessly. "He is our messenger."

"Yes." Christophe turned his fine brown eyes on Paula. "Paula and I saw him at the American Hotel on Monday. Lukas seemed surprised."

"Surprised?"

Benno's question hung in the air for several seconds.

"Mmm. He seemed to think Frank's friends outclassed him. And one of the men he was with disturbed Lukas." Christophe frowned quizzically at Paula. "What was that man's name—the one who's a page with, ah, with the other firm?"

She blinked, shifting her spoon back and forth. Kohl's employees weren't supposed to fraternize with Metter's people. She was certain Christophe knew as much, yet he was deliberately headed in that direction, steadily closing a net around Frank Lammaker. Why? Indecision thickened her tongue. Lying was out of the question, yet if she mentioned Willem Bill, Benno could become angry with Frank.

"Paula," Christophe prompted. "You remember. You told Lukas who that was."

"No," she said at last, inspired. "Sandi did. Someone called Otis, I think—a painter."

Christophe's lips came together, drawn down at the corners. She felt he could see inside her head. He definitely knew she was skirting the issue.

"You're right," he said smoothly. "Sandi did say that. But I meant the other man, from Metter's, is it? Yes, Metter's. You said he was a page named . . . ?"

Give up, she thought miserably. "Willem Bill."

"That's it," Christophe responded heartily, slapping the table.

Anna jumped, spilling the remnants of her wine and Benno instantly went to her aid, mopping with his napkin. Paula noted that as he leaned across his wife, he squeezed her arm quickly.

Slowly, inexplicably, irritation gnawed at Paula. She didn't know what line she'd expected Christophe to take. Certainly not a blatant attempt to put Frank Lammaker in a bad light with Benno. The effort seemed small-minded and pointless, unworthy of a man of Christophe's standing.

Benno finished tending the linen tablecloth and subsided into his chair once more. His dessert remained untouched while he faced Christophe, a fixed smile on his lips. "I don't know why Lukas should be surprised to see Frank at the American. Young people have always gathered there. Even in my time we did. Paula—" he turned to her and his smile softened "—I remember Anna and I and your—" He stopped abruptly, his mouth working slightly, before he pushed away from the table and stood. "Anna and I used to go there," he finished lamely. "Stay where you are, my love. I'll pour coffee.

He'd been going to say something about her father. Paula was certain "father" was the word Benno had choked on. She couldn't take any more of this. For what it was worth, she'd tell Lukas about Christophe's reference to Frank. If more information was needed, Lukas must find a way to get it himself. Let him sit through a tense meal like this. She had to get out.

"Anna," she said, trying to sound calm. "I'm sure you and Benno have things you'd like to talk with Christophe about alone. I think I'll take a walk before it gets too dark."

"No," Benno said quickly. "Absolutely not, Paula. Amsterdam is no place for a lovely young woman to walk alone at night."

She got up. "I'll be careful, I promise. I won't be long and I won't stray from the main streets."

Anna started to protest, but Paula was already backing away. In the hall she hesitated, wondering if she should take time to go for her coat. She did have to get out, to walk and think. Her long-sleeved dress and a brisk enough pace would keep her warm, she decided, opening the heavy front door. She closed it behind her and ran down the worn stone steps to the sidewalk.

A light wind snatched at her full skirt, swirling it around her knees. Paula crossed to the canalside. Herengracht was one of the only major canals where there were still privately owned homes. In the dusk, shadows of the narrow, tippy buildings wavered across rippling gray water.

Paula was glad to be in the fresh air. She loved this old city. Walking faster, she swung her arms and wished she wore pants and tennis shoes. Tonight she'd like to run, to forget all the barely restrained anxiety she'd left behind in that dining room.

Footsteps sounded behind her, rapid footsteps that soon become the even clip of someone running. She quelled the urge to look back, concentrating instead on keeping her own pace steady.

When a hand clamped her shoulder and spun her around she gasped, disoriented, and opened her mouth to shout.

Christophe smiled down at her, his eyes black and glinting in the coming night's light. "Why the hurry, Paula?"

Chapter Six

Paula's heart did nasty things. Deep breathing only increased her light-headedness.

"I'm sorry." Christophe bent closer. "I frightened you. Dammit, I'm sorry."

"You didn't frighten me," Paula managed, then laughed and pressed her chest. "You only made me feel I was going to die right here and now."

Christophe put a hand behind her neck. "I should have shouted instead of leaping at you like that. I was afraid I'd lose sight of you, so I just ran. Forgive me?" He had to feel her tremble. She hoped he wouldn't guess fright wasn't the main cause.

"Consider yourself forgiven," she said, inching away. "I suppose Anna and Benno sent you after me. They worry too much."

"Nobody sent me. I wanted to come." He rubbed her nape lightly. "But Anna was tired. She's probably glad to get rid of me early. I said I'd keep an eye on you and make sure you got home safely."

Paula wished his voice, the flawless English spoken with an incredibly sexy French accent, had no effect on her. She wished she didn't like the idea of Christophe wanting to join her, that she could summon a retort about how capable she was of getting herself home safely. "You're very kind, but I don't think I'm in mortal danger on a busy street like this" was the best she could muster. She wanted to see the look in his eyes—clearly.

"Young women should not walk city streets alone at night. Any city. Particularly streets as notoriously, ah, shall we say, colorful, as Amsterdam's?"

"But—"

"But," he broke in. "But this is a 'busy' street, Paula? Let's look around, shall we? You and I are the only humans in sight. One cannot know if there are others we do not see."

She shivered convulsively. *"Don't give him a chance to get you on your own,"* Lukas had warned. "I'll be fine." Her voice sounded as unsure as she felt.

"I think not." Christophe turned her around, guiding her south along the canal. "And you're cold. Here." He began to take off his jacket.

"No!" She held his forearm. "I'm fine, really."

Christophe rubbed her fingers, then gently pried them loose. "You're not fine, woman. Not fine at all." He finished taking off the jacket and draped it around her. "You shot out of that dining room as if you couldn't bear to be there a moment longer. If you'd been thinking rationally, and simply wanted what you said you wanted, a walk, you'd have taken the time to get a coat. Want to let me in on the problem? Was something said to upset you? Did I say or do something?"

She was out of her depth. "Nothing was said. I thought I might be in the way," she lied. There was no alternative but to lie.

Christophe appeared to consider. Paula waited, listened to water lapping concrete, concentrated on walking over the cobbles in her high heels. Caution was everything. She'd promised Lukas that Christophe would never know of their lunchtime conversation earlier in the week.

Finally Christophe said, "You weren't in the way, but good, I'm glad you aren't upset," and put an arm across her back to hold her upper arm. A long sigh moved his chest against her shoulder. "So we'll enjoy our walk. It's a beautiful evening and I haven't done this in too long."

Done what in too long? Paula wondered. Walked through the night with his arm around a woman? She doubted that was what he meant. "I love all the little lights on the bridges," she murmured and thought how much more romantic they seemed when she was held against the muscular side of an attractive man.

Christophe didn't reply. They walked on. Occasionally he gave her arm a gentle squeeze, but she sensed his preoccupation. Was he formulating his next line of questioning?

"We don't have to go on." Paula glanced up at him. "You'll be the one who's cold soon." His white shirt showed luminous, the top button undone, his tie loosened. "Let's get back," she insisted. Forgetting discretion in this setting, with this man, would be too easy.

"I'm a hot-blooded animal," he responded easily.

For an instant, Paula contemplated how hot-blooded Christophe might be under his cool Continental exterior. The pictures she formed, a complicated mix of how he would react when angry... what he might be like as a lover... made her glad he couldn't see her face. Hiding emotion had never been her strong suit.

"Paula," he said when the silence had lasted too long. "*Is* there anything you'd like to tell me... or ask me?"

Someone had sucked the oxygen out of the night breeze. She laughed and hated the sound. Why couldn't she just forget Christophe's real reason for being in Amsterdam?

For tonight, why couldn't she pretend they'd met under different circumstances, lose herself in the power that emanated from him, in the snap his energy lent to the air? He turned her on emotionally and physically. What she felt now was unique in her experience and she wanted it—all of it.

His hand moved downward to her elbow. "Is there something, Paula?"

Illusion had almost pulled her in. "No." Paula lifted her chin, expanding her lungs deliberately. "Nothing at all, Christophe." She glanced at his hazy profile, hesitating a moment, catching a hint of the subtle scent of his after-shave. *Be careful,* the inner voice reminded her too distantly. "What could I possibly want to say, or ask?"

She'd hoped to turn the tables on him. Christophe's relaxed laugh let her know he'd never be readily caught off guard. "I can't know what's in your mind, Paula, can I? But I can feel when a woman—or man—is uncomfortable. You became disturbed at the dinner table and I wondered why, if I could help. Forget it, please. A flight of fancy on my part perhaps. Have you been on the canals yet?"

His rapid change of topic surprised Paula. "Yes . . . no. You mean *on*, in a barge?"

"Uh-huh. I haven't taken a cruise here since I first visited with my parents. Let's do it. We're almost at a terminal." He was already steering her toward a brightly lit booth at the end of a dock. On one side swayed a glass-enclosed barge.

"Wait." Paula hung back, pulling Christophe to a halt. "It would take too long. Anna and Benno are bound to wonder where I am."

"You're with me." He smiled down at her. "I told them I'd look after you—" She could see his eyes clearly now and the smile didn't reach them. "And I will look after you, I promise."

Mesmerized, carried along by a potent blend of foreboding and fascination, Paula let him take her hand. What could happen to her on a little barge trip? They'd look at the sights, she'd field whatever course of interrogation he might be planning, then he'd take her home and say goodnight. The end. Or would it be?

She was uptight, Christophe decided, too uptight for a woman who insisted nothing was wrong. Her hand was stiff and icy in his. He had to go slowly with her or she'd shy away and clam up completely. He bought two tickets for the cruise, tucking her hand into his elbow while he fished for money. Somehow he was going to lull her, coach her into letting go. Then, if he was lucky, he might get at the truth about Paula Renfrew.

They walked wordlessly down the shifting wooden dock, and he helped her board the craft. "Go all the way to the back," he instructed automatically. "The view's better." She passed him and he smelled her perfume—light, gardenia or something. He looked down on the top of her head. The black hair, whipped into curls by the breeze, had a burnished sheen. God, he didn't want her to be involved in cheating the Kohls.

"This is something." She slid into a bench seat and he sat close beside her. "The skyline looks almost on fire from here."

"Yes," he said. He must keep her talking. "Good Lord, I just had a thought." Turning sideways, he hitched up a knee and held it with both hands.

Paula raised her brows expectantly. "What? You look… What's so funny?"

"Don't you ever tell Lukas or Peter we did this."

Her mouth tightened. "I hadn't planned to." She sounded frosty, Christophe noted, and immediately wondered why. "What makes you think Lukas or Peter would be interested in our taking a trip on the canals?" she added.

Could Lukas have warned her to be careful? Or Benno? Damn their asinine hides if they had. Christophe made himself smile. "Paula," he began. "I worked hard to become a transplanted Amsterdammer. Natives don't behave like tourists. If those two found out about this they'd never let me live it down."

She stared for an instant before her features softened and she grinned. "I have you in my power." She shook a finger at him. "Never give the opposition a weapon they can use against you."

Keeping the smile on his lips became harder. "And I thought you were a friend, Paula Renfrew. Or at least a friend in the making." Her comment could have been a meaningless figure of speech. But he didn't imagine the sensation that they were feinting around each other. He was sure she knew more than she should about him and his reason for being here.

Her mumbled "Mmm" gave no hint of what she was thinking. She stared through the barge's curved rear window. A swinging overhead lantern played shadows across her face. Her expression had become distant.

With a grinding shudder, the barge pulled away from its moorings and swung to the center of the canal. Paula peered upward. He looked at her face, then at the smattering of stars in a dark sky turned golden around the illuminated roofs of buildings, the spires and domes of churches and towers. Too bad they weren't like the other couples aboard, out to enjoy the night—and each other.

He spread an arm along the seat back behind her. She shifted slightly, but he pretended not to notice.

"Christophe." Her eyes, when she faced him, were deeply shadowed. "You said you stayed in Benno and Anna's backhouse before. I'm sorry to put you out of a bed. Peter mentioned a houseboat. Is that where you're staying?"

"Yes, it is."

"Really. Where?" Her interest was genuine.

"Oh, not far from here. On Singel. I can see the Mint Tower from my bunk and walk to the flower market in a few minutes. It's a great spot. The barge belongs to Peter. Lukas and I helped him renovate it years ago."

"Peter's?" She tilted her head. "Peter has an apartment in Lukas and Sandi's house. What would he do with a houseboat?"

"He used to live there and have his photographic studio there, too. Now he rents out the boat. Fortunately for me, it was available when I decided to visit this time. Would you like to see it? We could get off at the flower market and walk back."

Not subtle enough, he thought wryly. Her reaction had shown instant disapproval. "Not tonight, Christophe," she said without inflection. "I'd like to get off at Bloemenmarket, anyway, and head home. But I'd better not be too much later."

"Don't you trust me?" *Damn.* He shouldn't have tried that tack until he was more sure of his subject.

Paula met his eyes squarely. "Is there some reason why I shouldn't trust you, Christophe?"

"Of course not. I was being flippant." He'd have to give her that one... and be more subtle in future. "You lived in New Jersey. I don't think you told me the name of the town."

"Bayonne."

"And you gave up New Jersey and . . . Bayonne . . . for Amsterdam and strangers. An unusual choice."

"Why?" she asked sharply. "You chose your course in life, didn't you?"

He was taken aback by her vehemence. "Yes," he agreed, studiously keeping his voice level. "To a certain extent. But I always knew what I wanted to do."

"So did I." She laughed shortly. "I just wasn't born as directly into it as you were."

A chink had appeared in her armor and he lunged for it. "You were, in a way. You said your father was here before you and left. You followed in his footsteps. Why did he decide to give up?"

Her knuckles whitened where she clutched the lapels of his jacket across her breasts. "I never knew," she said tonelessly. "And once I realized he'd rather not discuss the subject, I stopped asking."

She sounded so convincing. He wanted to be convinced, but he couldn't be, not so easily. "Perhaps you'll find out one day, by accident. And perhaps when you do you'll tire of all this and decide to go home like he did."

"Never!" Was that fervor in her eyes, or anger? "This is my home now," she went on. "Everything that matters to me is here. There's no one to go back to in the States anymore."

His breath quickened. Instinctively he knew her passion could be her undoing. Making her angry might be the key. "Everything that matters?" He pulled the corners of his mouth down. "Why would a lovely woman, who could undoubtedly find something exciting to do with her life— something lucrative—choose such a dull career?" He ran his eyes over her slowly, knowing she'd see him assessing her.

''Diamonds aren't dull.'' Her cheeks were flushed now. ''Why would such an attractive man choose a career in a dusty field like banking?''

Breaking her down wouldn't be easy. She was too mature, too sure of herself. ''What can I say?'' He waved his free hand. ''You're right, of course. We all find adventure and stimulation in different ways.''

''I grew up watching my father work. He designed one-of-a-kind pieces and then threw away the setting molds. And all the time he talked about the diamonds he'd worked on here while I learned and waited for my chance—this chance.'' Her fingers dug deep into the fabric of his jacket. ''Dad's favorite piece was a marquis, six flawless carats for the sixth birthday of a European count's daughter...'' She'd averted her face.

Every muscle in Christophe's body tensed. *A marquis cut, six carats, flawless.* The exact description of the gem stolen shortly before Michael Renfrew's rapid departure from Amsterdam. Had he loved the stone so much because it had become his ticket to independence... and because he'd done the impossible: stolen it successfully?

''One day,'' Paula continued very softly, ''people will come thousands of miles, to have *me* turn their *dull* diamonds, as you seem to regard them, into perfect treasures. My name will be known in those quiet rooms around the world where people discuss who's the best finisher for their diamond.''

Her intensity threw him off for a moment. She sounded honestly involved in her craft for its own sake. But that wouldn't fit with his suspicions. He collected his wits. ''Aha.'' His voice betrayed nothing of what he felt. He smoothed away strands of hair from her cheek. ''I begin to see, I think. Paula Renfrew isn't a simple woman, at all.

She covets fame in her own way—obscure fame, but fame nevertheless. I like that.''

"You like ambition. You relate to what you perceive as your own kind,'' she retorted, then quickly lowered her lashes. "I'm sorry. That was snippy and uncalled for. How long do you expect to be in Amsterdam?''

Was she asking because she cared, Christophe wondered, or because someone else had fed her questions to which they'd like answers? Benno had been keen for him to come after her tonight. "No idea yet,'' he said. "How about you?'' Had this outing been a trap he'd fallen into?

"We've already covered that. I'm a resident now. What do you hope to accomplish while you're here?''

He knew he must appear impassive. Someone *had* primed Paula. "This is a routine visit.''

"Do you spend most of your time in Zurich, or making...routine visits?''

"My duties vary.'' At any other time he might have enjoyed the verbal fencing match. Tonight it made him edgy. He must stay with the subject of her father. "You ran the store after your father died. You didn't enjoy that?''

She opened her mouth, then turned away, but not before he saw the sheen in her eyes. "Not alone,'' she muttered. He had to strain to hear the words.

"You still miss your father?''

"More than ever, sometimes.''

Enough to want vengeance against people he may have said persecuted him? "Aren't you afraid being here may dredge up information that could prove painful?'' He held his breath.

"Like what?'' She swung to face him, staring hard. "He loved being here. Why should anything about that be painful?''

"Simple association can sometimes be overwhelming. That's all I meant." This time he looked away. He was hitting a nerve, repeatedly, but not getting any positive information.

Across the aisle, a couple kissed. Christophe could see the white arch of the woman's neck beneath the man's tanned hand, their lips moving leisurely back and forth, their flickering lashes. He pulled his arm from behind Paula and leaned forward to rest both elbows on his knees. Good God, he was shielding the couple from her view. Why? What was the matter with him?

His thigh touched hers and he felt her muscle tense, but she didn't move away. He glanced at her. Her features were set, her expression remote. A guide's voice droned on about the sights they passed. Christophe barely heard and knew Paula was also removed from her surroundings, except from him. They were acutely aware of each other.

"We aren't exactly burning verbal trails, are we?" he said when silence seemed to gape between them. "I make you uncomfortable. I knew it from the minute you walked into Benno and Anna's dining room."

"You were—are—wrong. I haven't had a lot of experience with social gatherings, that's all. I never know exactly what to say."

He cupped his chin and studied the shadows her eyelashes made on her rounded cheeks, the soft lines of her mouth. What he wanted to believe couldn't be allowed to matter now. His first priority must be to do what must be done with the Kohls' business, anything else was a distant second.

"We can get off at the next stop if you still want to see the flower market."

She sat straighter. "I'd love to. I went there in the daytime, but never at night with all the lights on."

"You're in love with beautiful things, aren't you?" He hadn't known he was going to say that.

A faint blush touched her cheeks and she said, "Yes," quietly. Her intensely blue eyes were on his mouth while her own lips parted slightly. His gut contracted, and he didn't know if he was glad or sad to feel the thump of the barge against the dock.

They climbed ashore on the other side of a bridge from the market. The street was crowded and noisy, the air pungent with a heady concoction of scents: spicy Indonesian food, the canal's mixture of oil and fumes, and, faintly, flowers.

"Stay close," Christophe instructed, wrapping an arm around her once more. She felt so good, so right. Duty could be a difficult son of a bitch. "Tell me more things you like. Paintings, theater, music? Keep talking to me. You make me nervous when you're silent."

She stood still. "You? Nervous? Come on, Christophe."

His jacket had fallen open. It took willpower to do no more than glance at the rise and fall of her breasts beneath her silk dress. In future he'd steer clear of cases involving beautiful women. "Well, maybe not nervous." He almost choked on the words. "But tell me what you like, anyway."

They walked slowly while she considered. "I like music, Dixieland jazz mostly. And I love to dance. Satisfied? I expect you hate both."

Christophe laughed heartily and it felt good. She was undeniably charming when she made one of her definite stands and then waited for an argument.

"What's so funny?" She kept a straight face.

He led her across the bridge to the first of the barges housing the flower market. "You." He matched her serious expression, then started to laugh again. "For a generally reserved lady, you can be pretty feisty. I don't hate jazz—or dancing. And I'd *love* dancing, as you put it, with you." He couldn't believe he'd said it, not Christophe St-Giles, not the man who never spoke without thinking first.

Paula's quick appraisal was wary. His open admission of more than a mild interest in her had broken through her guard.

"Smell the flowers?" he asked lamely.

"I smell garbage in the canal," she replied flatly.

He suppressed a smile. He liked her, truly liked her, and he wished he didn't. "Okay, keep those feet of yours firmly on the ground if you like. *I* smell flowers." Ahead, strings of lights sent shards of glittering color from the Bloemenmarket barges, across oil-coated water. For the rest of this evening he was going to let go and enjoy himself.

A passerby bumped Paula closer to him, and she made no attempt to draw away again. "Don't Amsterdammers ever go to bed?" she said breathlessly.

"Not if they can help it." He squeezed her arm. "That dress of yours deserves a flower—something to show off the color. What do you call that?"

She shrugged, suddenly relaxed and smiling, young. "I'm not sure. Aquamarine, maybe?"

"Trust you to come with a gemstone color. What kind of flower would you like?"

The lightness of the moment was infectious. She smiled, and he knew she'd fallen under the evening's charm. "I— you choose. I wouldn't know what to have. No one ever bought me flowers."

Her guilelessness made his heart tighten. "Right." He wanted to say many men should have bought her flowers, that men were fools, and that, nevertheless, he was glad they were.

He led her between stalls and across gently sloping boards to a tented barge. "Orchids . . . ? I don't think so. Too severe. I've never been big on roses. A gardenia?" He raised a waxen, ivory bloom to his face, then held it while she bent to smell. "Your perfume. Perfect."

She met his eyes, a little crease between her brows. He'd started out this evening giving her mixed messages. For the past half hour the message had been pretty straightforward—intense interest and close awareness of everything about her. She was trying to decide what to think. But maybe that wasn't all bad. So was he.

The bloom paid for, they returned to the sidewalk and he grasped her shoulders firmly. "Stand still while I pin this on." He lowered his head, blessing fortune for a chance to hide his face, and slid two fingers beneath the neck of her dress. Her skin was warm, smooth. Her breast rose and fell harder than it should. His own body's reaction was unmistakable.

He finished with the pin. "There." Now he had to meet her eyes. "Lovely." And he knew he wasn't talking purely about the flower. This evening hadn't gone the way he intended.

"Thank you."

Christophe barely heard what she said. A row of shops ran parallel to the flower barges, a narrow strip of rough concrete dividing the two. He felt more than saw a movement in a shop doorway.

He pulled Paula against him so hard that she gasped. "Put your arms around me," he ordered. "Pretend. Pretend anything you like but keep your head down and don't move."

"What is it?" she whispered into his shirt. "You're hurting me."

"Do this my way or one of us may end up really hurt. But perhaps that's what you want." Dimly, he cursed himself for the remark, but he had seen a figure, and the glint of something shiny. Whether or not she'd set him up, his first instinct was survival. Paula was rigid against him, trembling violently. "We're going to start walking. Keep your face turned to me. And if you shout you'll wish you hadn't."

She did as he instructed, moving with him, clinging like an absorbed lover. Only he could feel how weak she'd become, the way her body sagged slightly as if she might fall. He gripped her tightly. The shadow in the doorway moved, too, out and along the sidewalk. He was dressed in dark, probably black, clothing, a hat pulled low over his eyes—a tall, slender man who was almost invisible, except for the glint by his right thigh.

"Christophe, please." Paula's voice was muffled. "Let me go. Say something."

Let her go to leave a clear field for her friend with the knife, Christophe thought bitterly. Never. "Keep quiet," he ordered. "You're loving every minute of this, remember?" Why hadn't he seen it coming? He'd walked right into her trap. Why did this have to be the moment the crowds chose to thin? The only living souls he saw were a couple strolling ahead, two stall owners deep in conversation... and the dark shape slipping past shop windows.

If he could just make it back to the corner. Buses rumbled past there, and he could see clusters of people.

The figure darted from cover and Christophe tensed, ready for action. He started pushing Paula out of the way at the same moment as a crowd of teenagers barreled from a tavern onto the sidewalk, cutting the man off from

Christophe. He broke into a run, dragging Paula with him until they reached the corner and a bus just pulling out. He leaped, half carrying her, and made it aboard a second before the doors closed.

His breath came in gasps as he stared through the window at a man who pulled his cap farther over his eyes.

"Christophe." Paula held on to his arm and his shirt-front, no trace of color in her face. "Christophe, what's the matter? What happened out there?"

Either she didn't know a thing about what had happened, or she was an incredible performer. "I'm not sure. Probably nothing." He pushed her into a seat and sat beside her. Silence and a chance to think were all he wanted.

"You said something about what *I* wanted. I—"

"Let it go. I think we were being followed, that's all. I overreacted." He watched her face closely. Again she showed only the fear she had a right to show. He sank back and tried to relax. "It was just one of those things, I'm sure. Probably a potential pickpocket sizing up a couple who looked like good targets. Forget it."

But pickpockets didn't wait for crowds to disperse before they struck. Pickpockets loved crowds. And they rarely used knives.

Chapter Seven

Tuesday of the Third Week:

She was fed up. Absolutely, totally sick of the pointless circles her wits had scurried around since Saturday night.

Paula let herself out of the backhouse into the walled courtyard and took several gulps of early morning air. The day promised to be cool, like yesterday. Her tulips were still tightly closed, hiding, the way she was beginning to wish she could hide, at least from her own thoughts and feelings.

Damn Christophe St-Giles and his on-again, off-again attitude, his constant innuendos. And damn the way she couldn't forget him for more than a few minutes at a time.

She pressed her fingers to her face. More than two days had passed since she'd laid eyes on the man, and she still felt the cool firm lips he'd used—yes, used was the right word—on each of her cheeks a few seconds before he left her, utterly confused, at the Kohls' front door. *"Good night, Paula,"* he'd said, bowing faintly as he took back his jacket. *"Thank you for an interesting evening."* There had been no emphasis on the word "interesting," but Paula didn't miss his choice of an adjective, or the formality in his manner. What the hell did he mean by "interesting," anyway? And what had all his running and pushing and oblique accusations meant? On the way home she'd repeatedly begged him to tell her what had spooked him. He'd said, *"Forget it,"* so many times that she'd felt like wringing his self-possessed neck. Boy, she was sick of everything.

She let herself into the main house. Sunday had been a misery of waiting and worrying, trying to sort out the events of the previous evening, hoping in vain that Christophe would call or show up. Yesterday was worse. First she'd suffered Lukas's interrogation about Saturday, then Victor's explosion when she'd made a tiny mistake, and, finally, an emotion-charged episode with Kersten Gouda whom Paula had found crying in the staff room. The only bright spot had been her lunchtime expedition to buy the bicycle she'd coveted for days.

The bicycle, sleek and black, waited for Paula now in the basement stairwell of the Kohls' house. The need to gain confidence on her new steed was Paula's main reason for setting out for work at seven, an hour before she normally left. The streets shouldn't be too crowded yet. She also intended to arrive early to try talking with Kersten alone once more. The woman was troubled, but Paula hadn't been able to find out why, and she wanted to help.

Struggling, grunting, she hauled the machine to the kitchen level of the house. The Dutch penchant for saving ground footage by building upward, floor upon floor, might be charming to look at, quaint to the foreign eye; it was a pain when the fear of theft forced one to keep a heavy bicycle in the basement.

Halfway up the flight to the hall, Paula stalled, leaning against the wall. Good Lord, she thought, she was scared to death of riding this thing. "Onward," she ordered herself firmly. "If Amsterdammers can risk their limbs every day and manage to live, so can you, Renfrew."

She was puffing by the time she reached the entry hall. She needed this bike for more reasons than one. If she didn't get more exercise, her body would fall apart, anyway.

Paula had a hand on the front door when she heard a muffled sound from the living room. A clink, then shuffling…and something else. Soft crying? With one toe, she gently flipped out the bicycle stand, leaned the machine to one side and tiptoed closer to the living room. Madeleine didn't arrive this early. The Kohls rarely came downstairs before eight.

But someone was crying.

The clink came again, the sound of china on china, and Paula smelled fresh coffee. She approached the door and heard another sob. Anna was crying and drinking coffee when she should still be in bed. Paula's palms sweated. She couldn't leave not knowing what was wrong, yet she couldn't barge in on a woman who might resent the intrusion.

"Anna." Benno's voice, firm and consoling, startled Paula, and she took a step backward. For an instant she hesitated, then turned away. The couple's problems were their own affair. They would only be embarrassed if they knew she'd overheard. Not that she understood the stream of Dutch Benno used.

"Speak in English, Benno," Anna said clearly.

The effect of the request was to electrify Paula. She glanced quickly over her shoulder, expecting to find Benno and Anna staring at her. But the living room door still rested slightly open against its catch, a rim of light outlining the edge.

Paula stood motionless, scarcely breathing, waiting for them to call her and wondering what she would say when they did.

Benno spoke in Dutch once more.

"Madeleine may get here early," Anna replied in a shaky voice. "Use English, please, Benno. Just in case she hears us talking. She mustn't know any of this."

"Yes, yes, of course." Benno's reply was fainter. He must have moved to the other side of the room. "I don't know how much longer this will go on, my love, you have to try to be strong . . . for my sake."

Paula relaxed slightly. They didn't know she was there. But she was afraid to move. She wished she could materialize, bicycle beside her, on the sidewalk. Maybe creating lots of noise as if she'd just entered the hall would be best. She opened her mouth to call good morning, then couldn't bring herself to make a sound.

"Everything will work out, Anna. You'll see." Benno's voice became louder, and his footsteps. He was pacing. "Christophe is a good man. He wants what's best for us."

"Are you so sure?" Anna's sharpness surprised Paula.

"I have to be," Benno said. "If I could only convince him I'm right. Philip Metter is tied up in all of this—I know it. But Christophe keeps hounding me for more and more information about our people. He doesn't say if he's found out anything, or if he suspects someone specific, but I know he thinks the criminal is inside Kohl's."

Anna began to cry again, very softly. "Can't we send Christophe home? Please, Benno, tell him we don't want the loan anymore. Tell him we'll manage without it."

"Even if Christophe were the kind of man who could be sent anywhere, and he's not, I can't tell him I don't want the loan anymore because we can't manage without it."

Benno sounded desperate. "And before you suggest it, no other bank will look at us now."

"So what will happen? Oh, Benno, I can't bear what may happen."

"Shh. The thefts have stopped. We've had no complaints in five weeks. Whoever did this thing got what they wanted, whether it was simply the thirteen priceless gems they took or a chance to ruin our reputation. If the plan was to finish us, they won't succeed. Christophe wants full access to the personnel files and all our records. I'm going to give him everything—put our future totally in his hands. Any questions he asks, I'll answer honestly. Lukas must do the same. If we want to survive, we can't go on protecting our people from Christophe's scrutiny. We can trust him to be fair. I believe that. He'll rule out our employees as suspects because they aren't guilty. Then he'll have to look elsewhere. I don't expect him to prove anything except the innocence of Kohl's staff. When he's done that, I believe he'll approve the loan and our enemies will give up."

Anna sniffed. "How can you be sure there won't be more thefts?"

"From now on, Lukas or I will watch the stones packed and go with Frank to make deliveries personally, as it was done in my father's time."

"Then it will be as I feared," Anna sobbed. "Christophe will read the files. Then he will see you policing Frank. He'll know...think he knows..."

"Anna," Benno said patiently. "There is no alternative. And there is just the possibility that Frank did have something to do with our trouble. Not deliberately, but he's young, he talks. You heard that he's friendly with someone from Metter's. He could have given information without realizing—"

"No!" Anna shouted. "Not Frank. I know Frank had nothing to do with this, but Christophe will think otherwise. He'll read all those...those things from long ago and start to question Frank. And then...and then... Madeleine's Frank will run just like—" The rest of the sentence was lost in strangled noise.

Paula felt frozen; her hands had never been so cold. There had been thefts, and the resulting loss was great enough to threaten Kohl's survival. And Frank was suspected of being involved, and Metter's. Lukas's interest in Frank at the American Hotel made sense now, deadly clear sense. And the way Christophe made sure Benno knew Frank and Willem Bill were friends. She needed air, desperately.

"I won't let anything happen to Frank," Benno was saying. "I trust him, too, remember. I just wanted you to know the way Christophe's mind could work. We have to worry far more about our finishers. Someone made those copies of the stolen gems and they were good copies, Anna, so very good. If I know Christophe, finding that craftsman is on the top of his list. In the same way, keeping our invaluable artists happy is on the top of *my* list. I must try to make sure he doesn't offend their sense of honor."

Copies? Paula struggled to piece together what she was hearing. Copies were made of diamonds that disappeared. For what purpose?

"Benno," Anna began querulously. "Does Christophe think Paula's involved? Is that why he wanted to know so much about her before she arrived on Saturday? He did make sure we realized she was familiar with Metter's page."

In the silence that followed, Paula reached to brace herself against the banister. "*...or one of us may end up really* *hurt. But maybe that's what you want.''* Christophe's strange remarks the other night became significant. He *did* think she was guilty of something. And he also thought she was a part of whatever had sent him running through the night.

"Paula is talented," Benno said distinctly. "She also arrived in Amsterdam a few months before the low-grade copies rather than the real thing started showing up with our customers. I know what he thinks. He believes she could have something to do with planning the thefts. We spoke yesterday, and in that way he has of saying without saying, he suggested as much. He even explored whether she could have been the one who'd made the substitute pieces. Ridiculous. I told him she's good, but only nine, almost ten months good, four years away from completing her apprenticeship—"

Paula covered her ears. She must get out of here. Blindly she grabbed the bike and slid open the front door. Once outside, she closed it again, slowly, carefully, and stood on the wide top step trying desperately to collect herself. She would find Christophe St-Giles, confront him with his mad theories, make him agree to grant the loan and go away.

City noises had already begun. Trucks on their way to early deliveries made the street tremble. Through open basement traps, Paula heard the familiar sound of the water that sloshed between the pillared foundations of many canal-side buildings. A street-cleaner whistled while he pushed his broom, and a woman knelt on the steps of the house next to Benno and Anna's, scrubbing vigorously.

Fueled by resolution, Paula set off, wobbling wildly at first. When she'd said she hadn't learned to ride a bike she'd been almost honest. Her father had been too busy to take time to teach her, but her brother had occasionally held the saddle of his big racing model while Paula pedaled furiously, undaunted by numerous falls. Today, fury tinged with undercurrents of indecision took her mind off her inexperience. She pumped her legs as enthusiastically as she had with Grant all those years ago, though with less concentration, and the result was gratifying. She'd be a pro at this in no time.

Soon the exercise and the air rushing past her face felt good, calming. She must proceed cautiously, after all. An impulsive reaction to what she'd accidentally learned could be disastrous. If she wasn't very careful—and wily—Christophe would somehow deflect her before she could do anything to help Benno.

Paula rode on, heading first south along Herengracht, then east toward Dam Square. Christophe had picked her out as a criminal. *Criminal.* Paula stopped at an intersection, momentarily distracted. Lukas had been right in thinking Christophe St-Giles wouldn't bother with her unless there was something he thought she could do for him. But she was sure Lukas hadn't known the direction his old friend's suspicions were taking. Christophe *had* made a point of linking her to Frank Lammaker and Willem Bill in front of Benno. And he was forever asking questions.

Two women passed carrying baskets and talking volubly. Brought back to the moment, Paula checked for oncoming traffic and set off again. As she went, she tried to reconstruct the conversation during the canal cruise. A lot of stuff had been said about her choice of career being strange, or dull, for a woman. How long would she stay? Christophe had asked more than once—as if he thought she might trip and tell a different story eventually. Did he think that if she were a thief she'd be stupid enough to allude to plans for clearing out—presumedly with her loot?

Her front tire hit a groove between cobbles, and Paula turned the handlebars sharply to retain balance. Just for today, she'd make her way along a less-traveled route. She didn't need to worry about any cyclist but herself yet. The series of alleys she began to follow would take her around Dam Square and onto Rokin.

She was calmer now. Offense, as her father had so often said, was not necessarily the best defense. Her most sensible bet was to go about her day's work as planned and let Christophe make the next move.

The roar of an engine startled her. The noise rumbled along the walls each side of Paula. She glanced over her shoulder, then quickly back as one of her wheels slewed sideways. The approaching white car was small enough to pass her with ease.

Paula slowed and pulled close to the wall on the one-way street. The engine sound dropped back to a muted, regular clack. She looked back again and risked letting go of one handlebar to wave the old vehicle past. It continued to putter steadily, keeping the same distance between them. Shadow in the alley obscured the driver.

Uncomfortably aware of her own unsure progress and the measured pace of whoever was behind her, Paula riveted her eyes ahead on a point where the alley curved sharply to the left. Apprehension mounted, gripping her belly, gnawing at the muscles in her thighs. *Relax,* she told herself silently. Her experiences of the past few weeks, added to what she'd heard this morning, were making her jumpy. The car's driver was being careful. When they reached the next main road, he would go on his way.

Paula wasn't prepared for the screech of tires that blasted her ears a second later. Disoriented, she backpedaled, slowing down.

There was only another second, the second when she started to check behind again, then the car was there. A flash of white and a glare on windows, a dim impression of chrome. The rusted door handle was clear.

Paula screamed, turned sharply, scraping her body along sandblasted brick. "Don't!" she yelled. "Don't hit me!"

While she shouted, the car's side mirror slammed into her hip, caught beneath the handlebar and Paula shot forward, sideways, and down.

Then it was over. Stunned, she lay very still, the bicycle a painful heap on her legs. She was too shocked to move. The car stopped, backed up and idled beside her, its engine a steady drone. The sound of glass scraping through rubber told her the driver had rolled down his window, but he didn't speak, made no attempt to come to her aid. Without being sure why, Paula kept her eyes closed, her body inert until she heard tires rolling, picking up speed, squealing, first loudly, then fading, fading, until the alley was silent again.

Paula struggled to a sitting position, pushing the bike away. Her hair fell in a tangled mass over her face. She raked at it with shaking hands and felt blood and grit at her temple. The shaking became violent. Blood seeped through the knees of her jeans and oozed from grazes on her palms. Her throat burned and she retched, feeling as if her insides were tearing. She didn't vomit.

Breathing through her mouth, Paula waited for the nausea to pass and willed her mind to clear. No one came. No one had seen what happened. If she'd been killed, she might have lain on her concrete deathbed for hours. She'd chosen a passage between the windowless sides of houses and offices. A murderer's dream...no witnesses. Her attempt to stand failed, and she slid to the ground once more. That car had followed her this morning, she was sure of it, and the driver had blessed his luck when she took an unexpected turn. He, if it had been a he, had made his hit and gone on his way. She was supposed to be dead.

Within minutes Paula managed to get up. Shock had affected her more than injury. Gradually her heart slowed and she tested her legs, rotated her wrists. Bruises were going to be her distinguishing feature for a while, and, after a day or two, scabs, but no joints were swelling, everything moved that should move. *Thank God.* She automatically glanced skyward. Bruises and scabs she could take. She was alive, apparently with no broken bones, and that was a miracle.

Pushing her mangled bike with its bent wheels, Paula made slow, painful progress into Dam Square. Usually she sent admiring glances in the direction of the Royal Palace with its great green dome. Today she knew it was there, took some solace from being in the open among a smattering of people, and limped on, affecting nonchalance whenever a curious glance came her way.

Outside Kohl's she almost lost her nerve. She had no intention of discussing what had happened to her. Talk must be kept to a minimum. A dagger of fear pierced her. From now on she had to be vigilant, to watch and wait. Friends were no longer clearly discernible from enemies— enemies she hadn't known existed until today.

She shoved the bike among the collection piled inside the work entrance doors. Several employees rode in each day. The next trick was to get to the staff room, tidy herself and cover her tattered jeans with her long coverall.

Paula almost made it out of the changing rooms without encountering anyone. Kersten Gouda stopped her at the door and motioned her back inside. Paula groaned inwardly. She had troubles of her own and she hurt all over.

"Paula," Kersten said urgently. "Yesterday. You were kind and I was a fool crying like that. I don't want you to misunderstand. There is nothing wrong. Nothing."

Self-consciously Paula made sure her hair covered the wound at her temple. "It's all right," she assured Kersten, registering at the same time that self-contained women rarely cried for no reason. "I would never say anything, if that's what you're worried about."

Kersten smiled faintly. "I believe you. It was a weak moment, Paula. Do you understand that? There are those times when we cannot hide our feelings as we should."

A dim thought that this was one more puzzle, and she didn't want to deal with it now, added impatience to Paula's discomfort. "I hope you feel better now," she said, certain this was not the case.

"I..." Kersten's beautifully manicured nails twisted buttons on her suit jacket. "A long time ago I lost someone I cared about deeply. I never believed what the police said. They thought he wanted to go away, or that he'd been killed. But there was no trace of where he went and no body was ever found."

Paula no longer felt like escaping. She stared, fascinated, at Kersten. "Who was this?"

"I must not say." Kersten sat on a bench with a thump, presenting the top of her shining blond hair. "I must just wait and hope. Things have happened... I've said too much, but I wanted you to understand that I don't normally bring personal troubles to work. Yesterday was hard because it was the anniversary of our... It was a day that reminded me so strongly of what happened."

Impulsively Paula sat, trying not to wince at the pain in her knees, and put an arm around the woman's shoulders. "Don't tell me more than you want to. I understand you're unhappy. I won't mention this conversation, but if you ever want to talk to me, I'm a good listener."

"Thank you," Kersten said simply. "I knew you were kind."

Kersten got up and smoothed her skirt. She smiled before she left, and the sadness in her eyes tugged at Paula's heart.

After checking her appearance once more, Paula took the elevator to the workshop floor. Climbing stairs would be low on her list of favored occupations for a while.

She was late, but it didn't seem to matter. The steady hum of machinery comforted her and she stepped into the room, hoping to slide into her place without having to talk to anyone.

Christophe St-Giles lounged on her stool, a cigarette burning unattended between his fingers while he talked to Jacob and another polisher. Victor bent over his scaife, fierce concentration furrowing his brow.

Paula took in the scene and quashed an instant desire to flee. The desire drained away rapidly, to be replaced by slowly rising fury. This man, occupying her place as if he owned it, suspected her of dishonesty. He was steadily disrupting the lives of people she had come to love. And while he played Remington Steele to the diamond industry, she confronted the possibility that someone was trying to kill her and she didn't even know why, or whom to turn to for help.

"So the stones aren't marked to indicate who the craftsman was?" Christophe was asking. He showed no sign of having noticed her. "Doesn't that bother you? An artist signs his paintings, a writer has his name on his work."

Jacob, clearly expansive and enjoying the attention, gestured magnanimously. "In the trade we can recognize each other's work. Isn't that so, Victor?"

Victor grunted, but didn't look up.

"And a log is kept," Jacob carried on, undaunted. "Descriptions are carefully noted, together with the polisher's name. It is enough."

Paula walked behind the bench and stood between Christophe and Victor. Jacob nodded at her over Christophe's shoulder. Victor stopped working long enough to glare up at her. His glance held a venom that turned Paula's stomach. "You are late," he said, his eyes shifting to Christophe's back. Immediately Paula gained the impression that it was the Swiss, not her who had provoked the old man's ire.

"I'm sorry, Victor," she said, but looked at Christophe. He didn't turn around. "I had a little trouble on the way." Still Christophe kept his back turned. For a crazy instant she was tempted to thump him.

"Your troubles are no concern of mine," Victor said harshly, swiveling from his stool. "You are to be here on time, like everyone else. There cannot be favoritism because of...connections. The others will not like it." He stalked from the room, leaving Paula with her mouth open.

Another wave of nausea overcame her and she hurriedly sat on Victor's vacated seat. Unconsciously her hand went to her temple where an ache had started.

"Good morning, Paula." Christophe's voice was soft.

She raised her eyes to his face. He stood close beside her. Coming in after the accident had been a mistake. She should have returned to Herengracht.

While she watched, his pupils dilated. "What has happened to you?" he whispered urgently, bending closer, moving aside her hair. "What the hell has happened?"

"Shh." She glanced around, desperate not to arouse curiosity. Weakness turned her skin clammy. "A little fall, that's all."

His hand on her elbow almost produced a cry. She moved instantly, propelled on shaky legs toward Benno's office. Once inside, Christophe let her go and she faced him.

"Getting any *interesting* information?" she said through her teeth. This wasn't the way she'd planned their next meeting.

"Very interesting," Christophe said distractedly. He was looking at his fingers. Paula looked, too. Blood. She crossed her arms and felt dampness on her right sleeve.

"All right," Christophe said tightly. "What's going on? You're bleeding from your face and your elbow, at least. What sort of 'little' accident did you have?"

"I fell," she said evasively. Tension mounted steadily inside her. "I fell." This time she repeated the words more loudly. She was frightened—frightened. "A car hit me and I fell, I tell you. It meant to hit me. He wanted me to die. I know he did." Tears began to stream down her cheeks, and she couldn't check them. Christophe's face was a blur. He was pushing her backward into a chair, kneeling at her feet. "Did you know someone would do that to me?" The words wouldn't stop coming. "Did you ask for it to be done? You think I'm something awful. Did you get someone to hurt me?"

"Paula, hush. You're not making any sense."

"You want to prove I'm guilty of stealing. Then you won't give Benno the loan and you'll go back to Switzerland and be a hero with your family and their important bank because you'll have saved them money. You don't care about an old business failing. You'll say Kohl's can't protect their only asset, diamonds, and then make sure they go out of business. You'll make me have to go home—or get the police—or—''

His mouth, gently pressed to hers, brought her eyes wide open, cleared her vision instantly. She tried to pull back. He leaned closer, slid his hands beneath her arms to circle her body.

The kiss went on and on, soothing the pain from her head, numbing her aching bones. Slowly she lifted her fingers to his face, framed his high cheekbones, pushed deeply into his hair and held on tightly.

Christophe broke away momentarily. ''Are you quiet, now, Paula?'' He kissed her again as she stared back at him, dazed. ''I would never hurt you.'' Soft brushing, skin on skin, smoothness, the touch of tongue to teeth, mingling scents, one clean, hint of leather, male, the other gentle flower. Paula succumbed rapidly to her own arousal. A dozen small kisses outlined her jaw, the tender corners of her mouth, her brow. He held her as he might a troubled, fragile child, stroking, reassuring. He kissed her as only a passionate man kisses a woman he wants.

''Now,'' he said against her cheek. ''Let me hold you. I want to hold you, *chérie*. Perhaps I shouldn't, but I do.''

She turned her lips to his ear. ''This isn't right, Christophe. I don't understand anything anymore.''

''Tell me what happened to you.'' He kissed her mouth once more. ''Forget what we should or shouldn't do. Trust me.''

Of course, she thought, she would do as he said—trust. She had to trust someone. The words tumbled out, the overheard conversation at Benno and Anna's, the discovery that he, Christophe, thought she had done something dishonest, and the ride through the streets. When she told him about the hit-and-run accident a shudder shook him.

"Paula," he said softly. "Think. If I believed you were guilty of something and I was going to need you as a suspect, would I try to have you killed, or even seriously hurt? I would want to keep you in one piece. You agree?"

Yes, she nodded.

He eased off her coverall. Confronted by her torn jeans, he recoiled. "You will go home, Paula. I will take you and then you will rest."

"Anna and Benno mustn't know—or Lukas. They have enough worries. I'm only cut and bruised. I can say I fell from the new bicycle. They knew I was still learning to ride. Please, Christophe, don't tell them what happened."

"I won't." He was looking at her temple. His fingers were so gentle. "I won't as long as you do what I say from now on."

"Anything," she whispered and closed her eyes.

She felt his mouth brush her lids and wanted only to sleep—and know his arms were around her.

"The side mirror hit your hip." A broad hand covered her side. "The bone only, or soft tissue, as well? Do you think you might be hurt inside?" He unsnapped her waistband and she made no attempt to stop him.

"I'm sure it was just the bone."

He eased down the zipper and carefully peeled aside her jeans to expose a purple welt on pale skin above bikini panties. *"Mon Dieu,"* he muttered and let out a low whistle. "Perhaps we should take you to a doctor."

"No!" Paula grabbed his arm. "I'm going to be fine."

"You must be fine." His intensity silenced her clamoring nerves. He ran the tips of his fingers around the edges of the injury, and on, across her stomach. Paula watched, mesmerized, pain forgotten. "You must be fine," he repeated and bent slowly to touch warm lips to her belly.

"Christophe." Paula rallied, remembering their surroundings and the unanswered issues between them. "Thank you for being kind." She coughed on the words and cleared her throat. Hurriedly she fastened her jeans and pulled the coverall back on. "I feel better now. And I'm sorry for all the wild accusations."

His dark eyes never left her face. "But we've reached another level, haven't we, Paula? You now know things you must not reveal. I trust you to be careful. And you *will* trust me, correct?"

"Correct." She was emphatic. At least she hadn't blurted anything out about her agreement with Lukas. Immediately she remembered Lukas had also exhorted her to be careful. Working on appearing calm, she stood, and Christophe immediately stood with her. "I'm going home," she announced matter-of-factly. "A few hours sleep and I'll be fine. The car probably hit me accidentally and then the driver panicked." She paused, laughed. "And then *I* panicked. Stupid of me." What had happened to her resolve of earlier in the morning? Christophe was supposed to have made the next, she'd hoped, revealing move. She'd blown that.

"You're right, I'm sure. Will you have dinner with me on Friday evening?"

"Dinner?" she repeated and knew she sounded surprised. She was surprised.

"A peace offering." That wonderful smile could do magic. "You've had some bad moments because of me."

"Oh . . . yes, dinner." There would be a chance to talk about all their differences. "Yes. I'd like that. Thank you."

An hour later Christophe had helped her from the gun-metal Saab she hadn't known he owned and ushered her into the Kohls' house. Only Anna was at home. She listened to Christophe's edited explanation of the cycling accident and sympathetically echoed that Paula should go to bed. Within minutes, she'd done just that and lay with shades drawn, ice packs on the strategic sore spots on her body.

She'd agreed to go to dinner with Christophe on Friday. Her frown was directed at fuzzy lines of light on the wall. And he'd asked—no, instructed—her to trust him. *"Think,"* he'd said, *"if I believed you were guilty of something... would I try to have you killed?"* No, he wouldn't. But the truth held small comfort. No questions had been answered, and no statement made that he thought her innocent.

Paula pushed a pillow behind her spine to ease the hip. They had "passed to another level." She felt vaguely sick again. Unfortunately, Christophe's "other level" had nothing to do with the kisses she was never going to forget.

THE WOMAN WOUND AND UNWOUND the paper, pleating it, crushing it between her fingers, then flattening the sheet again.

"My God," the man said tightly. "My God."

"No." She tossed the paper aside. "Please. Sit down." With one hand she smoothed the padded top of a chest in a corner of the elegant living room. "We're getting close. I can feel it now. I wish it was all over, just as you do, but it will be soon."

He remained standing. "You dream. Oh, you dream. It's all starting again. I told you this would never work."

Slender fingers curled into a tight fist. "We have to do what the man says." She slammed the fist into her other palm. "I believe him. He knows every detail exactly as it happened. The last sighting before the disappearance, where the police looked, what the reports said, everything. He couldn't know these things unless he has direct sources."

"We should stop." The man finally sat on the chest. "If we stop now, we may still salvage something."

"Salvage something?" Her voice rose. "What about a man's life? Isn't that worth saving more than a few lumps of crystal?"

A deep sigh hissed past the man's lips. "I cannot argue about that. But how many diamonds will this 'friend' of ours need to complete the *rescue* he talks about? When will he have enough for his *cause*?"

"I don't know." She paced distractedly. "We need more stones, just in case. And a transfer has to be made exactly as he instructs. We've come too far to risk holding out now."

The man sprang to his feet. "More stones. Can't you understand we're being taken for a ride? This... this...whoever he is will take everything we've worked for and keep squeezing us for more."

"We can get more." All inflection had left the woman's voice. "I will continue to make the deliveries."

LATER, THE WOMAN stood on the gently swaying flower barge, surveying rows of plants in wooden trays. Each time she heard footsteps, she looked up expectantly. The man who called them had never said when the exchange might take place. It could be anytime. She could hardly believe after all this time the moment was so near. She could be looking into those dark blue eyes she'd never forgotten, returning the dear smile with its wry turned-down corners. Tears of longing welled in her own eyes, and she looked at the plants once more.

In one corner she spotted it—a dormant miniature rose bush in a clay pot. The packet she carried was small but distinctive, and the bare branches of the bush would provide little cover. She experienced a moment of fear. If someone else found the stone first . . . *"Do as you're told. Never question me."* The only time she'd argued with her contact, he'd shut her up with chilling authority. Her instructions were to lay the packet flat on the soil at the back of the plant and walk away.

Soon, too soon, she was stepping over frayed boards to the sidewalk and blending quickly with other shoppers. Again she found herself staring into faces. She saw no one she knew.

HE DUCKED to clear the awning in front of the barge and stepped swiftly aboard. Looking neither to left nor right, he made for the corner and slid his left hand behind the rose bush.

"You like the plant, sir. It's a little sad, but with love it'll do well. I'll give you a good price."

Damn. Constant irritations. His plans weren't going smoothly anymore. Slowly he withdrew his hand, the packet in his palm. "Perhaps it would take too much love." He smiled benignly. "More than I have to give. I'll look around and think about it." Something sharp had snagged beneath his ring; a thorn? He stiffened his features against a wince and whistled as he edged away.

Once on the sidewalk he made himself pause to light a cigarette. He thought he felt the stall owner watching him. Or was he simply getting jumpy? He'd started sauntering away before he felt stickiness in the palm still shielding the small packet. Nonchalantly he put his lighter back in his pocket, the diamond packet with it, and examined his hand.

Damn. Blood trickled from a puncture wound beneath his ring. The rose thorn was still embedded. He'd never liked roses.

Chapter Eight

Thursday of the Third Week:

"Finally," Christophe muttered, pulling farther into the shadows. Blessing good fortune and his own patience, he waited several more seconds in a doorway opposite the bar Frank Lammaker had just left. Finally the man was going through the steps Christophe had waited a week to see repeated.

Every afternoon for the past seven days, he'd positioned himself where he could watch Frank leave Kohl's. Every afternoon, Frank had emerged, no briefcase or bag in sight, and immediately boarded a bus. Until today.

Christophe gave Frank a short head start before falling in behind him. The weather was beginning to feel like spring and the messenger had changed into lighter clothes this time: sleeveless V-necked sweater over a long-sleeved shirt and gray pants. One more well-dressed young man blending into the late afternoon crush of homeward-bound workers.

At the next corner, Christophe hung back, watching Frank set off in the same direction he'd taken the previous Thursday.

Christophe broke into a run. He'd studied a detailed map of the city, planning his own strategy for this moment. Instead of getting into Vondel Park by the north entrance Frank had used before, he planned to enter the most easterly gate, skirt along a southern path and arrive on the far side before Frank. The only hitch would be if Frank and Willem had decided on a different meeting point.

By the time Christophe sprinted into the park he was breathing heavily. He'd seen how fast Frank was capable of moving. Every second counted. *God,* he prayed silently, *don't let them make any fresh moves.*

As on all the other afternoons since the first chase, Christophe's new Saab was parked in a side street angling off the cul-de-sac where Willem Bill had made his U-turn. Christophe hesitated at an exit a few hundred yards from the one Frank had taken. Once he left the cover of trees and shrubs, he'd be clearly visible to anyone waiting in the remote street.

He heard the high, tuneless whistle an instant before the sound of rapidly thudding footsteps. Frank and Willem were pulling a repeat performance to the letter. Cautiously Christophe peered through the gate. The car was there, its engine idling. He counted to ten and made a run for the Saab. As he went, he caught the glint of low sun on Frank's fair hair. The man was already bending to climb into Willem's car.

Christophe was inside his own vehicle, gunning the powerful engine to life, when Willem and Frank cruised past the side street. They returned, and Christophe counted to ten once more before slipping into gear and following.

They sped south, then west, gradually leaving behind the areas Christophe knew. Willem didn't hesitate once. He knew his course well.

A sudden left turn almost undid Christophe. He overshot, unable to stop in time, and missed the street the white car took. Cursing aloud, he turned in the middle of traffic, drawing loud horn comments from irate motorists.

Damn. All this and he was probably going to lose them.

He negotiated the corner, unconsciously leaning into the curve, and swore again. Willem Bill's car was parked half a block ahead, and the two men were on the sidewalk pulling possessions from the back seat.

Christophe drove past, staring ahead. From the corner of his eye, he saw Willem lead the way up a flight of steps.

When he'd allowed an interval to pass, Christophe drove back and slowed opposite a white stone house sandwiched between almost identical pink facades in a terrace of clearly expensive homes.

He locked his elbows, gripping the steering wheel tight and let out the breath he'd been holding. Seventy-nine. No need to write down the number of the house, or the street name: 79 Overstraat. He'd remember.

Smiling faintly, he depressed the accelerator, changed gears and pointed the Saab toward the city center.

Friday of the Third Week:

"We want to know all about it, don't we, Sandi?" Peter Van Wersch held out a chair for Paula. "Are you sure you're comfortable, Paula?" He fussed while a waiter seated Sandi.

Sandi leaned forward and touched Paula's hand. "Are you all right, Paula? I couldn't believe it when Anna said you'd gone back to work today. You mustn't overdo. That's why Peter and I hatched a plot to spring you for lunch."

"And it was a lovely plot," Paula said, appreciatively checking the plant-strewn decor of a sumptuous restaurant overlooking Amsterdam's Central Station. "Almost worth getting knocked off a bicycle..." She bowed her head and reached for her napkin, furious with herself for making a stupid slip.

"I thought Anna said you fell," Sandi commented quietly.

"That's right," Paula agreed quickly—too quickly. She breathed deeply and met Sandi's gaze squarely. "I fell."

An awkward silence followed, broken by the waiter taking their order and returning with cocktails. Peter and Sandi were watching Paula intently. This was why she'd made such a lousy poker player. Every emotion showed on her face.

"Something's wrong," Peter said at last, his blue eyes unwavering. "You're not telling us everything about this *accident* of yours."

Paula thought fast. "My beautiful bike is ruined," she said, a laugh catching in her throat. "All that money down the drain. It would cost as much to fix it as to buy a new one."

Sandi made a clucking sound. "You're safe, Paula. That's what matters. If you try again, get more practice first."

"You must have had some fall," Peter said as if no one else had spoken.

Paula stared at him, a sinking sensation in the pit of her stomach. "It wasn't pleasant."

"But you totaled your bike? Paula, a simple fall shouldn't do that much damage to the machine, unless you went off a bridge or something."

He wasn't going to be deflected. Paula laced her fingers tightly together. Confiding in someone would feel so good.

These were her friends. Why shouldn't she tell them what was happening? Even if they couldn't help, they'd support her and she wouldn't feel so alone. For all Christophe's show of concern—and passion—other than calling once to ask how she was, he'd ignored her since Tuesday.

"A car hit me."

She'd spoken so softly that she wondered if they'd heard. Immediately she hoped they hadn't. Christophe had warned her to keep her own counsel.

"Why didn't you say that before?" Peter frowned at her. "How did it happen?"

"I don't know." She felt sick yet again. If the questioning went on, she'd be forced to relive the horror she'd been through.

Sandi had covered her mouth. Her eyes were huge.

"A car just hit you?" Peter shook his head. "It ruined your bicycle and caused you to cut your arms and legs and your head? Just like that? And you don't know how it happened? Come on, Paula. We warned you not to try riding in Amsterdam when you have no experience. For God's sake, don't try it again, practice or no practice. Your nerves are bound to be shot now."

What did it matter if Christophe had warned her to say nothing—to "be careful." He didn't own her. If she didn't get help from someone she trusted, she'd never get to the bottom of what was happening here.

Peter sat beside her, his elegant body inclined in her direction. Paula slid shaky fingers into his, and he immediately covered them with his other hand. "Peter," she said. "It happened in an alley on the other side of Dam Square. I'm probably paranoid, but I almost thought he meant to do it. There was plenty of room for him to pass, but he hung back, then speeded up and hit me. I was lucky—he only winged my hip and caught the handlebar.

My wheels went sideways when I started to fall and his rear tire must have gone over them."

"Paula," Sandi whispered. "What are you saying? You believe someone *tried* to hurt you ... ?" The green eyes filled with tears, and Sandi started to cry. She fumbled with the neck of her blouse.

Peter rubbed Sandi's back. The concerned expression on his slender face was new to Paula, who always thought of him as an irrepressible clown. She'd been right to speak up. She was certain of it now.

"Is there anything else, Paula?" Peter asked, his hand still on Sandi's shoulder. He massaged the base of her neck. "Why would anyone want to hurt you? It doesn't make sense."

"Sandi," said Paula gently. "You and Peter are my friends. There are some other things I'd like to tell you. Maybe we could help each other sort them out. But you can't tell Lukas, you know—that I've mentioned them, rather. You don't need me to explain how upset he is. If he finds out what happened to me...after...well, after some other things ... he's likely to go on overload."

She had their full attention. Sandi sat very straight, mascara smudged beneath her eyes. Peter took a slow swallow from his drink and lit a cigarette, never looking away from Paula. His blond hair had slipped over his brow, but he didn't seem to notice.

"What other things, Paula?" He squinted through smoke.

Her nerve faded. Impulsiveness was a luxury she couldn't afford. "Maybe they'd be better not mentioned," she said and sipped from her own glass. "Forget it." Now she sounded like Christophe.

"No," Sandi interjected sharply. "Tell us, now. I want to know. Lukas would want to know. We aren't children who can be shielded.'' She glanced at Peter, her pale skin flushing. "Peter, please, whatever you learn here must go no further."

He pushed the small finger of the hand holding his cigarette back and forth across his brow. "You've got my full attention, friend—and my loyalty—as always."

"Go on, Paula," Sandi said. Their meals arrived but they ignored them.

Paula launched into a full description of her accident and worked backward, explaining some of the conversation she'd overheard at the Kohls'. At that point, Sandi became deathly pale again and Paula noticed she plucked nervously at a button on her jacket. Perhaps Lukas didn't tell his wife everything. Paula almost wished she'd never begun her story, but there could be no stopping now.

"You mean Kohl's is in trouble?" Peter commented thoughtfully. He raised his brows in Sandi's direction. "There've been thefts? Why didn't you and Lukas tell me?" Paula didn't miss the hurt in his eyes, and instantly her heart went out to him. She'd never considered he might know nothing of his friends' business trials.

Sandi stroked his forearm. "We couldn't talk about it, Peter. We shouldn't be talking about it now. This thing with Paula brings us into a new dimension, but nothing else can be allowed to change. There must be no talk, no gossip. You understand how important reputation is in the diamond market."

"You thought *I* might share your problems with others?" Peter's tone was aggrieved. "You really believed I would take pleasure in my two best friends' pain and use it as a casual conversation-maker?"

Paula hated the turn this conversation was taking. "I'm sure Lukas and Sandi didn't think that," she put in hastily. "Benno and Lukas hoped to get their loan and put everything right without anyone finding out about the thefts."

"And how do you know that?" Peter watched her intently. "Did you learn that outside Benno and Anna's door, too?"

She blushed. "No. It was mentioned, but I already knew. Lukas told me about the loan. And I didn't plan to listen, Peter."

A small sound escaped Sandi's throat. Peter touched her hand, then turned her face toward him. "Are you all right?"

Sandi wordlessly nodded her head.

Paula rushed on, filling any possibility of an awkward silence. She explained Lukas's concern over Christophe's sudden interest in her. The words tumbled over one another. Soon she'd retold Lukas's theory that Christophe intended to deny the loan Kohl's needed and that he was determined to find concrete reasons to do so. Christophe's deliberate tying of Frank Lammaker to Metter's and then the dinner at the Kohls' when Christophe raised her own connection to Frank and to Willem Bill were soon added to the information she unloaded, with an increasing sense of relief.

"Is there more?" Sandi had pushed her full plate aside.

"Only that Christophe took me on a barge trip and then behaved very strangely. He ran and hauled me aboard a bus as if someone were following. Then he wouldn't tell me why."

"I wonder what the point of that was." Peter speared a forkful of omelet and ate slowly. He swallowed. "Sounds wild. Anything else?"

"No. I don't think so." Had she done the right thing in telling all this?

"This is a nightmare," Sandi muttered. "I never thought we'd go through something so awful."

"I shall speak to Christophe," Peter announced, smacking down his fork with enough noise to attract attention from nearby diners. "I shall talk to him and find out what's happening."

Paula and Sandi clutched his arms simultaneously. "You won't." Sandi's order shocked Paula. "You will say nothing, you understand? Nothing, Peter."

"But, I—"

"Nothing," Sandi spat out. "This is why Lukas and I have been alone in this—with Benno and Anna, of course. We cannot afford to risk any upheaval now. Support us, Peter. Love us and understand our difficulty. Please, do not interfere."

He bowed his head and said, "I cannot understand Christophe. This is the man Lukas and I shared everything with. We shared our best and worst times. Are you sure I can't talk to him? You know he's on my houseboat and I see him some evenings. I could stop by and just chat—steer the conversation and see what happens."

"If you do—" Sandi's voice was urgent "—you could bring about our end. Lukas doesn't understand him anymore, either. That's why he's so hostile. But Christophe holds all the cards. We must play his game his way."

Paula watched Peter, her stomach tight with apprehension.

He stubbed out the cigarette he'd left burning in the ashtray and patted Sandi's hand. "I understand, darling. Of course I do. Whatever you say is the way it'll be. As long as you promise to tell me if I can help."

Sandi relaxed visibly. "I will, Peter. You're a dear. I've wanted to tell you, but Lukas and Benno are so determined to keep our trouble within the family and I have to respect their decision. Paula—" she dropped her voice even lower "—do you really think that car driver intended to hurt you, because if you do—"

Paula broke in quickly, "No, no I don't. I think too much has been going on, and after overhearing Anna and Benno I was upset and my imagination ran away with me. Why would anyone want to hurt me?"

"You're right." Sandi found a kleenex and blew her nose. "I feel better. Thanks for agreeing to do things my way, Peter."

He shoved back his hair. "Not a word from me, I promise."

"I won't say anything, either," Paula said fervently. "I'm just glad we all know what's going on." And she was. A few more days of solitary struggling with her thoughts and fears and she might have gone mad.

"Listen, both of you." Sandi made fists on the table. "Benno and Lukas have decided on how they want to handle things. I think it's best they don't know we've had this talk. At least for now. We will be here and ready if and when they need us—agreed?"

"Agreed," Paula said.

"Agreed," Peter echoed.

"FRANK WILL COME to pick me up." Madeleine Lammaker spoke happily while she flicked a duster over polished surfaces in the Kohls' living room. "I have a—a—date," she laughed, "as you, Paula. Frank is taking me to the fancy restaurant in Rembrandts Square. He is a good boy." Her English was sketchy, spoken slowly and with a heavy accent.

Paula sat on a carved oak chair, watching the plump woman's happy, expressive face. "I like Frank," she said simply. "You're lucky to have him." *And if you knew what he's suspected of now, you'd be destroyed,* she thought miserably.

Pale eyes met hers and shone. A heavy network of wrinkles on Madeleine's face belied her serene air. Her life could not have been an easy one. Uncomfortable with the knowledge she couldn't share, Paula got up and went to peer through the windows. The less she concentrated on Frank, on anything to do with the cloud of distrust steadily gathering on the horizon of her world, the better. She felt sad about what might be lurking in Madeleine's future.

The canal was crisscrossed with ripples running against one another. Like deep green crumpled satin, it reflected the last remnants of day in the darkening sky. The Kohls had gone out for the evening and Paula had opted to wait for Christophe in the main house, rather than have him come to the backhouse. She knew her reason. The thought of his being there, among the few possessions she valued, seemed too personal, made her feel vulnerable. She shrugged. Maybe he wouldn't even show up. He hadn't made any attempt to confirm their date.

"When do you leave?" Madeleine asked behind her.

"Eight, I think," Paula said absently. The afternoon had dragged by, her thoughts turning into a festering mass of indecision as her appointment with Christophe got closer. This invitation was one more part of his strategy. The indelible memory of his blistering kisses aside, Paula had no illusions about the depth of his interest in her. It went no further than the limit of his calculated use of her. As Lukas had so kindly pointed out, Christophe St-Giles was a man unlikely to be short of feminine company.

Madeleine had spoken again.

"I'm sorry, Madeleine," Paula apologized. "I didn't hear that. And why are you still here, anyway?" She checked her watch. "It's almost eight."

"It is easier for Frank to pick me up here than go all the way home. He was busy after work, but he should be here soon. I might as well work until he arrives."

Paula opened her mouth to comment when Christophe's Saab slid into angle parking beside the canal. He got out, tossed down a cigarette and ground it underfoot. Paula stepped back but not before he'd glanced at the window. She smiled and waved.

"Bye, Madeleine," she called, rushing from the room. "Enjoy your evening."

"Bye," she heard Madeleine echo.

Paula was already yanking open the front door. She barreled into Christophe and he laughed, catching her against him to keep their balance. "What's the hurry? Missed me, huh?"

The rush of hot blood to her face only added to her chagrin. "I've got a thing about not keeping people waiting," she responded lamely. She could hardly admit her stomach was one big knot at the thought of spending an evening with him. Or that she wasn't sure what percentage of the knot was made up of anticipation, what of apprehension. She also couldn't tell him that if she'd allowed one more second for reflection before running from the house, she might have chickened out of going with him at all.

Christophe had chosen an Indonesian restaurant in the trendy Jordaan district. Jaya's owner hovered over his staff and clients with the concentration of a man whose mission in life would fail if a single unsatisfied stomach left his simply decorated premises.

For two hours Paula bravely sampled dish after dish, all delicious, all filling. Christophe's absorption in the food, and his capacity, made her determined to keep eating enthusiastically.

"You're slowing down. Had it?"

Paula heard amusement in Christophe's voice and realized she'd been staring for a long time at the skewer of spicy chicken she held. "Whew!" she sighed. "I guess so. But it was a beautiful dinner. Thank you."

"I like it here," Christophe replied, taking the skewer from her fingers and deftly chewing off a grilled pepper. "The place is unpretentious, but the food's great."

He finished eating and paid the bill.

Outside, he placed a hand loosely at Paula's nape and asked, "How about some dancing?"

Paula hesitated, deciding what to say. Throughout their meal, the conversation had been innocuous—Christophe had seen to that. Nothing heavier than the spring's influx of tourists had been discussed. There was no guarantee that he would be more forthcoming while dancing, but he might.

"Big decision, Paula?" He opened the car door and lifted her skirt clear of the door. "I thought you told me you liked dancing—to Dixieland." He shut her in and walked around the hood, bouncing keys in one palm.

He was right, she had said she liked to dance. And she did. And she'd like to dance with him. "Let's go dancing," she said as he climbed in. "You may have to make allowances for my battered knees."

"How are the bruises coming?" He maneuvered from a parking area in the center of the street and started back the way they'd come.

"Fine," Paula replied. "Just call me scabby. My elbows haven't looked this way since I was the neighborhood's ten-year-old tomboy."

He glanced sideways at her. "I can't imagine you as a tomboy, Paula."

The way he had of looking at her, his simple comments, wielded a power he couldn't possibly guess. She clasped her hands together in her lap.

"You were frightened that day." He stopped for a light, then leaned forward to check in each direction before turning left. "I meant to ask you. You didn't happen to notice the license, did you?"

"License?"

"The plate on the car."

She grimaced. "No, dammit. I was so rattled that all I remembered afterward was a rusty door handle and scratched white paint. And it was a small car. I don't know much about European cars, so I can't even tell you what make it was."

He didn't answer immediately. "A white car?" he said at last. "Small?"

"Yes." Paula shifted, tired of the subject. She wanted to forget the incident. "And I'm sure the driver was as scared as I was. He probably thought he *had* killed me and made a run for it out of instinct."

"Brave of him," Christophe muttered.

And something you would never have done, Paula thought instantly. "We can only operate within the range of our physical and emotional capabilities."

"You're philosophical tonight."

He became silent again, and Paula was grateful he'd dropped the subject.

"Where are we going?" she asked abruptly, recognizing the Singel Canal. "I didn't know there were any good jazz places along here—not where you can dance, anyway."

"Ah." In the light from the dash, she saw the shadow deepen beneath his cheekbone. He was smiling. "The very best place to dance to jazz is right here." They drew up between two trees planted in tiny squares of earth beside the canal.

Paula sat still until Christophe opened her door. He took her hand and helped her out. "Watch your step," he said. "The gangplank's a bit mossy. Don't slip."

"Christophe, stop." She planted her feet. "I thought you said we were going dancing. This is Peter's houseboat, isn't it?" Even in the darkness, fresh paint gleamed on the deckhousing of the converted barge.

"Yes. It's also my home—for now. And I have an excellent selection of jazz records and more than enough space for one couple to dance."

Every instinct in Paula's body went on alert.

"Do I frighten you, Paula?" Christophe asked softly. "Are you afraid to be alone with me?"

Egotistical bastard. "Hardly. Surprised, that's all. Lead on."

His muffled chuckle filtered to her as he led the way across the shifting plank. Paula narrowed her eyes at his broad back. M. St-Giles was a fascinating, powerful man. He was accustomed to getting his own way. If he thought his charm, physical as well as verbal, would lull her into pouring out facts he wanted to know, he was about to be disappointed. She didn't know anything that might be of use to him; he, on the other hand, could help her considerably—by agreeing to get out of her friends' lives. And she wouldn't be resorting to seduction to reach her goal.

Half an hour later, nestled against plump cushions on a low corduroy couch, a glass of brandy in her hand, Paula felt less secure. Christophe was sorting through piles of records reading titles aloud to himself in French, discarding some, removing others from their jackets. "I must confess," he said without turning, "these are Peter's. I borrowed them."

Paula tensed. "For this evening?"

"We-e-ll—yes. Honesty's the best course, right?" Smiling brown eyes quickly met hers.

"You assumed I'd agree to come here with you?"

He put on a record and watched until the needle met the first groove. "Let's say I didn't intend to give you a chance to refuse." His grin was just short of wolfish. "Do you mind?"

She should mind, but she didn't. Paula wasn't about to tell him so.

Christophe took her glass and set it aside. "Shall we try some of that dancing?"

He pulled her into his arms and moved effortlessly to the slow beat of an old blues piece Paula didn't recognize. It was beautiful, the horn work heart-wrenching in its clarity. Christophe was beautiful, tall, straight, his muscles flexing beneath her hands, against her breasts, her thighs. A heavy ache started deep inside her. The rhythm was insistent. Christophe moved with it, became a fluid part of the music, wrapped her tighter, his chin on top of her head.

"Peter knows I was taking you out this evening."

His breath moved her hair. "Yes." She looked up and immediately wished she hadn't. Christophe's face was inches above hers.

"Does he mind, do you think?" Firm lips spoke against her temple before moving down to the side of her neck.

Half Paula's attention responded to Christophe's roving mouth, half to his question. Would Peter wonder at her motive for seeing Christophe? Sandi had begged both

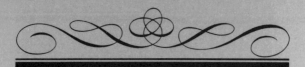

YOUR
PASSPORT
TO
R♥MANCE

HARLEQUIN

VISA
FOR FREE GIFTS

**VALIDATE
YOUR
PASSPORT
TODAY!**

Send us your Visa and get
4 Free Books, a Free Tote Bag
and your Extra Mystery Gift!

GO FOR IT

HERE'S YOUR TICKET TO ROMANCE AND A GEM OF AN OFFER!

1. Four FREE Harlequin Romances

Book a free getaway to love with your Harlequin VISA. You'll receive four exciting new romances hot off the presses. All yours, compliments of Harlequin Reader Service. You'll get all the passion, the tender moments and the intrigue of love in far-away places...FREE!

2. A Beautiful Harlequin Tote Bag...Free!

Carry away your favorite romances in your elegant canvas Tote Bag. At a spacious 13 square inches, there'll be lots of room for shopping, sewing and exercise gear, too! With a snap-top and double handles, your Tote Bag is valued at $6.99 — but it's yours free with this offer!

3. Free Magazine Subscription

You'll receive our members-only magazine, Harlequin Romance Digest, three times per year. In addition, you'll be up on all the news about your favourite writers, upcoming books and much more with Harlequin's Free monthly newsletter.

4. Free Delivery and 26¢ Off Store Prices

Join Harlequin Reader Service today and discover the convenience of Free home delivery. You'll preview four exciting new books each month — and pay only $1.99 per book. That's 26¢ less than the store price. It all adds up to one gem of an offer!

YOU'LL GET A FREE MYSTERY GIFT TOO!

USE YOUR HARLEQUIN VISA TO VALIDATE YOUR PASSPORT TO ROMANCE — APPLY YOUR VISA TO THE POST-PAID CARD ATTACHED AND MAIL IT TODAY!

Paula and Peter not to intervene with Christophe. The warm breath was at her throat now; strong hands but gentle came to rest under her arms, thumbs slowly stroking the sides of her breasts. She had to keep a clear head, to remember she was with a sophisticated man, a practiced lover doing what came so very naturally.

"Paula." He brought his face close to hers. "Are you and Peter... Have you and Peter been more than just friends?"

"No." Her own husky whisper brought a deeper flush to her cheeks. Sometimes the body didn't heed the brain. "Peter is a good, good friend—nothing more." Why couldn't she just want to have *this* man as a good, good friend? Why did she want much more with Christophe?

He stared down into her eyes. "I'm glad. I like Peter, too, but some things come ahead of that kind of friendship." His hips and thighs guided their dance, an old dance, the oldest—the movement of their bodies, molded as one, surrounded them in a sexual force field. Paula's breathing speeded. Christophe's hands moved from her sides, to her bottom, pressed her urgently against his thrusting arousal.

"I want to make love to you," he murmured the instant before their mouths met. He held her against him with one hand, with the other he unbuttoned the front of her dress and pushed it aside. His tongue slipped past her teeth, reached and Paula reached back. Her womb pulsed, the muscles in her thighs, her buttocks. Unable not to, she slid a hand from his chest, down, over his belt to touch the hardened part of him. His groan made her smile against his mouth and their kisses became more frenzied.

"Paula, Paula." He nuzzled her head back. "Come to bed." He'd pushed her dress from her shoulders, slid down her bra straps. "Sleep with me tonight." He smoothed lace from her breasts and bent to kiss her throbbing flesh.

Paula moaned softly, far back in her throat. He pushed her gently onto the couch and half covered her with his big body. "Say something, Paula." One large hand slid beneath her dress and up her thigh. "I want you."

"I want you too, but—" Her words were cut off by his next kiss, deeper and deeper, more and more demanding.

When they came up for air he said, "But what?" and his hand moved higher, pressing between her legs.

"No!" Paula wriggled. Christophe mumbled incoherently into the cushion beside her neck and gripped her hip.

Paula cried out, jackknifing to sit, shoving him away. His fingers, digging into the bruise, had brought a sharp pain . . . and the harsh return of reason.

Christophe sat upright on the couch, staring. "What? What is it, for God's sake?"

She started hauling her bra back into place and buttoning her dress. "We don't even trust each other," she said dazedly. "I won't be used, or use you that way. Maybe in time being together will be right, but not now." This was awful. She'd allowed the unthinkable to happen, let him get close enough to her to switch off coherent thought and action.

"God." He leaned against the couch, eyes closed, his chest rising and falling rapidly. "You've got fantastic timing, lady."

Once her clothes were straightened, she smoothed her hair awkwardly. Her mouth felt swollen. With trembling fingers, she reached for her brandy and swallowed enough to make her cough. "I'm sorry," she said when Christophe had been silent a long time.

He didn't reply.

"I didn't expect that to happen. I . . ."

"Didn't you?" He looked at her, the softness erased from his eyes. "You aren't a child, Paula. You knew what could happen...but maybe you're right—you didn't have to expect it." He lifted his own glass and reached a cigarette from a box on a glass end table.

For the first time, Paula was aware of the slight motion of the houseboat. This one was sumptuously furnished, its overhead decking raised to a height even a tall man would find comfortable. She hadn't seen the rest of the boat and wondered exactly where the sleeping quarters were. Immediately she decided they were bound to be too close. The sooner she extricated herself from this mess, the better.

Christophe was smoking, watching the tip of his cigarette turn red when he drew on it. He appeared composed again.

"We allowed ourselves to get carried away," she began tentatively. "What happened had nothing to do with people—just mood, a man and a woman—"

"You're right," he cut her off impatiently, leaning to rest his elbows on his knees. "I tried to push you too far, too fast. Forget it."

A small light came on in Paula's brain. "Forget it. *Forget it?* Is that how you cope with any conflict? *Forget it?* I won't, not this, or a lot of other things you could easily explain to me."

He squinted sideways at her. Every feature held a wariness. "Such as?"

"Why did you haul me aboard that bus the night we went on the canal?"

"I told you. I thought I saw someone following us. Forget—"

"*It!*" she finished for him. She was tired, bone aching tired. "Okay. You aren't about to tell me anything about your investigations here in Amsterdam. Why should you—you don't even tell Benno."

He stood with enough force to splash Paula's drink over her hand. "I told you to back off and leave things alone. I told you to trust me. There's nothing you can do about Benno's problems, so stay out of them."

Paula swallowed painfully, rubbing at drops of brandy on her fingers. She thought a moment and said, "I'm not trying to interfere in anything that doesn't concern me. What I say to you I say because I think you're a good man, a caring man. Benno is becoming ill over this difficulty with the firm. He needs the loan your bank can give him to make good the losses he's sustained. Please, Christophe, will you let him have the money and give him credit for being able to make sure there are no more thefts?"

Christophe sat again, bringing his fist down against the table in the same motion. The pistol-shot sound of his ring on the glass echoed in her brain. "It's not enough that Benno and Lukas won't give me full backing," he fumed. "I have to have a foreign do-gooder poking her nose into my business. I'm doing what has to be done. I don't have to explain any of this to you, but I will say one thing—think about it. If I don't get to the bottom of those thefts, two things will happen. One, there will be no loan, and two, the thefts will start again. Do you understand?"

A stinging sensation crawled up her back, and heat into her face. She felt horribly foolish and embarrassed. "You think I'm a meddling airhead."

"I think you don't know what you're getting into. Remember your *accident*, Paula. It was probably just that, but do you know for sure? Could it be that you've trodden on other toes with your probing and someone's trying to frighten you off?"

Other toes. "I take it I've totally alienated you simply by being worried about Benno? I'm not going to say I'm sorry, because I'm not. These people have been good to me and I care about them." She stood. "It's late. I'd better get home."

Christophe rose and stood in front of her. He wound a curl behind her ear. "I came on too strong, as usual. I *am* sorry. Will you forgive me?"

"Yes." But not completely. "I'm sorry, too. I don't often lose my temper, and when I do it's never effective."

"I'll drive you home." He picked up his jacket and found his keys. "But you are going to have to promise me to stay out of what I'm doing here."

"I . . ." Paula closed her eyes and made herself wait before replying. She would do what she had to do. "Thank you for a lovely evening. I'd rather get a taxi home, if you don't mind."

"I do mind. That's out of the question." He was determined to call all the shots.

"Christophe," she said clearly. "I'm going to take a taxi. They pass along here all the time."

"You'll let me drive you." He took her elbow.

Paula shrugged free. Not shouting or showing her true feelings was taking superhuman effort. "Good night, Christophe. Thank you for everything. Please—don't push this any further."

She left him, closing the door without looking back, and walked ashore. All she needed to rattle her nerves to shreds again was another drive in the close confines of a small car—with Christophe.

Paula set a brisk pace. People still strolled the canal-side, and she saw a taxi weaving a path among them. Her waving arm was ignored and she realized the cabbie already had a fare. She walked on, looking back several times to make sure Christophe wasn't following. He was nowhere in sight, and she didn't try to fool herself that there was no disappointment mixed with her emotions.

She headed in the general direction of home, constantly checking for a cab. None had shown by the time she had to turn away from Singel onto a street that would take her to a point on Herengracht, a dozen blocks from the Kohls'.

Once away from busy Singel Canal, Paula found herself alone in the dark streets. Her heels clipped a staccato tattoo on the sidewalk.

Slowly at first, then increasingly rapidly, her heart began to pulse in her throat, sound in her ears. At a scurrying noise she cried out, then shook her head in self-derision when two cats scampered across her path. She was a scared ninny.

Paula began to hum, then stopped, irritated to realize the tune was the one she and Christophe had danced to. She should have let him drive her home. Refusing had been pigheaded. Her high heels were a nuisance, but she broke into a trot.

Halfway along the next block she stopped. The echo she heard seemed a beat slower than it should be for her own feet. Maybe Christophe had followed her, after all. She turned, a smile on her face, and saw no one. She *was* jumpy. Amsterdam was an active city, all right, but everything she read suggested there was nothing to fear if you stayed out of the wrong areas.

Slowly, deliberately keeping her pace steady, she crossed the silent street.

The prickling sensation that began at the base of her spine, crept upward, vertebra by vertebra. Her own footsteps tapped, slender heel tips nick-nicking cobbles. The other feet that had started moving behind her made the unmistakable sound of a man's leather-soled shoes.

Chapter Nine

Paula ran. So did the other. Horrified, she slowed to look back, still sidestepping. The shadow was a distance behind her, but it loomed tall—a man—and he was chasing her.

Panic ripped at her throat. She was a fool, a fool. Her own pride had brought her this terror.

The middle of the street. If she ran down the center of the pavement she'd feel safer. Damn her flimsy shoes. There was no time to take them off. *Yell!* she ordered her pounding brain. *Scream!* She opened her mouth but no sound came out. Rape victims, black shapes facing away from television cameras, said they couldn't scream. *Rape.* Paula choked on jarring sobs. Where was he? Why didn't he just grab her and get it over with? She'd never outrun him.

If a car would come, she'd be picked up in its headlights. No car would come.

She darted to the other sidewalk, her chest one racking pain. Shadows from narrow alleys between buildings sliced across her path. Each black wedge lived, had substance. Again and again she flinched, waiting for impact with each dark barrier, only to run on and face another.

The strap of her purse slipped from her shoulder. Paula grabbed it and caught her heel at the same time. Stumbling, flailing, she lunged into a wall and dropped the purse. She rushed on without it. The footsteps were closer, right behind her. He had to be there now, inches from reaching out to grab her.

Ahead yet another alley shadow loomed. Burning sweat ran into her eyes. She made as if to run on, then veered abruptly into the tiny passage, fled, elbows bent, fists clenched, into its waiting nothingness. If she could make it to another street, maybe a busier street, she might lose him.

She saw the wall seconds before she would have smashed into it.

"Help!" Even she barely heard her cry. She'd run into a blind alley. The only way out was the way she'd come. The way the man was coming. Chest heaving, she turned. The shadow wasn't running anymore. He walked on feet that seemed quieter, not hurrying, closing in.

There was nowhere to go.

Paula flattened against the wall, pressed her palms into its brick surface and waited. The man's silhouette loomed against the fuzzy shaft of light from the street.

She wouldn't just stand there and do nothing. Awkwardly, keeping her eyes on the advancing form, she dragged off one shoe, then the other. She threw one aside and spread her feet, bracing, holding a shoe aloft, its heel poised for a sweeping jab.

He stopped.

Paula rubbed the sweat from her eyes with the back of a forearm. "Okay," she whispered, "come on." She heard his breathing and the tiny flicker of resolve died.

He dropped abruptly, catching Paula off guard. For seconds she couldn't see him. Then he leaped up before her, grabbing her wrists, wrenching away the shoe. It hardly made a sound as it ricocheted off the wall and disappeared.

She had never known such fear. She opened her mouth but again no sound would come.

"Be still," the man hissed. His head was close and she saw his pale eyes glint through slits in a ski mask.

"No!" she shouted, surprised at the noise. "No!" And she kicked at him with her bare feet.

"You will be still and quiet." The voice, heavy with a Dutch accent, was accompanied by cold sharp pressure on the front of her neck.

A knife. This man was going to kill her. Paula struggled with the fuzz creeping into her brain. She mustn't faint.

More footsteps sounded, more running. Paula moved, trying to see over her captor's shoulder.

"I said, be quiet," he ordered. "Or you're dead. Believe me, lady, you will feel, but where I cut you will make no sound."

Paula closed her eyes.

"Listen carefully," the deep voice ground on insistently. His breath fanned her face. "If you want to live, Paula Renfrew, get out of Amsterdam."

For an instant she didn't notice. Then her eyes were wide open and staring. He'd used her name. This wasn't an accidental encounter arising out of being in the wrong place at the wrong time. He *knew* her.

"Do you understand what I say?" he persisted, pressing the knife harder.

"Who are you?" Paula asked. "Why are you doing this?"

"That isn't important. Let the past die. What happened years ago is finished. We want it to stay finished. It's all over and done with. *Do you understand?*"

She understood she wanted out of this alley. Paula nodded, then stifled a cry when she felt the knife break her skin.

"Good," he said, backing away. "That is very good. Make your excuses for leaving. What you say to your friends means nothing to us. But make it convincing, then start to withdraw. Go home to your safe place in America and forget what took place here."

When he'd put several yards between them, he turned and slipped swiftly from the alley and out of sight.

She was going to faint, Paula thought, groping against the wall, lowering herself to sit in a doubled-over heap. Violent trembling shook every muscle, and her sobs, when they came, hurt her chest. Cautiously she touched her neck and felt a drizzle of blood. Her teeth chattered uncontrollably.

"Is there someone in there?"

A man's voice boomed hollowly to her. She shrank farther back, trying to stem the croaking noises she made.

"Answer me." This time the voice was closer. "Where are you?

"Paula? Oh, my God, Paula."

Strong arms that made no attempt at care, gathered her up and hauled her to the sidewalk. Christophe, minus his jacket, his hair a disheveled mess, stared into her face. "What's happened to you?" He looked down. "Where are your shoes? Speak to me, dammit."

All she could do was cry.

Christophe pulled her farther out until they were beneath a streetlight. He pushed back her tangled hair and lifted her chin, searching her eyes, touching her cheeks. His hand stopped in midmotion. "Your neck," he whispered. "Your neck's cut. How . . . ?"

"Hold me," she moaned at last. "A man followed me. He had a knife."

He gripped her upper arms, shaking her slightly. "Don't fold up on me, Paula. You can't let go yet. Did he . . . did he . . ."

She shook her head slowly. "Rape me? No. He just said a lot of things I didn't understand and cut my neck. I want to go home."

Christophe took a handkerchief from his pocket and bent to examine the wound. "It's small," he said. "Antiseptic and a dressing will fix it. Are your shoes in the alley?"

At her murmured "Yes" he retrieved them and helped her put them on. He jogged down the block to find her purse.

"Thank you," she said brokenly when he returned, grateful for the arm he put around her.

"Come back to my place," he said. "It's closer and I can fix that nick for you."

"No," Paula said. "Thank you, but I want to go home."

Christophe didn't argue except against her intention to continue walking. He lifted her easily, carried her back to where the Saab was parked and settled her inside.

The drive to Herengracht and the Kohls took less than ten minutes. Outside the house, Christophe switched off the engine and turned to Paula. "I started to follow you as soon as you left, then lost you. First I thought you'd taken that one taxi—it slowed, but then I realized he must have had a fare. I caught sight of your dress, but you were a long way ahead. I should have made you let me take you home, used force, if necessary."

She edged closer to the door. Bits and pieces of something nebulous began to take shape in her mind. "I must get into the house," she said.

"Okay." Christophe was out of the car and opening her door before she could say anything more. "Benno and Anna will be in bed by now. I'll play Florence Nightingale to that neck and make you a hot drink. Then you can give me a blow-by-blow description of tonight's fiasco." While he spoke he helped her to the sidewalk.

"Thanks, Christophe," Paula said evenly. "For everything. But you've done your bit. Now I just want to stick on that dressing you talked about and collapse for the night."

"But I thought you'd want to talk . . . ."

"I don't" she said more shortly than she intended. She tapped his shoulder lightly to soften her manner. "Not now, anyway. We'll talk when I've stopped quaking like a scared kid. I'll call you, okay?" She started up the steps.

"Wouldn't you like me to stay with you until you're calmer?"

She'd like what was best for her, Paula thought, keeping her face averted. "Don't worry. I'm fine. We'll be in touch."

She did give him a quick glance as she closed the door. His face was upturned but she couldn't see his expression. That might have told her a lot, she decided.

Inside the door she kept the light off and waited until the Saab roared away.

Someone had told that crazy man where to find her this evening. He'd been waiting for her, assured she would eventually come from the houseboat.

Only one person knew she was going out with Christophe tonight: Christophe.

Chapter Ten

Sunday of the Fourth Week:

"Good grief." Peter yawned, peering at Paula with bleary eyes. "What time is it?"

"Almost three in the afternoon," she said dryly. "And it's Sunday, in case you've forgotten that, too. Should I come back when you're more rested?" Two sleepless nights had left her incapable of diplomacy.

Peter straightened with evident effort and opened his door wider. "Come in, smartass. You're certainly in fighting form." His eyes narrowed as she passed him. "You look like hell," he said slowly.

"Thanks." Paula flopped full length on his leather couch, shoving several cushions beneath her head. "You don't look so hot yourself."

"Hard night," he said, smiling as he made his way to the abbreviated kitchen in the corner of his big living room. "I'll make us both coffee. We could obviously use it."

Paula sat up and glanced apprehensively in the direction of Peter's bedroom. He caught her look and shook his head. "I don't have company, love, so relax."

She was too tired to blush. "I've got to talk to you, Peter."

"Talk away, darling. I'm all ears."

"Peter, this isn't a joke."

"Oh, I know—believe me, three o'clock on a Sunday afternoon tells me this is going to be serious stuff."

"Dammit," Paula muttered, exasperated. She got up and went to lean on the counter separating the kitchen from the rest of the room. "See this, Peter?" She tilted up her chin. "There's a cut under this dressing."

He poured boiling water over coffee in its filter before glancing up. "Let me guess," he said. "You got so upset you decided to end it all?"

Paula rounded the counter and stood next to him. "Close, Peter, close. Except someone else decided to end it all for me."

He stared, his lips slowly parting.

She touched the dressing. "A man in a ski mask followed me into an alley on Friday night and held a knife to my throat."

The kettle clattered to the stove. Peter grabbed it before it could tip off a burner and fall to the floor. "Good God, Paula. You aren't serious."

"Oh, Peter, Peter." She rubbed her eyes wearily. "I haven't slept in two nights. Coming here this afternoon is the first trip I've made out of the house since Friday and all the way I was looking over my shoulder."

"Sit down now," Peter said, taking her hand and leading her back to the couch. "Sit there and tell me everything. And unwind, would you. I'm here. Nothing's going to happen to you."

Unfamiliar tears burned her eyes and she lowered her head. "It's all going to sound pretty mad." She sat close beside him, her fingers entwined in his. "I went to dinner with Christophe. I thought it might give me a chance to talk him into giving Benno and Lukas their loan. Afterward we went back to his houseboat—your houseboat. My mediation efforts didn't go well and I left.''

"Alone?"

"Stupid, right? I wouldn't let Christophe drive me home. Anyway, I couldn't get a taxi and some creep followed me.''

"And held a knife on you." Peter's grip on her hand tightened. "Did he do anything else to hurt you?"

"No." She looked up into his bright blue eyes. "I was afraid that's what he wanted, too. It wasn't. Peter, he knew who I was. He'd been waiting for me. He must have known exactly where I was and that I was going to leave alone."

Peter bit into his bottom lip. He got up and began to pace. "What are you suggesting? Are you saying Christophe had something to do with this guy frightening you? Why would he do a thing like that?"

"To make me back off. He knows I'm aware of the thefts and his own plan to make life impossible for Benno and Lukas. He came rushing up immediately after that joker with the knife left. He poured on the concern, said he'd followed me as soon as I left the boat but lost me. I don't believe him.''

"No, Paula, no." Peter shook his head slowly. "Christophe wouldn't do a thing like this. There's got to be another explanation. Did the guy say anything? You said he knew who you were.''

Paula buried her face in her hands. She needed sleep. "He told me to leave things alone, or something like that," she said between her splayed fingers. "Get out. It's all over. That kind of stuff. He told me to go back to the States. And he threatened to kill me, Peter." She dropped her hands between her knees and Peter stopped in front of her. "He said he'd cut me where he'd stop me making any noise," Paula finished.

Peter looked pale. "The bastard. He's got to have something to do with whoever stole those stones. Maybe because you've been seen with Christophe and he's effectively put a stop to their scam—at least for now—they hope to get at him through you. Who knows?" He rubbed his forehead in frustration. "They've singled you out for some reason. It begins to look as if the car thing was deliberate, too. We all agree Christophe's motive for being so hardheaded is his need to make his reputation even bigger with daddy and the uncles. But he wouldn't sink so low as to do these things to you, Paula, believe me."

What Peter said made sense. Relief warmed every aching part of Paula. Whatever Christophe might do to gain his own ends, he wouldn't hurt her. Of course he wouldn't. How could she have been so foolish? But being seen with him might be the cause of her problems.

"Peter," she said, "you're right. Someone thinks I'm a threat. I'm going straight to Lukas. He has to know about this. Or maybe I should speak to Sandi first—"

Peter hauled her to her feet. "Neither," he said flatly. "I know you're concerned about Kohl's. I'm more worried about you. Maybe it wouldn't be such a bad idea for you to take a vacation until the dust settles."

"Leave Amsterdam?" Paula said disbelievingly. "Allow these . . . these whoever they are to frighten me away from what I've wanted all my life?"

"Only for a little while." Peter went to rattle around in a cupboard. He produced two mugs and poured coffee.

Paula took the mug he offered her. "I'm not going," she announced. "And Lukas and Benno need to know what's happened. I think you've hit the nail on the head. I'm probably being victimized as a way of trying to get at Christophe. He needs to realize that and so do Benno and Lukas. They all have to be on guard for more trouble. As for me, I've already received their ultimate threat. I don't know what else could happen to me."

Peter pressed his lips together and absently tapped his fingers against his mug. "Okay," he said quietly. "You came to me because you say you trust me, right?"

"I do." She nodded emphatically.

"Do you trust me enough to do what I ask? I've known all these people a lot longer than you, and I think I'm in a better position to figure out the best course to follow."

"What are you thinking of doing?" Paula asked. She waited while he considered. The seconds seemed like minutes.

"Lukas has too much on his mind," he said at last. "And Sandi. And I don't know how much more pressure Benno can take. Christophe's the one I have to talk to. Me, Paula, not you. *I'll* talk to Christophe as soon as the time seems right. Meanwhile, you're to stay away from him. Don't call him. Don't accept calls *from* him if you can avoid it. If you see him when you're at work, make an excuse to duck out. Sit tight, you understand? You've gone through enough as it is, and you certainly don't need to take any more chances."

"You're sure I shouldn't at least speak to Lukas?" Paula persisted uncertainly.

"I'm sure. It could be enough to send him after Christophe in a way that would make sure Kohl's doesn't get a guilder from St-Giles. *That* will be the end for our friends, Paula. Don't do it. Leave everything to me, please."

Several hours later, Paula let herself into the backhouse. The phone was ringing. She walked around it, willing the noise to stop. The caller was likely to be Christophe. She'd agreed to follow Peter's instructions to the letter, and the last person she could risk talking to so soon was Christophe. The ringing stopped. Paula sighed with relief and headed for her loft bedroom. She wasn't alone anymore. Now she had Peter to help her.

Her foot was on the bottom step when the phone jangled again. She backed to the wall and waited. Each blast of sound made her wince and the ringing went on and on.

She couldn't live in fear. In a rush, Paula covered the few feet to the phone and snatched up the receiver. "Yes?" she said sharply.

"Paula, is that you?" A man's voice whispered.

The all too familiar fear made her clutch the receiver hard. "Yes."

"This is Lukas. Don't talk—listen. Meet me in the workroom as fast as you can get there. Don't tell anyone where you're going. I need your help."

"Lukas..." she began, but a steady buzzing told her he'd hung up.

Paula hovered over the phone, trying to decide if she should alert Peter. Lukas had instructed her to tell no one. And he'd sounded desperate. She grabbed her purse and fled, not stopping to think until she'd got off the bus at the corner of Rokin and arrived at the work entrance to Kohl's in already gathering dusk.

The door was ajar.

Lukas must have been so distracted that he'd forgotten to lock it. Normally during nonbusiness hours she would have expected to ring, then wait for the alarm system to be turned off before she could enter.

She must get to Lukas. Inside, she took the steps two at a time and almost fell over a barricade across the second flight. Two boards, crossed, held her back. A paint can and brush stood behind them. Paula raced down again and wrenched aside the elevator's grill door.

The old car clanked slowly upward. Paula pressed her hands against the side walls in the tiny cubicle, tapping her toe with impatience. She passed the second floor and looked upward as the third began coming into view. One more to go.

The elevator stopped.

"Come on, come on," Paula groaned. "Don't foul up now, you old beast." She punched the button for the fourth floor. Nothing happened.

Paula flexed her fingers, trying to remain calm. She pressed the button for the fourth floor again, then every other button. There was no response, only the gentle creaking of the ropes and wires above and below her.

"Lukas!" she yelled, craning, trying to see upward. "Lukas! Down here. In the elevator. Lukas!" He must hear her. "Lukas!"

The lights went out.

Paula screamed and immediately covered her mouth. The power had failed. What was the matter with her? A simple power failure had stopped the elevator— No, the elevator stopped before the lights went out. She would not panic. She *would not*. Common sense, not panic, would get her out of here.

Opening the door would be tricky, but not impossible. Reaching the third floor from her position was out of the question, but she could open the inner grill and reach down to work the latch on the second floor's guard door.

She worked the stiff grill open and dropped flat on her stomach, stretching to feel for the handle she needed. Her fingers found only metal bars, each one the same as the next. Her arm wasn't long enough, and even if she dared risk trying to climb down, there wasn't enough room. Unless someone came along, she was trapped. Where was Lukas? If he'd come and gone already, no one was likely to show before morning.

Paula sat up and scooted into a corner. Lukas wasn't here. If he were, he'd already be on the stairs, making noise, something. She thought of his call. *His* call. The hoarse whisper on the phone could have belonged to any man. What a fool. She'd walked straight into another trap.

The sound of the third floor safety door opening brought Paula to her feet. "Lukas, it that you?" She laughed and cried at the same time. "Thank God. I thought I was stuck in here till morning."

There was no reply.

"Can you get the lights on?" she yelled. "Or find a flashlight? There's one in the staff changing rooms. In the first cupboard inside the door."

A crash reverberated through the car and it began to rock. Paula was thrown against a wall. More thunderous blows to the roof of the elevator followed. She slid down to sit, her skin crawling while she strained to make out some shape, any shape in the darkness above. "Lukas," she whispered, knowing whoever was doing this to her wasn't Lukas.

The hammering increased, punishing her eardrums until she hunched on all fours, shielding her head, pressing the insides of her wrists to her ears. Why hadn't she called Peter? He'd have come with her, or more likely, stopped her from coming at all.

Paula curled into a tighter ball. She heard her own sobs, a harsh, croaking noise. Where was Christophe now? What was he doing this very moment? Her thoughts made a quiet place in the middle of her anguish. She wanted him. With Christophe she'd always feel safe. The admission shocked her. Several seconds of silence passed before she realized she was no longer rocking. The banging had stopped.

Slowly, Paula sat up again, pushing her damp hair away from wet cheeks. She settled back into the corner, hugging her knees. What would they do to her now?

The next sound was of footsteps clipping carefully downstairs, then the front door latch clicked.

Paula rested her head back. So this was her lot tonight, to be scared into close hysteria and then left alone in the dark.

"Christophe," she said brokenly and closed her eyes, seeing his face in her mind. She felt again his powerful arms, gentle hands, the soft touch of his mouth. Whether she liked it or not, love could come without bidding and regardless of what Christophe thought of her, she was falling in love with him. And Peter was right, for her own safety she must stay away from the man. *Dammit.*

The seconds crawled by, and the minutes, blending into great endless hours. Paula heard the clock on a nearby tower strike twelve. She shouldn't sleep in case someone came back, in case...

CHRISTOPHE POURED A STIFF SCOTCH and returned to the couch. He closed the file he'd been reading and tossed it to the growing pile on the deck. Beside him lay a much shorter stack.

He crossed his arms and drank, staring blindly at one of Peter's blown-up black-and-white shots. Again he thought of Paula Renfrew, as he'd thought of her a thousand times before in the last two days. She'd insisted she'd contact him. The message had been implicit: don't call me, I'll call you. He sniffed and picked up one of the files beside him.

Benno and Lukas had finally shaken loose on all records. He'd spent the afternoon with personnel data and hadn't exactly found earthshattering material. Still, there

were some possible leads here, some titillating bits and
pieces.

"I'll call you," Paula had said. He glanced at the phone.
So why didn't she? Hell, he was getting a case on the
woman, and he couldn't allow himself the luxury. The hit-
and-run deal, the attack on Friday night—what did they
mean? What conclusion was he supposed to draw from
them? Paula had come right out and asked him to back off
from his investigations here. Could she be part of a larger
network of criminals who had started out using her as a
decoy with him, then turned on her when she failed to
make progress? Was her life in danger? His insides contracted and the reaction sent off a warning flare in his
mind. He was beginning—scratch beginning—he already
cared about Paula and he must stop. Persecution and pro-
tection made unlikely bedfellows. There was only one thing
that could make it worse... No. He didn't love Paula, he
was attracted to her. Christophe drank again. Balancing
protecting her with finding out what she might be guilty of
should be enough to keep his mind and body away from
other possibilities with her.

The file in his hand was Frank Lammaker's. Nothing
here he didn't already know. Christophe set it down and
picked up Kersten Gouda's. He'd almost discarded it, but
something kept drawing him back to the scribbled notes,
most in Benno's handwriting, about the woman. She took
her vacation time all at once, usually in midwinter, and
headed for the south of France. Her vacation address was
noted. Christophe stared at the hotel name again. He knew
the place and it was expensive, a little rich for most diamond pages, he would have thought. But she could have
resources outside the obvious.

He glanced to the top of the page, to Benno's entries
from his initial interview with Mrs. Gouda. Evidently she'd

been very forthcoming with information about her personal status. The wife of a policeman missing for some years, she believed at that time he'd been abducted. She refused to accept the opinion of his chief that he had simply decided to disappear, that people didn't stay abducted for long without someone hearing something. Kersten, then thirty—Christophe checked the date and noted that she must now be forty-four—had stated confidently that she was sure her husband would eventually contact her and need her help.

Christophe began to close the file. Kersten Gouda was certainly an interesting woman, but not remarkable for his purposes. He slapped the folder wide open and stared at the address beneath Kersten's name: *79 Overstraat*. He'd missed it! After days of searching telephone books, a dozen trips past the house to see if he could observe someone coming or going, and one risky direct approach when there'd been no reply to his ring at the door of 79 Overstraat, he'd almost allowed the occupant to slip through his fingers.

Kersten Gouda lived at 79 Overstraat. He whooped and flapped the file back and forth. Pieces were sliding together.

Grinning to himself, he put Kersten's records with Frank's and picked up Victor Hodez's. The diligent Victor had been a contemporary of Paula's father, Michael. He, too, had been a suspect in the theft of a large gem, then cleared by Michael Renfrew's rapid defection. Christophe flipped through the stack of papers on Victor. He'd started with Kohl's as an apprentice and come through the rough period of the theft to rise to his present position as head polisher. Apart from that one incident, his history was squeaky clean.

Christophe sifted through several record books to a scuffed volume from thirty-five years previously. All employees from that time were listed. He found Victor's name under the apprentice classification, and Michael Renfrew, together with a notation that he left without notice. A Lars Hugo was another contemporary of Hodez and Renfrew. Hugo had left after his apprenticeship to take a job in Antwerp. A fourth young man, Leo Erkel, rounded out the number. Erkel's entry had elicited an exclamation point after "Has decided to finish out apprenticeship with Metter's." Christophe shook his head faintly. That must have pleased whichever Kohl had been in charge at the time.

Another book held descriptions of stones and the names of craftsmen who worked on them. Another column stated buyers' names and date of sale. He easily located entries for the thirteen stolen stones Benno had tried so hard to cover. Christophe checked the finisher's initials for each one, hoping his latest hunch would check out. It didn't. Four different men had worked on the stones. Damn. He lit a cigarette and stretched his limbs. Where was the common thread?

The last file on the couch was thin. *Paula Renfrew*. He flipped open the top cover without lifting the folder. Paula's picture, clipped to a letter, lay on top. Slowly he raised the photo to eye level, studied the lovely, uncomplicated face. In black and white the gentle curves of her features were accented, and the thickness of her lashes, the way they shadowed her eyes. He read the letter quickly. It was the first she'd written Benno, asking for a job.

Christophe stood and walked to a window on the canal. Paula Renfrew did have a connection with the diamond thefts. No way could he persuade himself out of the obvious. He looked back at the pile of personnel records. How did these people fit together? With a long sigh, he leaned against the window. This operation could probably use the expertise of the entire Interpol, Scotland Yard and FBI organizations; there were certainly enough trails to follow and loose ends dangling to keep more than a platoon of trained men busy.

He looked at Paula's picture again. This beautiful woman—for him, this increasingly desirable woman—had been at the center of every overt act since he'd arrived. If only he could stop himself from wishing they'd met when neither had more to gain or more to lose.

Chapter Eleven

The man threw himself on the bed. "How do you know this?"

"He told me," the woman replied.

"You've had another contact?"

She sighed. "We'll keep having to deal with this man until we get what we want."

"But he cut her neck? My God."

"He said her neck had been cut accidentally, not that *he* cut it."

"My God," the man repeated and gripped a bedpost above his head with one hand. "We've got to get out of this. She might have been killed. Murder would only accomplish one thing—we'd almost certainly be caught."

"She wasn't killed and we aren't going to be caught." The woman sat on the edge of the bed. "And maybe the scares she's had will keep her out of our hair."

"The car was stupid, too." He scooted around her and stood. "That was stupid and unnecessary. A sure way to point in certain directions if she decides to go to the police."

"Evidently she's too concerned about her benefactors for that." The feminine laugh was unnaturally high.

"Anyway, I can't worry about her now. We've got other problems."

"What problems?"

"We've gone through all but three stones. He wants another tonight, which will leave one and the pear-shape. We need more diamonds just in case."

"Let him have the pear." The man's voice dropped.

"No," his companion stated flatly. "We keep that as our trump card, if we need it. That gem is enough for any man's ransom, if it comes to that."

"Ransom," he snorted. "I think you finally used the right term for what we've been paying, only we've gone beyond that, haven't we?"

Pale skin became paler. "Meaning?"

"Meaning why not be honest with ourselves. We're being blackmailed now. We can't go back and there's no end in sight. He'll squeeze us forever."

She started to cry soundlessly.

"Don't." He put a hand on her shoulder. "Don't cry. I'll do what has to be done, but slower from here on. One stone at a time.

Monday of the Fourth Week:

Paula listened to footsteps on the stairs. Dawn had long ago sent meager dustings of pale gray light into the elevator. She could read her watch, and it was time for the first Kohl employees to arrive. Still she was afraid to shout.

She stood up, straightening her sweater and brushing her jeans. She found a comb in her purse and dragged it through her hair. What happened to her from now on could hang on how well she calculated each move.

Whoever was climbing the stairs started to whistle, and Paula almost collapsed with relief. Frank Lammaker. Only one man around here had that tuneless whistle and insisted upon using it endlessly.

She cleared her throat. "Frank." Her first call was tentative, then she shouted, "Frank! The elevator's stuck. Can you get me out of here?"

Several seconds passed before the car jerked and moved upward. Paula shook back her hair and hitched her purse strap over her shoulder. *Look normal,* she instructed herself, preparing to smile. Frank mustn't know she'd spent the night there. No one else should be involved in what was happening—not if she hoped to extricate herself from danger, *and* help Benno. She had to appear nonchalant to Frank, then make it to the bathroom—quickly. Next on the agenda would be a call to Peter.

"How long have you been in there?" Frank asked, peering down as she came into view. "Why didn't you yell before?" He swept open the fourth floor doors, laughing, his blond curls still tousled from walking in the wind.

Paula liked Frank. Without any proof, she was certain he was innocent of any wrongdoing against his employers. "I was only in here a few minutes," she lied, stepping out, trying not to let her stiffness show. He would assume she'd entered through the retail showrooms as most manufacturing employees did early in the morning.

"You should have hailed old Victor. He's always up there at the crack of dawn." Frank looked at her closely. "You okay? You look pretty ragged around the edges."

"I'm fine. Stayed up too late last night." Of course Victor would be in by now, but he also used the stairs and she hadn't heard him. Maybe he'd come early while she'd dozed without knowing it. "I tried calling Victor, but you know he's going deaf, don't you?" Deception upon deception, but what choice did she have anymore?

"I wonder who switched off the power to the elevator?" Frank said almost to himself.

Paula wiped her palms on her jeans, thinking madly. "The power panel's in the hall outside the showrooms, next to the one for the lights. Anyone could have done it by mistake." She was going to have to watch every word. "I'd better get moving, Frank. Victor gets on my case if I'm late."

Frank rolled his eyes. "Victor gets on everyone's case for something. Hey, how about lunch? You do look a bit like a wilted hothouse flower at the moment. Come out with a bunch of us to the Pilsener Club. Great place. Great beer and food."

"I don't know." Paula could think of nothing but the bathroom now. "Maybe."

"Great," Frank said, starting up the stairs again. "I'll come and find you when I've finished my morning deliveries."

Paula hung around long enough to check the lower flights. As she'd suspected, the crossed boards and paint can were gone.

Half an hour later she was feeling better. She blessed her resourcefulness in always carrying a travel toothbrush and small quantities of the basic makeup she used. Given the ghastly night she'd spent, sleeping in snatches, only to awaken with violent starts, she looked fairly human. Bustling, making much of gathering odds and ends from her bench and announcing she had to speak to someone downstairs, Paula made it through the workroom and out from Victor's eagle eye without his comment.

Calling Peter from Kohl's was out of the question. Dressed in her blue coverall, she ran along Rokin toward Dam Square and found a booth.

There was no reply at Peter's home. Paula searched the phone book and found the number of his studio. He answered at the first ring.

"Peter," she said urgently. "I want to bring you up to date so you'll know what's happened if something...if anything...Peter, I want to make sure I'm missed if I disappear."

Dead silence met her comment.

"Are you there?" she asked sharply.

"Yes," Peter said and she heard him swallow. "Did something else happen?"

Paula expelled a shaky breath. "When I got home from your place I received what I thought was a call from Lukas. He asked me to meet him in the workroom of Kohl's. Then I was trapped in the elevator all night. I just got out."

"Good God," Peter said explosively. "Lukas wouldn't trap you in an elevator, Paula, or anywhere else. Why should he? This is getting crazy. We're going to the police."

"No," Paula insisted. "If we blow this wide open, where will Benno and Lukas be, then? They'll be lucky to see Christophe's dust as he leaves town, sans the loan. St-Giles wouldn't touch them for sure, then. And afterward the whole of Amsterdam would know what's been going on. They'd be finished."

"Okay, okay," Peter said testily. "But we don't need a second Joan of Arc. Martyrs are out of fashion. Let's talk this through and decide what to do. First, why would anyone do this to you?"

"To remind me I'm supposed to get out of town? To frighten me enough to make me hurry?" Paula suggested.

Peter clucked his tongue thoughtfully. "Shouldn't have thought it necessary so soon after the little knife number. Oh, hell... I've got it."

"What?"

"They're watching every move you make. You must have been seen coming to my place yesterday. Only when you rang the intercom outside the front door there would be no way for a watcher who wasn't close to know it was my bell and not Lukas's you pressed. Of course they'd think of Lukas first."

Paula thought an instant. "But even if I *was* going to Lukas, so what?"

"If they decided you might be spilling the beans about the threats against you—getting Lukas on your side—they might want to change your opinion of him. Make you think he was responsible for the threats in the first place. They might even hope to plant the idea Lukas is involved in the thefts. Or, if they know Christophe is hot on their trail, and we're both pretty sure they do, these turkeys could have it in their heads to use you to set Christophe and Lukas against each other. But I'm sure of one thing, Paula, they desperately want you out of Amsterdam as soon as possible."

"I think so, too," Paula sighed. "And I'm not going."

"Are you sure it wouldn't be best."

"I've never been more sure of anything, Peter. Just the fact that something about me keeps them stirred up is valuable. They're going to make a mistake and reveal themselves. Wait and see. I'm right."

Peter didn't answer for a while. "I hope you are right," he said finally. "I'll get to Christophe as soon as the time seems right. I don't want to deal with him unless I'm sure we can both be rational. Paula, anything happens, *anything*, and you tell me, promise?"

"Promise," she agreed fervently.

"What are your favorite flowers?" he asked.

Paula blinked. "Flowers? Oh . . . all kinds. Gardenia . . ." she hesitated, feeling Christophe's presence all around her. "Roses, I guess." Another reminder of Christophe was the last thing she needed.

"Typical woman." Peter laughed. "I'm going to send you some. You deserve a treat. Just make sure you don't stick yourself on a thorn. With your track record—"

"Thanks, Peter," Paula broke in dryly. "Talk to you soon."

By eleven-thirty, Paula was longing for her lunch date with Frank and his friends. A chance to be with young, uncomplicated people sounded heavenly. She needed an opportunity not to think of anything heavier than what beer to order.

"Still eleven-thirty I believe, Paula."

Victor's voice had an ice-water quality. She looked up guiltily from her watch. "Eleven thirty-one," she corrected, smiling.

His expression remained deadpan. "Hmm. The young find it hard to concentrate these days." He bent to his work once more. "What happened to your neck? Cut yourself shaving?"

Paula had to laugh. Victor had just made his closest attempt at humor in her experience.

"You should watch out," he added. "You might cut your whole throat."

The smile slipped from Paula's face. *If you only knew,* she thought. "I'll be more careful next time, Victor." What should she say when someone asked what she'd done. "I caught the skin in the zipper of my windbreaker," she said. Victor grunted, accepting the explanation. Lying was becoming easier, and she hated it.

Promptly at twelve, Frank stuck his head through the door. "Ready to go, Paula?" He kept a wary eye on Victor, who didn't appear to hear.

"You bet," she said with alacrity, stopping her wheel.

"Great. Meet you out front when you're ready."

Paula hurried into the empty staff room and opened her locker. She'd give almost anything for a change of clothes.

The door opened and closed behind her. Paula slipped off her coverall before turning around.

"I'm still waiting for that call." Christophe stood with his hands sunk in his pants' pockets. "Remember the call you said you'd make to me?"

She hung the coverall inside her locker and fished out her purse. *"Duck out if you see him at work,"* Peter had warned. With Christophe looming between her and the door, ducking out would take swift maneuvers. "How are things going, Christophe?" she asked with as much lightness as she could muster. "Figured out which of us is the arch criminal?"

"Dammit, woman." He reached to grab her wrist and pull her close. "We're past the game-playing stage here. The last time I saw you, some madman had made a pretty good attempt at sticking a knife in your throat. You weren't so flip then. What happened to calm you down?"

"The guy was a mugger." She tried to jerk free. "He lost his nerve. I got lucky, I guess."

"A mugger who told you to get out of Amsterdam and didn't try to steal from you?"

Paula thought fast. "He must have seen I didn't have a purse and he just said a lot of stuff because he was mad."

Christophe's face was a rigid mask, his eyes brown steel. "Why are you avoiding me? I've had plenty to worry about since Friday night, without you adding to the pot."

He worried about her. Paula closed her eyes a fraction, gathering her composure. Whether she wanted to or not, she cared about his man, but she'd be a fool to imagine he felt the same, or to forget the enormous barriers separating them.

He tightened his hold on her.

"You're hurting my wrist, Christophe," Paula said, speaking as evenly as she could manage. "Let me go, please. I've got a date."

"No." He released her wrist and immediately clasped her in his arms, holding her hard against him. "I'm not letting you go without a lot more conversation, Paula."

She only struggled once. He was too strong for her. "Get this over with." Her hands came to rest on his shirt-front between the lapels of his jacket. She fastened her gaze on his striped tie and tried, uselessly, not to feel the hard lines of his body against hers.

"We felt something special together the other evening, Paula."

He was a master of understatement, she decided. Her flesh had already begun to ache. "Brandy and music are a heady combination," she said, not daring to look into his eyes.

"Not good enough," he said softly, backing against the door, pulling her with him. No one would be able to open it until he moved. "You aren't the type of woman to... I don't think just any man with a bottle of brandy and a few jazz records could turn you on."

Her head snapped up. She made fists against his chest. "You don't know what type of woman I am. If you did, you'd know—" She clamped her mouth shut. He'd know she was in love with him? Had she really almost said that?

"I know you're in trouble," he said promptly.

No beat in the conversation had been missed. She'd done nothing to give away her feelings. "My trouble is you," she said. "You're a lot of people's trouble around here. Go home, Christophe St-Giles. And give the good people who thought you were a friend the chance they need."

He regarded her levelly. "You are certainly convincing. And I want to believe you're for real. God, how I want to believe it."

Her heart sank. He still suspected her of involvement in those thefts. But there was another element. His voice had a real note of regret when he said he wanted to believe her.

"Nothing to say?" he persisted. "Are you sure there isn't something you'd like to tell me—something you'd like help with? I would help you, Paula, and I know it would be worth it—to both of us."

"Stop it!" she blurted, her heart breaking into rapid thuds. He was staring at her, his eyes narrowed. "We've got nothing else to talk about." She had spooked without being sure why.

Christophe saw her eyes widen and glanced at her neck. A hard pulse beat there. He'd frightened her. He didn't want that. He couldn't bear... Why did she have to be mixed up in something illegal?

Her body leaned into his, slumping. He supported her weight. The poor little devil had got into more than she'd bargained for and now she was caving in. Absurdly he wanted to keep holding her up—forever, if possible. She'd buried her face in his shirt. "Look at me," he said firmly, intending to try again to draw her out. She did as he asked, and he stared into depthless blue eyes fringed with lashes spiky from tears. "Oh, Paula, damn you," he groaned and pressed his lips to hers.

He heard a sob catch in her throat and drew back. Her eyes were closed and he kissed her lids, the salty, wet lashes. "You know what you do to me, don't you?" Again he checked her expression. This time it held pain, pain he instantly shared and felt strike deep at his insides.

"Let me go, Christophe," she whispered.

He kissed her again, sliding his hands beneath her sweater to span her supple waist. Her lips parted and she stood on tiptoe, clung to his neck, ran her fingers through his hair. The force of their coming together exploded the last fragments of his reason. He wanted her. He wanted her desperately. And she wanted him. Raw heat burned him, driving, thrusting him against her firm belly. Her tongue was in his mouth. He met it, then withdrew, took her bottom lip gently in his teeth.

"Paula. We need to be together."

"I know," she said softly. "I know."

Together, he thought, they needed to be together, alone and far from here, from the distrust threatening to rob him of a woman he was never going to forget. He'd like to take her away, forget the whole shooting match in this miserable city he was coming to hate. They'd make wild love all day, all night; come out of their nest only when weakness threatened to kill them both. His attempt at lightening the train of his thoughts only made his muscles more rigid. He couldn't take much more.

"*Merde.*" The pressure of the door handle cracked into his spine. He released Paula and she shot away, turning her back. "Paula." He lifted a hand toward her, then dropped it to his side, resigned, and rubbed a thumb across his mouth a second before pulling open the door.

"Geez." Frank Lammaker squeezed through the narrow space Christophe allowed him. "First stalled elevators, then doors that won't open." He fiddled with the lock and glanced at Christophe. "Did you have trouble with this thing?"

"No," Christophe said shortly. What did elevators have to do with it, he wondered. He didn't miss the knowing look in Frank's eyes. The other man knew there was nothing wrong with the door, or its lock.

Frank leaned to see around Christophe's shoulder. "Paula," he said. "You ready?"

Desperation threatened to undo Christophe. He flexed his fingers helplessly at his sides. He didn't want her to go, but he couldn't stop her.

"Coming," Paula said. Her voice was unmistakably husky.

Christophe turned in time to see her finish running a comb through shining hair. He shoved his hands into his pockets, willing his nerves to quit jumping.

Paula walked past him without meeting his eyes. Frank led the way from the room, but not before he'd cast a curious glance from Christophe to Paula's bowed face.

"Paula," Christophe said quietly. She stopped halfway through the doorway and faced him. He looked at his shoes and took a deep breath before saying, "Please think before you do anything."

Their eyes met. She didn't reply, didn't have to. Her mirrored emotions sent him all the messages he feared and hoped for: indecision, suspicion, pain . . . and so clearly—desire.

Chapter Twelve

"How many kinds of beer are there?" Paula asked, keeping her smile in place with difficulty.

Frank's friend Willem Bill waved his hands expansively and said, "Dozens, a dozen—who knows? Pick your poison. Light or dark, from a bottle or a barrel."

Paula liked the dark-haired young man with his animated brown eyes. "From a barrel," she announced, determined to enter the spirit of the occasion, "and light." She couldn't forget the look in Christophe's eyes as she'd left him.

A flaxen-haired young woman to her right touched Paula's arm. "Aren't you going to ask?" she said.

"Ask what?" Paula replied, puzzled.

"Why we call these pubs brown pubs? Tourists always want to know." This was Willem's girlfriend, Ghislaine, a fledgling actress.

"Ghislaine," Willem turned back from placing their order. "Paula lives here. She isn't a tourist, my love."

"I know what she means," Paula interrupted. "Newcomers. And I don't know why they're brown pubs."

The torrent of Dutch that followed made Paula laugh. Frank's "bunch" of friends, with the exception of Willem and an apprentice finisher from Metter's, were writers, painters and theatricals, twelve highly strung men and women in all. Evidently each had something to add to the explanation of why De Pilsener Club and hundreds of similar establishments in Amsterdam were labeled brown pubs.

Finally, Frank stood up and demanded silence. Shouts gradually subsided into snickers and he announced, "They are brown either because the floors and tables and most other parts of them are brown wood, or because the wallpaper is never changed and cigarette smoke turns it brown. Take you choice, okay?"

A disgruntled chorus went up and the dispute continued, occasionally translated into English when someone remembered Paula didn't speak Dutch.

She drank her beer in preoccupied silence and ate little sausages and lumps of cheese on toothpicks, dipping each one into hot mustard. As her thoughts deepened, she mentally drew apart from her boisterous companions. When would Peter talk to Christophe? Peter believed in her innocence; maybe he could convince his old friend.

A glint caught her eye, a bright flash from the other side of the smoke-filled, dimly lit room. Paula screwed up her eyes. The smoke stung and she was tired. The flash came again and this time she located its source, a stone in a man's ring reflecting the flame of a candle on his table. He sat alone, turning a glass of jenever around and around. Paula stared at the ring, and the hand, large and knotted, gripping the glass.

Even before she glanced up, she knew he would be watching her. Pale eyes bored into hers and Paula recoiled instinctively. The man wasn't old, or was he? A tall, wiry body, close-cropped, iron-gray hair and impassive features made his age difficult to estimate. With an effort, she

turned her attention to Frank. "We mustn't be late getting back," she said tightly.

Frank patted her hand. "We just arrived," he said, a
note of concern in his voice. "Are we too loud for you?"
He indicated the rest of the group. "We're always like
this."

"I love listening to you," she assured him honestly. "It's
just..." She glanced past him. The man still watched her
unflinchingly. Hair raised on the back of Paula's neck.
"There's a man over there who gives me the creeps. He's
staring and I keep getting the sensation I know him."

Frank started to swivel in his chair.

Paula gripped his forearm, shaking her head faintly.
"Don't look, please. I'm being silly. I never saw him before in my life."

He ignored her and turned around. "Willem," he said
over his shoulder, then swung back and dropped his voice.
"Isn't that some head honcho from Metter's over there?"

Willem dragged his attention away from Ghislaine and
checked in the direction of Frank's jabbing thumb. A sour
twist turned his pleasant mouth down. "You could say so.
Our polisher extraordinaire. The charming Leo Erkel
himself. If the rest of the employees held a least-liked, most
admired contest, old Leo would win hands down. The
guy's a genius with the nature of a rattlesnake. He lies in
wait, then strikes when you least expect it."

"Ignore him, Paula," Frank muttered when Willem was
once more engrossed in Ghislaine. "I've noticed him in
here before, and he always looks that way."

There was no ignoring Leo Erkel, Paula soon decided.
No matter how hard she worked at becoming part of the
table talk and pretending the man wasn't there, she felt his
eyes on her. When he got up she was instantly relieved...until he returned within minutes.

She clock-watched and tried to appear involved, willing the hands of her watch to move.

The heavy curtain covering the door billowed, and a wedge of smokey light appeared briefly while a hunched man entered. Paula stared, slowly reached to squeeze Frank's wrist. "It's Victor," she hissed. "Frank, you didn't tell me Victor came here for lunch." She hesitated before answering her own remark. "He doesn't. He never leaves Kohl's in the middle of the day."

Frank groaned. "Of all the lousy luck."

Victor peered around the room, allowing his eyes to adjust to the gloom. The next instant he was at Paula's side, bending over to whisper, "Come with me now. What do you think you are doing here?" He threw Frank a venomous glare, then pointedly ignored him.

Quelling embarrassment and indignation, Paula made an excuse to Frank and the others and followed Victor outside, where he immediately faced her. "How could you be such a fool?" he demanded. "To come here, with those people?"

Paula could only stare askance.

"This is where Metter's employees come every day. There is a feud between their house and ours. Mr. Kohl, old Mr. Kohl and young Mr. Kohl do not like—no—do not allow their employees to be with these people."

Paula barely contained the urge to tell Victor the Kohls couldn't control their staff outside work. "I didn't know, Victor." She managed to keep her voice level. "No mention of our work or the business was made. Most of the people I was with aren't even in the diamond trade. If it's such a sin, why does Frank feel comfortable?" She instantly regretted the last question.

"Frank isn't my concern," Victor said coldly. "*You* are. You are my apprentice and I will not have the work I've

put in with you wasted because you choose the wrong
company.''

"Why should going out to lunch with a few friendly
people waste the work you've done with me?'' She was
becoming exasperated.

"If you are . . . If Mr. Kohl decides not to allow you to
continue with us... Paula, listen to me carefully. There are
things I do not think you know. It's time you did.''

Paula pushed her hair back. A cool wind flattened her
cotton sweater to her back. "What things don't I know?''
A curious, tentative excitement snagged her stomach.
Victor had a trusted position with Kohl's. Perhaps he could
tell her facts that would help her present impossible circumstances.

He took her elbow and backed her against the dark
windows of De Pilsener. "First, it is important you not
draw undesirable notice to yourself, Paula. Coming here
was a great mistake. You are being watched.''

Her scalp tightened. "Go on.''

"Next, the reason for your being in Amsterdam is
known, although not, I think, exactly what you intend to
do.''

He'd lost her. "I'm sorry, Victor.'' She shook her head.
"I don't understand what you mean.''

"You don't deny that you know your father left
Amsterdam accused of theft? That he stole a single perfect diamond and got away with it?''

She opened and closed her mouth, aghast.

"No. Of course you don't deny it,'' Victor went on, apparently taking her silence for agreement. "I knew what
happened at the time. Nothing was proved for sure, of
course, but when Michael left without warning, we all
knew—it was assumed—that he was indeed the guilty one.
When you were hired I was surprised. But I know the older

Mr. Kohl's kindness. He would want to give you a chance. But I don't think he realizes you know what happened to your father, does he?''

Paula found her voice. ''I don't know what you're talking about,'' she began slowly. ''My father never stole anything. He was the most honest man I ever knew.''

''Paula.'' Victor touched her arm awkwardly. ''I understand how you feel. Michael told you what happened, didn't he, and he insisted he was innocent? You came here to...to what? To clear his name? To seek revenge? Whatever you had in mind, give it up. This is a tight industry, and as soon as people in it find out what you're doing they'll close ranks on you. I'm just grateful someone mentioned where you were coming today. You must stay away from any element that could draw undue attention to you and concentrate on your craft. One day you will be a credit to Kohl's, my girl.''

The blood in her body seemed to have drained to her feet. Her head was light. ''This is bizarre.''

Victor ignored her. ''I only hope I'm not too late. Our diligent hunter from Zurich also followed you here. He's across the street now, waiting to see what you do next.''

Christophe had followed her. Paula struggled not to search him out.

''I knew something was wrong as soon as he showed up in Amsterdam and then stayed, looking at books, poking around. Whatever is making Benno Kohl and his son so changed these days has to be St-Giles's fault, and I've noticed his interest in you. I believe there must have been enough trouble for the firm to need financial help...'' He paused as if making a decision. ''There could have been more thefts, and this Swiss is trying to find out more about it before he will agree to a loan. I can only guess at these things. But if I am right, and if he has also discovered your history, Paula, he could suspect you of being involved.''

She laughed bitterly. Victor had fitted the pieces together with deadly accuracy. But he'd also given her the missing piece in her own study—the real reason Christophe suspected her. "I tell you this, Victor." For Paula, spring's caress had deserted the wind. She crossed her arms tightly. "I've never heard the story you tell about my father. Why would I? He didn't do what he was accused of. And now I *will* find a way to make sure everyone else knows it.''

Victor clamped a hand on her shoulder. "Do nothing until this man Christophe is gone from Amsterdam. If you insist on probing, and I think you should not, at least wait. But that period of all our lives we shared with Michael is closed. I do not believe he would wish you to involve yourself. And now—we must hope it isn't too late to deflect this Christophe. In a few moments, we will walk past him and pretend to be surprised. I will deal with things.''

"I can't." She was suddenly desperate.

"You can," he insisted. "I will tell you one more thing and then we will go quickly, before our time here appears too long to explain. Robbery at Kohl's is more than a figment of my imagination. Word has it that a number of stones have been taken. Big stuff. You must not talk of this—to anyone. Benno and Lukas know about your father and I'm absolutely sure now that M. St-Giles does, too. The coincidence of your presence is too great. You are bound to be suspect. *I* know you have nothing to do with these thefts and that's why I'm here, to help you. I saw St-Giles ahead of me as I arrived on the street. I'm sure he's watching you.''

Victor paused, scrubbing at his jaw. "What is best?" he muttered. "What is best? Perhaps you should go to your home in America where you will be safe. Amsterdam could become too dangerous for you. A foreigner in trouble with Dutch law is really in trouble.'' He considered, frowning deeply. ''For now, we will *accidentally*, bump into our friend.''

They started walking and Paula sighted Christophe. He was buying flowers from a woman with a basket of bouquets and appeared absorbed. She tried to breathe slowly, counting, inhaling, exhaling.

Within yards of Christophe, Paula halted, transfixed by a car at the curb. It was small and white, its paint scratched. A Volvo, she noted. Her anxiety deepened. She glanced at the handle on the driver's side and knew she had seen its rusty surface before. Paranoia had taken over. Paula caught up with Victor who had stopped to wait for her. She made herself smile. There must be thousands of little white cars with rusty handles in Amsterdam. This one didn't have to be the one that had hit her.

''Well, well.'' Christophe looked up as they approached. ''What a surprise, Paula. And you, Victor. I hardly recognize you away from your wheel.''

''M. St-Giles.'' Victor bowed slightly. ''I, too, am surprised. I didn't know so many people knew this little street. Are you, er, are you going to De Pilsener Club?''

Paula couldn't believe his approach, to actually bring up the place she wasn't supposed to have visited. Perhaps Christophe hadn't seen her go in or come out. Oh, she was fooling herself, she decided angrily.

Christophe finished paying for the flowers. ''For a friend.'' He showed the brilliant assortment of blooms. ''I often walk around here. I know the area from when I spent a year in the city.''

''You would do well not to frequent De Pilsener,'' Victor advised in a low voice.

"Why?" Christophe raised his brows. "It's one of the best brown pubs in town."

"Ah, yes," Victor agreed. "But as I just told Paula, Philip Metter's people gather there almost every day and Mr. Kohl doesn't like us to be close to them. Paula didn't know. Fortunately I discovered she'd been invited there and I came to take her back. She understands now—don't you, Paula?"

She nodded, feeling stupid. "Victor is very good to me."

"I'm sure he is," Christophe said before adding to Victor, "Thank you for warning me. Why don't you leave Paula with me? We have a few things to discuss. I promise I'll get her back safely."

Victor's eyes found Paula's. He opened his mouth as if he would say something, then only shrugged. "If you insist. Will you be all right, Paula?" he said with emphasis.

She felt a warm rush of gratitude and sympathy toward the old man. "I'll be fine," she reassured him. "I'll see you soon."

Standing at Christophe's side, she watched Victor's retreating back with a sense of panic. What "things" did Christophe want to discuss with her?

"You okay?" Christophe asked, his voice oddly lacking its usual authority.

Paula avoided looking at him. "Fine, thanks."

A burst of noise from the door of De Pilsener Club preceded the eruption of Frank and his friends onto the sidewalk. Waving and shouting, Willem and Frank, with Ghislaine between them, crossed directly to the white car. Paula's lungs felt compressed. She glanced at Christophe, but he was gazing across the street.

Paula looked, too, and saw the tall form of Leo Erkel lope from the pub. He collided with Victor and sent up a loud oath.

"Aha, Leo." Willem, poised beside the driver's door of the little car, laughed, hands on hips. "Swearing at Victor? Your friend must have been beating you at your beloved cards again. How many times must we tell you not to bet with a friend if you want to keep him?"

Frank and Ghislaine ran to shove Willem into the car, Frank with a worried expression on his face. Paula heard him tell Willem he'd regret his meddling, that they might both regret it.

Again she became engrossed in the Volvo. She didn't want to believe Willem or Frank would hurt her, yet...

"What is that man's name?" Christophe asked suddenly.

Paula snapped her attention to his face, then to the direction in which he stared. "You mean the tall one putting on a cap? Leo Erkel, I think Willem said. He's the head polisher for Metters'." Erkel had turned in the same direction as Victor but walked several yards behind. If, as Willem suggested, these two were friends, they weren't pleased with each other today.

"Too complex," Christophe murmured. "In English they say something about tangled webs and deceit. I think I begin to understand."

"What do you understand?" Paula asked. Willem's car sped away, and she was left alone with Christophe.

"Let's start back," he said, automatically putting an arm around her shoulder.

Paula lifted his hand and put a few feet between them. She wasn't playing games anymore. Now Christophe would learn that she knew exactly what he thought about her and why. Let him try grappling with surprise, she thought, too angry and confused to enjoy the prospect. She half ran and he strode beside her.

Christophe reached for her arm but she shook loose and hurried on. "You knew what was said about my father, all the lies about his being a thief, and you started your tidy case against me. You needed a scapegoat for the recent robberies from Kohl's, an excuse to say the firm is losing its touch and shouldn't be trusted with a loan from your precious bank. An outfit that employs the daughter of a man they're sure once stole from them cannot be taken seriously. And the fact that I must be the one responsible for the second batch of thefts seals your opinion." Tears sprang into her eyes, and she wiped them furiously away. "You were only too willing to think I was my father's daughter." She rounded on him, breathing heavily. "You never knew my father. He was beautiful and honest. A quiet man everyone respected. Now I know what he carried around with him all those years, and I hate the people who did that to him. You should be helping me find them, not trying to persecute me."

Christophe moved a step closer. With the fingertips of one hand he smoothed tears from her cheeks. He still held the riotous bouquet.

"Paula," he sighed. "I'm almost as convinced as you that your father wasn't guilty. And I'm sure I can prove it. But doing so and making sure we both end up alive may not be easy."

He thrust the flowers into her trembling hands.

Chapter Thirteen

Christophe didn't speak again until they were within yards of Kohl's. He'd held Paula's elbow firmly as he rushed her along. "Now." He stepped into a doorway, taking her with him. "I have to meet with Benno and Lukas. I may or may not be able to get back to you today. But I *will* make a chance to talk soon, okay? Can you live with that?"

"Tell me what you'll be doing," Paula demanded. He'd spoken of fear for their lives, and now he wanted her to wait quietly like a good little girl.

"You'll just have to trust—"

"Don't," Paula broke in. "Please don't ask me for any more blind trust. I'm fresh out."

He held her hand and brought it to his lips, keeping his eyes on hers. "It's safer for you to know as little as possible for a while," he said urgently. "That way you're less likely to give off vibes the wrong people can pick up."

"I'm not a kid," Paula insisted. "Please don't treat me like one. Who *are* these 'wrong' people? Will you tell me what you know, what you think? I'm going slowly—no, rapidly—mad. You don't think Frank did have anything to do with it, do you? I don't see how." She thought of the white car but said nothing.

"I'm not ruling anyone out yet," he said, glancing anxiously over her shoulder. "Look, I'm working on a lot of conjecture. A few hard facts mixed in, but not enough. This afternoon may tell me a lot—I expect it to. I promise I'll at least touch bases with you before the day's over. Beyond that you'll have to—"

"Trust you," she finished for him. "All right, Christophe. I don't have much choice. But if I don't hear from you today, I'll be looking for you by tomorrow. And I can't wait forever for some answers. I've got this weird feeling time's closing in on me." She gave an involuntary shiver.

Christophe hugged her quickly. "Not weird, *chérie*, accurate. It's closing in on both of us."

BENNO AND LUKAS STOOD side by side at the window in Benno's office. The air felt funereal as Christophe closed the door behind him and waited for one of them to acknowledge him.

After several seconds, he cleared his throat. "We had an appointment, I believe," he announced.

Lukas turned first, and Christophe took an involuntary step toward him before checking an urge to throw his arms around the other man. Lukas Kohl was beaten. Defeat had erased the light from his eyes, the confidence from his handsome features. His shoulders sagged in a way no suit would be expensive enough to conceal.

"Lukas, I—" Christophe searched for the words he wanted. "You don't look well, my friend." He flinched as he said it. They had been friends, but the time seemed so very long ago.

"You'd better sit down," Benno said, approaching his own chair and gripping the arms while he lowered his bony frame. "We'd all better sit. There's much to talk about,

Christophe. I don't think you'll want to continue with your plan for this afternoon.''

Christophe sat slowly in a chair opposite Benno and looked inquiringly from Lukas to Benno.

Lukas sank to the edge of his father's desk and crossed his wrists on his thigh. "There's *no* point in doing what you suggested.''

"Why not?" Christophe asked. "Somewhere between that room—" he indicated the workroom "—and the buyer, those stones were switched. I haven't been through the procedure. You have. So many times you could easily be missing something that will seem obvious to me. So we act out the process, step by step, and see if we can find the link, the second when this...this sleight of hand...was possible on each occasion. And it was done in a second—I'm certain of that.''

"Too late." Lukas found a cigarette and Christophe half rose to light it for him. "It may be too late for everything, Christophe. There's a possibility, if you could arrange a lot of money for us fast, that we could…" He shook his head. Smoke seeped through his almost closed lips.

Christophe inhaled the strong scent of the Gitane and something else—fear? If fear had an odor, it was in this room. He kept the lighter in his hand until he'd lit one of his own cigarettes. Emotion must be kept in check, he reminded himself. *Let them do the talking.* The Kohls must give all the information in this exchange, while he listened and analyzed.

"Lukas, tell him." Benno shrank back in his chair and closed his eyes. "Tell him exactly what's happened. What he does then is up to him.''

"Yes," Lukas said softly, "it will all be up to you Christophe, *my friend*.''

Christophe rested his elbows on his knees, made a steeple out of his fingers and positioned it against his lips. Smoke from his own cigarette made him squint, but he watched Lukas closely.

At last Lukas said, "They changed the rules on us," and laughed bitterly. "Another flawed stone has turned up in the hands of one of our oldest and most respected customers."

"I see." Christophe flicked ash into a brass ashtray. "I wondered how long it would be before this happened." He sought Benno's eyes. "All the more reason to do what I had in mind. We must move quickly."

"You don't understand," Lukas snapped. He slid from the desk and walked to the door and back. He stopped in front of Christophe and spread his arms wide. "I told you they changed the rules on us. This stone didn't go through the usual channels. I bought it myself in Antwerp. It was sold before it arrived in Amsterdam. The buyer had specified his needs, and I merely had to find the right product."

Christophe narrowed his eyes. "What difference does...? Oh, I see. You mean this stone required no work here. Kohl's simply bought it on behalf of someone else and delivered it."

"Yes," Lukas said shortly.

Benno drummed his fingers on his knees. "Lukas, Christophe doesn't understand these things. The diamond was already essentially finished, yes, but it required some work before delivery, otherwise there would have been little need for us in the transaction—except for the buyer needing our access to trading circles in Antwerp. We were both go between and final finisher in this sale."

"Then I don't see what was different," Christophe said.

Lukas exhaled slowly. "Everything else was different," he said. "The stone was with us for a much shorter time than most. It wasn't cleaved here, or offered for sale here. It never entered the strong room after it was finished. Christophe—" He rubbed his eyes. "I bought the thing in Antwerp. I arranged for it to be shipped here. It arrived. When it arrived, it was the same stone I'd bought. I saw it wrapped for delivery *and I took it myself*, for God's sake. The pattern has been broken, and everything that has gone before means nothing in your investigations anymore." He turned to Benno. "Father, tell him what it has come to if we are to survive."

Benno rubbed his chest absently. "We have only one chance, Christophe. Cut our losses and try to rebuild."

"Benno—" Christophe begun.

The old man broke in quickly, "No. Let me finish. I know what you're going to say. Call in the authorities. No. In our business we take care of our own problems—when and as best we can. Then you will say you cannot help us because this will keep happening and St-Giles is not a charitable organization.

"I do not ask for charity. From now on, we will change our procedure. The buyer will be expected to pick up his purchases here. All we need is the capital to build back our stock."

Christophe stood and ground out his cigarette. He'd been right, dammit. The rotten little hunch he'd hoped would prove wrong was dancing into the light. "I hear everything you say," he said evenly. "And I get the picture. I still want to watch the way you've dealt with gems until now. It's getting late. Let's go."

Without waiting for replies—or arguments—he opened the office door and stood back until Lukas, Benno following slowly, led the way into the workroom.

For the next hour they traced and retraced the progress of a stone from workroom to delivery pouch. A gray tinge hovered around Benno's mouth when they finally climbed into the firm's small van and wound through the streets to the Kohls' house. There, Benno played the part of a jeweler's employee likely to accept the small package from Frank, whose place Lukas took. Christophe stood by in what would have been the guard's position. He no longer concentrated on the charade. *Damn, damn.* He *had* to be wrong. He *had* to have missed something.

"Well?" Lukas touched his arm, and Christophe jumped. This was the first voluntary contact Lukas had made with him since his return to Amsterdam. *"Well?"* Lukas repeated.

Christophe stared at him for a moment. "Yes," he said, rousing himself. "I think I've seen just about all I need to see. But I'd like to run through the stuff at the building one more time."

Lukas said in a steely voice, "My father can't take much more. This is killing him."

Christophe nodded faintly. "It'll soon be over."

Lukas's eyes held his a fraction too long for comfort before he waved Benno back into the van.

Another hour later, Lukas looked up from a glass-topped case in the strong room and removed his loupe from his eye. "What are we accomplishing here?" he asked wearily.

Benno sat behind the case, an array of diamonds displayed on their opened tissue packets in front of him. "Have you seen enough, Christophe?" He remained stoic, letting Christophe know he was prepared to keep this up as long as necessary if it would help Kohl's.

Christophe made up his mind, and a heaviness formed in his heart. "Yes, thank you. You would now pack away the stones not purchased, correct, Benno?" He waited for the affirmative flicker in Benno's eyes. "These—" he indicated several packets, already closed and stacked to one side "—would be sent by messenger to their new owner, when?"

"Immediately," Benno replied, beginning to slip the folded white sheets with their sparkling treasures inside back into small wooden file boxes. The boxes he put into a safe behind him.

"The stolen diamonds were always among the ones selected?" Christophe indicated the three packages still on the case.

"Of course." With evident asperity, Lukas pushed aside the velvet mat he'd been using under the stones and handed his father the three packets. "They were sold before they were switched, remember?"

"I remember," Christophe said levelly.

Benno finished locking the safe and they exited the two doors, parallel, which were the only way into and out of, the basement room. A space of approximately an inch separated the massive sheets of metal. Before closing the second door, Benno used a key to engage an alarm. Another alarm protected the outer door.

Christophe stood a while, looking at the fortification. *Foolproof?* he pondered—yes, absolutely foolproof.

PAULA PULLED HER FEET beneath her on the couch. Christophe had arrived half an hour earlier, and apart from giving her an absentminded greeting—in French—and accepting the drink she'd offered him, he'd been silent. He sat, or rather stretched, his head tilted back, his legs straight, at the other end of the couch. He balanced his untouched drink on one thigh and stared vacantly at the beams high above.

She plucked at a loose thread in her sweater, gathering courage to prompt him. After she'd arrived home from work, Peter had called and she'd told him everything was under control, that Christophe would make sure nothing else went wrong. Peter had sounded unsure. He'd warned her to be cautious. Dear Peter. Paula smiled to herself. She was grateful he worried about her, but she must follow her own instincts and they told her Christophe would take care of any problems.

Enough waiting, she told herself, reaching to rub his shoulder. The distance between them must be closed. From now on, whatever was to be faced would be faced by them—together. "Tell me about it," she said, still rubbing.

Christophe lifted his head and drank some Scotch before looking at her. Paula's heart constricted. In his eyes she saw pain.

"There's been another robbery," he said at last, and drank some more. "This time the thief used a different method."

"Another...?" Paula withdrew her hand and covered her mouth. "Oh, no."

He offered her the glass and she sipped. "It's all going to be such a bloody mess," he muttered.

"You won't be able to give them the money, will you?" Paula asked in a small voice. "Kohl's will be finished."

Christophe shrugged. "Possibly. A lot depends on... The next couple of days will decide everything."

Paula blinked back tears of frustration. "I wish I could help."

"You probably already have."

"I don't see how. What was different about this theft?"

"It doesn't concern you, Paula." Christophe sighed deeply.

"It does," she insisted. "And I want to know."

"The stone was sold before it arrived at Kohl's. Does that mean anything?"

"No—no, I guess not," Paula said slowly. "Wait! You mean it was bought for someone sight-unseen?"

He sat up and faced her. "Yes. Do you know anything about that kind of transaction?"

"Not really. Only I remember when we worked on a stone that had been bought in Antwerp expressly for a jeweler in Amsterdam."

Christophe moved closer. "Do you remember anything about it—the stone, I mean. That what's his name—Jacob—told me each diamond is different and finishers remember them."

Paula closed her eyes to concentrate. "Slightly more than eight carats, brilliant cut, minor natural—that's a tiny flaw—that Victor took care of. Flaws like that are often eliminated during cleavage, but some...."

Christophe shoved the glass into her hands. "I've got to go," he said, grabbing his coat on the way to the door. In the act of reaching for the handle, he turned back. "I ... I care what happens to you. Wait for my call, please."

She felt the rush of the night air, smelled flowers in the courtyard. "Christophe, wait!" The door slammed, and she heard his running footsteps before Benno and Anna's basement door opened and closed.

"Wait," she said disgustedly. "Wait and trust, wait and trust."

The rest of the Scotch went down her throat before she realized she'd upended the glass. Paula coughed. The stuff burned.

At midnight she trailed to the loft, carrying the phone, its long cord snaking behind her. She lay down fully dressed. If Christophe needed her, Paula would be ready to go.

The city's bells tolled one in the morning, and she watched the lighted panel on her clock blink away the seconds.

When the phone did ring, her brain went into shock and she lifted the received in slow motion. "Yes," she whispered.

"How about a provisional date?" Christophe asked.

"What?" Paula struggled to sit up. "What did you say?"

"A provisional date for Wednesday night. If everything goes as I expect, I'll take you dancing for real this time, and we'll celebrate."

Paula's nerves jumped. His flat voice sent ice into her veins. "You've found out something else, Christophe," she said, breathing hard. "And you don't like it. Tell me what you know now. What are we going to celebrate?"

"If I find what I expect to find in the next couple of days, we'll celebrate the uncloaking of our thief. The only problem is—what will we all decide to do about it?"

Chapter Fourteen

Thursday of the Fourth Week:

"Thursday," Paula said. "Amsterdam never sleeps." Laughter spattered in bursts through the club Christophe had chosen for their date. Couples alternately slunk or gyrated around an eight-sided dance floor.

Christophe shifted his morose gaze from the champagne he swirled in his glass to his watch. "So it is," he remarked without interest. "Thursday for two hours now."

Paula slumped in her chair, mentally and physically exhausted. As Christophe had promised, they'd spent the evening dancing. That's all they'd done. Between numbers, executed by Christophe with as much enthusiasm he might have been expected to show had his partner been a blown-up dummy, they'd sat in a darkened alcove while she valiantly attempted conversation. Christophe had grunted, ordered more champagne from time to time, presumedly for their "celebration," and eyed her speculatively whenever he thought she wasn't watching him.

"Christophe," Paula begun hesitantly. She rocked her head from side to side, her eyes closed, gathering strength and courage. "Christophe, are you going to tell me *anything*?"

"How's the champagne?"

She shoved the glass aside. "I've had it. I don't know how the champagne is. I don't remember what I ate for dinner. I'm not even sure what kind of music is playing. All I know is you've been giving me the cold shoulder all night and I don't understand why. You invited me out, remember?"

"I'm sorry you've had a rotten time."

"Dammit all!" she exploded. "What is it with you? You're as uptight as hell. Just answer my one simple question, will you? What gives? Did you find out what you expected? *Do* you know who's behind the thefts from Kohl's?"

"Maybe." Christophe set down his own glass and stared at her yet again. His eyes had a penetrating quality Paula found magnetic and infuriating at the same time.

"Maybe?"

"Okay, yes. I know who stole those diamonds."

Paula wiped damp palms on her skirt and leaned closer to him. "Tell me."

"I'm not sure I'm ready." He took his time lighting one of his wretched cigarettes, drawing deeply, checking the tip.

"That's it, Christophe." Paula's head began to ache. "I can't take any more of this. You've been sending me mixed messages for days. I thought we'd decided to trust each other. So why don't you share what you found out?"

"Perhaps I'm still waiting for something—like the reason for the robberies."

This time Paula stared. "Money," she blurted. "Why else would someone steal priceless gems except for money?"

He shrugged. "Let's go back to your place. The noise here is getting to me."

They left the club and drove home to Herengracht in Christophe's Saab. He dogged her through the Kohls' basement and across the courtyard to her backhouse as if there were no question of his not going with her. Paula's tension grew second by second. He wasn't enjoying this any more than she, yet he trudged on like a man following a script he had to perform. What was in his mind, she agonized. What did he intend to do next?

"Don't you ever wish for privacy?" he asked when they were inside with the door closed.

Paula faced him, hands on hips. "I've got privacy," she said, confused. "This is my place. I pay rent for it."

"But you always have to come through Benno and Anna's house. That would drive me nuts."

"I seem to remember you telling me you stayed here for several weeks once. Did it drive you nuts then?" She hated the way she sounded. He was deliberately baiting her.

"We always used the gate from the alley. Lukas lived out here, too, and Peter when he didn't have another place and while the barge was in pieces."

"Benno prefers to keep the gate permanently locked for security reasons," Paula said. All she wanted at this moment was for Christophe to go away. "And I'm perfectly comfortable going in and out through their house. They don't keep tabs on me."

"No," Christophe remarked offhandedly. "Do you have any coffee?"

"I don't—" She bit off the blunt refusal forming in her head. Patience would be her ally now. "I'll brew some. Take off your jacket and relax. I don't like seeing you so uptight."

From the kitchenette, Paula watched him, helplessly fascinated by every move he made. He took off his jacket and rolled up his sleeves. Light reflected along the moving muscles in his powerful forearms. He loosened his tie and caught her eye. She looked away and clattered the coffee-pot over the tiled counter, found a filter and some mugs.

"Where'd you get the roses?" he asked suddenly.

For an instant she couldn't think what he was talking about. Then she remembered and said, "Those—Peter sent them to me. He's a nice man." Since Christophe hadn't mentioned talking to Peter about her problems, she must assume he hadn't. Best continue to leave the timing of that to Peter—if there was going to be a time now.

Christophe gathered fallen pink petals. "Roses," he murmured. "Lovely and dangerous. Look, but don't touch or they may hurt you. Like some people."

Paula busied herself with the kettle. "Peter said something like that. You must think alike," she said and wondered what Christophe's comment really meant.

"Peter's always going to be special to me," Christophe said. "He seemed glad I was seeing you tonight. He stopped by today. If it wasn't for him, I'd think I didn't have a friend left in this city."

What about me? Paula longed to ask. "Lukas is bound to be cool—and the rest of his family," she said instead. "They'll get over it when they accept you only want what's best for them."

He was staring at her again. Paula closed her mouth firmly and finished making coffee.

When they sat side by side on the couch, she tried again. "Christophe, you said you'd let me know what you found out."

His striking face could be so hard, Paula thought. Christophe's fist, firmly placed beneath his chin, let her know he didn't intend to include her in anything he might have discovered. Awkwardness sent its sting across her skin before she saw something else in the way he had arranged his features. Hurt? Uncertainty? He glanced sideways at her, and she had to stop an impulse to reach for his hand. Had the corner of his mouth quivered—jerked almost imperceptibly?

The next idea to hit Paula brought tears to her eyes. She blinked them away and went to the kitchen for more coffee. Christophe was close to the end of this assignment. How could she have been such a fool? He would finish here, then leave, and he was nice enough not to want to hurt her. Her attraction to him was pretty obvious and not reciprocated. He was suffering the pangs of a kind man uncertain how to let a woman down gently.

Instantly Paula made up her mind what to do. "Boy, am I tired," she said, yawning and returning to sit on a chair opposite the couch rather then beside him. "It's after three." She slid back the sleeve of the loose sweater she'd put on over her dress and looked pointedly at her watch.

The clatter of Christophe's mug on the table startled her. She met his eyes and recoiled. So dark, they appeared black, all expression erased. "Christophe..." she began and paused to swallow. "Christophe..."

"You want me to leave, Paula? Is that what you're saying?"

Two days ago he'd said he cared what happened to her. They'd touched. She'd been sure some deep attachment had started growing between them. She even thought she...she'd thought love might be what they felt for each other.

"I guess so," Paula heard herself say. "Tomorrow's a workday." Emptiness threatened to bring the tears she could not allow in front of this man.

"You're sure?"

Paula bowed her head. Christophe was a mystery. What did *he* want? For her to invite him to sleep with her? She felt blood rush to her cheeks. He'd have let her know if that's what he wanted. "I'm sure," she murmured without raising her face.

His jacket rustled as he put it on. When she smelled his after-shave, she knew he stood only inches from her.

"Good night, Paula," he said quietly.

Now she looked at him. She *did* love him. She could tell him and let him decide with to do about it. Paula opened her mouth, then averted her face. "Good night," she echoed. Christophe was too mature to laugh at her declaration, but neither of them deserved the discomfort it would bring.

His kisses were swift, finding the corner of her mouth, moving over her cheek to the dip beneath her ear, lingering gently against her neck. He held her briefly, tightly, and when he let go, she stumbled slightly, and he grasped her elbow. "I'm sorry," he said, meeting her eyes one last time before he strode outside.

"I'm sorry." "I'm the one who's sorry," Paula said aloud. That final glance had been easy to read. He regretted he couldn't be more, feel more for her. Whatever he'd wanted in a woman, she didn't fill the bill. He'd decided to work his way through the rest of this assignment alone and retreat. No doubt the future of Kohl's would be settled in a few days, and either she'd have a job or she wouldn't. She could probably find another position easily now, but she cared desperately what happened to Benno and Lukas—and all the people who'd become a part of her life.

For a long time she stood inside the door, her arms crossed. She cared about Christophe and always would.

Ignoring the dirty coffee cups, she climbed to the loft and pulled off her sweater. Christophe St-Giles came from a different world. Someone of ordinary means with aspirations to be a craftswoman for the rest of her life was unlikely to do more than arouse mild interest in him. Wealth and power were his past, present and future. He'd been alone with her tonight and hadn't even attempted to make love. She touched her neck. If she'd responded to him when he held her he'd have stayed. He couldn't offer her anything more than this night, but she could have chosen to take it rather than nothing.

Someone knocked the door sharply. Paula held her breath. Christophe. He'd come back. She ran her hands over her hair, deciding. If she let him in, he was bound to stay the night. Then would she be able to let him go in the morning and not break apart?

She couldn't leave him standing there. Paula ran downstairs, turning on the living room light as she reached the bottom.

A square of paper, one corner still underneath, lay close to the door. She picked it up and opened the door at the same time. The night was still. Paula stepped outside, searching the short path to the main house. The courtyard was empty. He'd come with his note and left rapidly, not wanting to face her again.

Misery overwhelmed her. Whatever happened, this episode must be forgotten, and in future she'd be more wary. Paula unfolded the paper, expecting to see his apology repeated. "If you want to help me save Benno, come to Brouwersgracht. Now. The barge at Palm Straat bridge. For Sale sign."

Christophe needed her. All the silence, the waiting and watching throughout the evening had been because he was trying to decide whether to ask for help. Now something awful had happened—she couldn't guess what—and he'd run back with the note. He'd given her the choice. She could go to him and share whatever risks he faced, or stay safely where she was.

Paula rushed upstairs for her sweater and headed to the street.

She knew the route. Lukas and Sandi lived on Brouwersgracht. Palm Straat was some blocks northwest of their house. Paula ran, grateful for her low-heeled shoes. Dawn couldn't be far away, but the moonless night still closed in around her like a black, oppressive bowl. Shapes of parked cars loomed, and trees. A cat spat as Paula sped into its path. She felt no fear. Christophe would be waiting.

On Brouwersgracht, the distance between the canal and houses was narrower than on Herengracht. Brouwersgracht, home to many young professionals, had once been lined with warehouses. Now the rickety structures were transformed into apartments and the occasional single house. The buildings seemed to shift slightly, blacker than the black sky, their roofs murky outlines. Paula felt safer close to the canal. Barges creaked and scraped at their moorings, and she smelled oil on the sucking water, and tar, and, subtly, the scent of air cooled and cleaned by night.

Yards short of the intersection with Palm Straat, Paula slowed and began checking each barge she passed. She peered closely at swaying vessels, searching for a sign. Christophe had meant a For Sale sign would be visible. Boat after boat, closed curtains at the windows of raised deckhousing failed to display the message she needed. Her heart began a slow, hard thump. Ahead the curved railings of a bridge crossed the canal at Palm Straat. Paula hurried on and saw the sign. An old barge, its bow obscured beneath the bridge, sported a luminous white board on a frame atop the long cabin. The lettering she needed to see stood out boldly.

Cautiously she stepped along the edge of the street until she located a warped board sloping to the vessel's deck. For the first time since he had read the note, Paula hesitated. No light showed in the cabin's old-fashioned round portholes. Where was Christophe? She took in her surroundings. No other houseboats were moored nearby. The closest buildings felt derelict.

At her first step on to the plank, boards gave. Paula jumped swiftly to the deck. A door, closed by a bar dropped into a hook on each side, led to the cabin. Christophe had to be here. She couldn't have arrived first.

A flicker caught her eye, and she stared hard at the closest porthole. The glass was an obsidian mirror. Then she saw it again, a rising glow that quickly faded. Candlelight. Christophe was already inside. Thank God he'd asked her to come. The bar on the door must have slid back into place without his knowing. He'd have been trapped.

Paula struggled to raise the heavy bar and hook it aside with a length of chain. Apart from this hardware, the rest of the barge appeared about to disintegrate.

The door opened outward and Paula's throat instantly seized. A sickening stench came from the cabin. She put a hand over her nose and mouth and held the doorjamb with the other. "Christophe?" she whispered, edging inside. "Christophe, are you here?"

Only a faint sloshing noise greeted her. The candlelight came from a nub waxed to an old saucer and placed on a low shelf near the door. Paula took two more steps inside and stopped, horrified. Her feet and ankles were submerged in water. "Hello," she said more loudly, then pressed the hand tighter over her mouth.

The eddying wash around her feet felt thick. Paula took the candle and looked down. She made herself breathe through her mouth. Sludge, littered with rotting garbage, slithered back and forth almost to her calves.

Paula turned back to the door, lured by the open air and meager light the street offered. Why hadn't she brought a flashlight?

As if her thought were heard, a blinding beam hit her squarely in the face. Paula dropped the candle, vaguely heard it hiss and die while she held parted fingers in front of her eyes. "Turn it off," she said. "Move the thing."

Abruptly the beam swung upward, painting the cabin an eerie, shifting gunmetal and yellow, and showing Christophe's solid body framed in the doorway. He walked toward her.

Paula smiled at him, held out her hands. Relief hit her like a warm cushion.

Christophe didn't smile. "You had me fooled," he said.

Paula dropped her hands slowly.

"It was my own fault," he said. "I believed what I wanted to believe. There was never any absolute proof you weren't involved." He motioned her across the narrow cabin.

"Stop it," she cried, backing away. "Stop it. You're frightening me." She caught a heel and fetid water wetted the hem of her skirt. "Christophe!" Paula screamed as her elbow struck the opposite bulkhead.

He waded toward her, oblivious to the wash soaking his pant legs. "I believed your whole act. And what I found out on Monday night seemed to back it up. Or it didn't disprove it, anyway. I had everything worked out and you weren't a part of it. But I was wrong, wasn't I?"

Paula couldn't speak.

"Where is it?" Christophe said. "Give it to me."

When Paula uttered a word it came out as a croak, "What . . . ?" She tried again. "What are you talking about?"

"Surprised, huh? Didn't you think your friends might double-cross you. You should have. They already threatened you, didn't they? You were supposed to put me off, persuade me to leave town, but you failed." He was very close now. "One big black mark against you. Then you were warned to leave Amsterdam yourself and you didn't. Another black mark. Why didn't you go? Too greedy? You had to force one more theft, didn't you? And you came here to make the drop. Only your partners set you up."

Tears clogged her throat, but her eyes were strained wide open and dry. "Who set me up—how?"

"I was warned."

"How?"

"I had a call before I left to pick you up last night. The gentleman didn't identify himself. He said you'd leave for an appointment as soon as I was out of the way and he told me you'd come here. He also said I'd understand what he meant by an *appointment*. I watched to see if you'd leave your place once I'd gone. Paula, I hoped you wouldn't, but you did and I followed. No wonder you could hardly wait to get rid of me."

"No." Paula looked him directly in the eyes. "You're wrong, Christophe."

He placed a hand each side of her shoulders. "You asked me to leave. You couldn't wait for me to go."

She flinched. "You're mad. After the way you treated me all evening, I'd had it. I thought you couldn't stand being with me, so I put you out of your misery." Damn her shaking legs. She *would not* let him see how scared she was. "And after you'd been gone a while I got this—see?" Her fingers closed on the note in her pocket. She withdrew it and flapped the paper at Christophe.

He waved her hand aside. "Forget it." His voice was barely above a whisper. "No more stalling tactics, Paula. Neither of us is leaving until I get what you intended to deliver here."

"I don't—Christophe!"

A muffled boom shook the boards beneath their feet. With a sickening roll, the barge listed to starboard and the door smashed shut.

Christophe spun away, then fell against her. "My God!" he yelled. "This thing's going to sink! We've got to get out of here!"

Paula knew what the next sound was before its dull clang faded.

"The bar," she groaned. "The bar's dropped over the door. We *can't* get out."

Chapter Fifteen

Water swirled around his thighs. "Son of a bitch," Christophe swore. "He found out what I knew and did this to me."

"Christophe!" Paula was clinging to his jacket. His body trapped her against the bulkhead.

He swore again, silently this time, and staggered away. "Keep calm," he ordered when he leaned beside her—feeling anything but calm. "I think that was an explosion in the bilges, and if it was, we could go down fast."

Paula grabbed his hand. "Look," she said, nodding to her right. "The water's coming in here."

He leaned around her, slid the flashlight beam along the side until he saw a swell forcing masses of bubbles immediately below the surface. "That's what I was afraid of," he said, fighting down panic. "The bastard knew what he was doing. He made sure this tub was well vented, then blew the bottom out. No chance of any air pockets slowing down the process with a good hole in the hull up here."

"The other side," Paula gasped. "We have to make it out of this slime. Come on, but be careful. It's slippery."

He glanced at her face. Her skin gleamed white, but her expression was determined. Whatever she might be guilty of, she had guts. "Yes," he agreed. "Keep holding my hand and forget everything but a handhold over there."

They waded up the sloping deck. The barge listed slowly, but not slowly enough. Christophe shone his beam ahead and clasped Paula's hand tighter. Second by second the port side of the vessel rose. At almost the same speed, the water gushed through the half-submerged starboard gash.

"Hold— Oh, no!" Paula shouted. Muscles in his arm stiffened against her weight as she fell to her knees, slithering, until her skirt ballooned on the wallowing surface.

Christophe felt his own feet slide. "It's okay," he said. "We'll make it." He bent his knees, finding better purchase, and hauled Paula out of the sucking murk.

The flashlight picked out a hook on the port bulkhead. He struggled on to grab it with two fingers, half expecting the thing to break loose. The hook held. "We're there, Paula," he said and thought, *where, where are we? We can't get out*.

"My God," she whispered. "This is hell. Look at the water. It's coming in so fast. We can't have long to make it out of this thing."

Her control gave him courage. "At least we're not tipping much now. This thing's sliding toward the middle of the canal."

"Sure," she said quietly. "Probably the way it was planned. Deeper water out there."

He looked at her, his stomach tightening. She was a bright lady. "Keep an arm around my waist," he said. "I'm going to work my way to the door just in case the bar missed."

The door was only feet away. Within seconds, he turned to Paula and shook his head. They were locked in.

"The portholes," she said and immediately grimaced. No man, or woman, could get through those small apertures.

He edged back to the hook, guiding Paula with him. "You'd think a good punch would make a hole in this worm-eaten stuff." The wood he touched flaked beneath his fingers.

She was quiet, staring at him. Slowly her lips parted. "Hit it with the flashlight. Make a hole and we'll rip out enough boards."

"It would take too long," Christophe replied. Regardless of what she might have done, he wished he could save her from this. He rubbed her arm and tried to calculate how much time they had left.

"Give me the flashlight," Paula demanded, and he handed it over without comment.

The light swept back and forth through the interior. "There's got to be something," she muttered. "Something we could use—Christophe—" Her voice rose. "Keep a tight grip on me."

He did as she asked while she stretched and groped. "Got it!" she exclaimed, holding a container above her head while she struggled beside him once more. "Where's your lighter."

"Lighter?"

"To blow this up with."

"Blow what up, Paula? Explain." The boat lurched and his heart matched the motion.

"Damn," she muttered. "We need something to tie this to the porthole. My dress is wet. This sweater would only melt or something."

"Paula, what are you trying—"

"We're going to blow the port out with this aerosol can. Then we should be able to make a big enough space to crawl through. Quick. Help me."

For an instant he didn't understand. When her thought became clear, he whistled. "Smart woman." He yanked off his jacket, transferring his wallet to a back pocket. One fear-powered tug tore his shirt-sleeve from the shoulder. Thank God it was cotton, not silk, he thought. "Give me the can." He knotted the fabric swiftly about the cylinder and tied the bundle to the porthole bolts.

"The lighter, the lighter," Paula begged. "Quickly. The water's coming in faster."

The flame of his lighter caught brightly at the cotton, then smoldered and died. Christophe cursed and tried again. "Come on, come on," he muttered through clenched teeth. This was their last—their only—chance.

"It's not going to work," Paula moaned. "There won't be enough heat to set it off."

He'd almost forgotten the gun. "Dammit," he said. "I *must* be mad. Get behind me. Move back carefully and cover your head." Carrying a weapon wasn't his habit. The last-minute decision to keep one in the Saab, and to bring it with him to the barge tonight, could save their lives. "Cover up!" he ordered.

The small gun he pulled from his pocket felt foreign. Christophe braced an elbow on the bulkhead, steadied his right wrist on his left forearm and took aim. He ducked his head as he squeezed the trigger.

The bullet missed.

His own expletive shocked him. He gritted his teeth. "Keep your head down," he ordered. And the second shot found its mark. A sharp crack sounded and a brief red glow penetrated his closed eyelids. Slivers of glass pricked his arms and he smelled the acrid scent of burned powder.

"You did it. Oh, thank God," Paula cried. She clawed past him and started pounding and pulling.

The port rim had blown out with the glass. Christophe threw himself at the jagged hole, dragging at boards that ripped away in strips. Frenzy fueled their strength. The gap grew, widened, and he stopped Paula's frantic tearing.

"Out!" he yelled. The barge shifted abruptly. They were both clinging to the opening, their legs submerged. "Hold my belt and I'll go first, then pull you."

He made it to sit on the hull with Paula, clutching his thighs now, still dangling into the cabin. More of the barge than he expected still showed above the canal, but it would soon disappear.

Paula let go of him with one hand and fumbled at her waist.

"What's the matter?" he yelled. "Come on!" He leaned to grasp her beneath the arms.

"No," she gasped, looking up. "Not until you read this. It'll be gone by the time we're all the way in that water."

"Come on, Paula. Not now."

She clung to the side, refusing to budge. "You've still got the flashlight. Read it." Something white showed between her fingers and the boat's dark wood.

"You're going to kill us both." He wound his legs around her body and took the paper she offered. The flashlight must be tossed when they swam.

"Read it," she implored.

Blood thundered in his ears, but he did as she asked and immediately threw the flashlight away to drag her bodily into his arms.

She muttered, "Christophe," as he balanced on the camber of the hull, holding her against him. They hit the water flat and he kept one arm around her, pulling hard with the other, terrified the suction of the sinking barge would drag them down.

Lagging pressure tugged from below, but he fought against it, made headway, first slowly, than with increasing speed. "I can swim by myself," he heard Paula gasp. He ignored her. She stroked with her free arm and kicked hard, helping their progress.

Christophe's hand scraped the slime-coated wall of the canal and he bobbed up, paddling, his breath raking past his throat. "We made it, Paula."

A shudder convulsed her body. He couldn't see her face clearly. "Yes." Her voice was barely audible.

With Paula beside him, Christophe swam along the wall, searching for a way up. He found a trailing rope, probably one of the barge's snapped mooring lines, hanging limply from a post above. "Don't let go of this," he told Paula and shinnied up the wall. Lying flat, he stretched down until he could hold her wrists and help her climb. She scrambled to the street, bumping a knee or elbow with every move.

Paula stood a little apart from him, watching the glimmering hull roll gently. Dawn's gray had begun its stealthy creeping into the sky. In the pale light he saw the droop of Paula's shoulders, the way her skirt clung in sodden folds about her legs. She swayed slightly and he reached to pull her against him.

"You don't believe me, do you?" she said. Her shivers coursed into him. She was crying.

"Yes," he said. "I do believe you. We were both set up. And if we'd died out there, it would have been my fault."

"I don't see why," Paula murmured, trembling violently now. Tentatively she pushed her hands under his arms and gradually tightened her grip until she dug her nails into his back. Her gentle crying became wrenching sobs, and he knew she'd used up all of a very big reserve of courage.

"It's going." With one finger, he turned her chin toward the canal. The last inches of the old hull slipped from sight. Ripples arched outward, huge bubbles flew to the surface, then nothing. The surface closed silkily over their robbed tomb as if it had never existed.

Paula pressed her face into his soaked shirt. "It *was* deliberate, wasn't it?"

"Deliberate and clever," Christophe replied. "You have to know what you're doing to sink something on cue like that. He vented the hull, then placed his bomb or dynamite, or whatever he used, in the right spot to make sure the barge would go down in the direction he wanted. Like you said—into the deeper water in the middle where it wouldn't be found for a long, long time. Only we got out."

"Why did you say it was your fault—or would have been your fault if we'd drowned?" Her fingers found his mouth. She stroked it slowly while she looked into his eyes.

The ache in his limbs had nothing to do with cold or fear. Some reactions were beyond control. "Because I should have trusted my instincts . . . about what I'd found out and needed to do about it, at once . . . and about you. My heart told me you were innocent and I knew as much in my head, only I've always got to be so damned sure. I never know when to give in and be human. I wait and see, and this time my waiting nearly killed us both." Concentration was tough. Exhaustion battled with his desire. Christophe knew exhaustion would have to be allowed to win.

"Why *did* you wait?"

He'd tell her everything in the next few hours, he thought, everything. Including the reason for his hesitation. "We'll talk," he said. "I'll explain what I know—

and I don't know. The next couple of days won't be easy. We're going to need each other.''

An ocher cast behind the warehouses promised sun. He must get her home and go back to his own place.

"Christophe," Paula said. "Why did they try to murder us?"

"I think, because of what I *don't* know yet," he said, pushing back her streaming hair. "And that's what scares the hell out of me."

Chapter Sixteen

Seven hours later, Paula entered the Kohls' basement. In one hand she carried the small, severed head of a tulip. The front doorbell rang while she climbed to the main level of the house.

She heard Benno say, "Come in," and knew she would see Christophe enter the hall.

"Paula?" Benno turned at the sound of her shoes on the marble. "Are you ill, my dear?"

He would wonder why she wasn't at work, she realized. She looked past Benno to Christophe. His dark eyes stared back and he smiled, a small, strained smile intended to reassure her. "Paula isn't ill, Benno," he said. "Just tired. But we'll talk about that."

Benno lifted his palms, shaking his head. "Is Paula to be with us also this afternoon? What can you have to say to us all, Christophe?"

Christophe offered a hand to Paula and waited until she took it. "Is everyone here?" He sounded weary and Paula wished they could leave, now, be somewhere together and be quiet.

"They're here, Christophe," Benno said, indicating the living room. "Although I can't imagine what you hope to accomplish."

He fell silent and Paula began to feel sick. No sound came from the big room. The others must be sitting there, thinking, worrying. She shoved her fist into her pocket and kept it there, mashing the tulip petals.

"Let's get this over with." Christophe stood back for Benno to pass and moved his hand to Paula's waist.

She took in the still tableau awaiting them: Lukas standing, hands behind his back, before the brass-encrusted fireplace, Sandi sitting very upright at one end of the damask couch. Anna leaned forward slightly in a small chair, her fingers curled around its carved arms. Paula yearned to tell the older woman everything would be all right. But she couldn't. Nothing would ever be the same for any of them.

"Christophe's here," Benno announced superfluously and with false heartiness. He slapped Christophe's shoulder and frowned at Paula as if he hadn't remembered she was there. "And Paula," he added faintly before going to the rosewood trolly with its array of silver and crystal. "Paula's going to be with us, too. What would each of you like to drink?"

Paula looked up at Christophe. "Is this the only way?" she implored. "Please, are you sure we should do this?"

He rubbed her nape absently. "You know the answer to your questions, Paula. I don't think we'll be wanting any drinks, Benno. Sit down, please."

"I expect magic tricks next, Christophe," Lukas said cynically while his father sat down near Anna. "I didn't know you had such a flair for the dramatic, and much as I like a good show, I do have work to do. Could we get on with whatever you have in mind?"

"Lukas," Anna said in a small, reproachful voice. "Don't insult our guest. Christophe wouldn't ask us all here if he didn't have something important to say." Dark blotches beneath her eyes accentuated her colorless cheeks.

Sandi hadn't spoken and Paula noticed the way she clenched and unclenched her laced fingers in her lap.

"We should get to the point quickly," Christophe said. He made no attempt to move from the middle of the room, and his hand remained at Paula's neck. "When I finish, I hope someone will help me fill in what I've missed. You will, won't you, Lukas?"

Paula's heart began to palpitate uncomfortably. She looked not at Lukas but at Benno. In the past few weeks she'd watched him grow markedly older. He had to be strong now.

"Lukas—" Christophe went on when the younger man failed to reply. "I didn't want this to happen. I still don't. Perhaps it will all turn out to be a mistake, but I don't think so. Do you remember that first interview we had in your father's office?"

"Which one?"

"I think you know which one, friend. The one when you said the facts would make it appear you were stealing from yourself." Christophe's fingers tightened on the back of Paula's neck.

Lukas shrugged and lit a cigarette.

"That was clever of you," Christophe continued. "At the time it was enough to push me in the direction you wanted—away from Lukas Kohl. But you weren't kidding, were you? You were the one who stole those stones. Who else could possibly have done it?"

"Christophe!" Benno broke in. "What are you saying? How dare you?" He half rose, then collapsed into his chair, his face ashen.

"Why not make this easier," Christophe suggested. "Explain how it happened, Lukas. All of it."

Paula put an arm around his waist and prayed. If only Lukas *would* explain it all, including the mysterious missing element that could still creep up to finish them.

Lukas drew leisurely on his cigarette, eyeing Christophe narrowly. "You have all the answers, Christophe. I wouldn't dream of upstaging you."

He sensed there was something Christophe still groped for, Paula thought desperately. Lukas intended to hold out as long as possible, to play for time and a break.

"As you prefer." Christophe bowed slightly. "Sit, Paula. We may be here longer than I expected."

Automatically she sat on the rug beside his legs, loath to be out of his reach.

"*You* switched the stones, Lukas," Christophe said. "Exactly as you suggested. I thought it was so days ago. After our little run-through on Monday I was sure. There was no other way. Each theft went the same. You were in the strong room with the customer. You waited until he selected a stone you'd had copied and while he examined another one, you made the switch from your pocket with the packets set to one side on the counter. I remember saying the act was a sleight of hand—a magic trick— something that happened in a second. That's the way it was, correct?"

Lukas's cigarette burned down between his fingers. Ash dropped to the rug, but he didn't appear to notice.

Christophe shifted his weight. "The little ploy with the so-called change in system—the stone stolen a few days ago—didn't fool me. Again you insisted you must be the most obvious suspect because you'd dealt with the transaction. And this time you said you delivered the thing yourself. That threw me for a few seconds because it didn't tie in with your effort to implicate Frank Lammaker. I hoped for a while I'd been wrong about everything."

"My God," Lukas breathed. "You *are* wrong. You have no proof of anything. You're bluffing and trying to climb out of a hole by pinning something on me. What are you afraid of? Going back to Switzerland a failure?"

"I'm not planning to go back to Switzerland," Christophe said. "But that's not the point here."

Paula's stomach contracted. Did he mean he was staying in Holland?

"I don't have to pin anything on you, Lukas," Christophe continued. "You've done the job for me. You and Sandi." He directed the last comment to the silent woman on the couch.

"Leave her out of this!" Lukas shouted, his composure visibly shattering. "She has no part in it."

"Christophe," Anna broke in. "Do we have to go on? Just tell us what's happened and we'll try to forget it."

Benno patted her hand. "Hush, my love. Don't get upset."

"I thought that last stone would be unloaded quickly," Christophe said. "On Monday night, late, I started watching for you to get rid of it, Lukas. At first I was afraid I might be too late—that it was already gone. I followed you all Tuesday and waited near your house in the evening. When Sandi left around ten, I followed. I saw her put a packet between the pages of a telephone directory in a booth in Dam Square. What I didn't allow for was the group of people who poured off a bus between you and me, Sandi. When they'd gone, so had you and so had the package. I never saw who picked it up. But you'll tell me, I'm sure."

"Sandi," Lukas said, crossing to sit beside his wife. "He knows nothing. He's fishing in the dark, darling. We should leave."

"You will not leave, my son." For an instant, Benno's sharp command froze the room's occupants. "What's begun must now be finished. Go on, Christophe."

Christophe took Lukas's place by the fireplace. "For a while Frank Lammaker seemed to be our man."

"No," Anna cried.

"No," Christophe agreed. "Frank is clean. He's quite a special young man. He wants to write—did you know that?"

Anna shook her head, brushing tears from her cheeks.

"He does," Christophe went on. "And he wants to be a part of the art scene in Amsterdam. Not so hard to understand in one his age. He really has outgrown the stunts he pulled as a kid. His clothes and entertainment are what he spends his extra money on. He augments his salary from Kohl's by working as a night janitor in a department store. His employee discount there also helps buy his clothes. He and his mother live simply. Much of what he earns pays for private tutoring to bring his academics up to scratch."

"And his attachment to Willem Bill?" Lukas rejoined. "What of that? Our people have never mixed with Metter's employees."

"What of his *attachment*, Lukas?" Christophe crossed his arms. "Convenient for you, but it means nothing as far as Kohl's troubles go. Willem also writes—and goes to classes after work. They led me to another suspect—Kersten Gouda." He laughed hollowly. "That possibility had me excited for a while. Willem and Frank went to Kersten's apartment regularly, and I thought I had a neat little conspiracy worked out."

Lukas pushed an arm through Sandi's. "You're quite the sleuth, Christophe," he said.

Christophe pinched the bridge of his nose. "A lot of things about Kersten puzzled me. Her standard of living, the wardrobe she wore to and from work."

"Oh," Paula stared at him, remembering. "I wondered about that, too."

"Means nothing," Christophe said. "It's Kersten who tutors Frank and Willem, and a lot of others, in her home. She's proud and doesn't want anyone to know the way she makes additional money, or why. Her fault is pride, if that's such a fault—nothing more and certainly not vicious. Not a crime that could bring the world down around the heads of people who have loved her since she was born." He eyed Lukas significantly.

"What does all this have to do with us?" Lukas said. He'd slumped against the couch back. Paula didn't remember the lines around his eyes and mouth being so deep, or the silvery glint at his temples.

"I gave you a chance to save us all this, Lukas," Christophe said, pacing to lean against the door. "You insisted I tell the sordid little tale, so hear me out. Kersten's husband left her years ago. That shamed her and she missed him—still does in a way. She even continues to hope he'll come back. And in the meantime, she buys pretty clothes and takes exotic vacations to snatch back a little of the romance she had for so short a time. And she pays for these pleasures with what she earns, honestly, at Kohl's and through tutoring many young men and women in her spare time."

"Fascinating," Lukas said sarcastically. "Everyone loves a martyr."

"Lukas, be quiet." Sandi's voice, its brittle cadence, electrified the atmosphere.

"So you see," Christophe continued, pointedly ignoring Sandi, "I'd run through the most convenient suspects and Paula became more and more the candidate of choice—as Lukas intended she should, if I didn't bite on Frank. Frank was to appear the obvious first choice, since the stones were substituted after sale and he was responsible for delivery. Without Frank, I had to look again at Paula and wonder if she was truly like her father. Was she both a thief as he was supposed to have been, and bent on avenging him? Someone copied those gems, and I tried to figure out if she was capable of that yet.

"You didn't waste any time telling me about her father, Lukas. But I still can't believe the man you once were, the man I knew, would deliberately endanger an innocent woman's life to steal from his own family. And where is the money, Lukas? *Where* is it? I have the necessary resources to find out if you've made any big deposits. There are no records of any."

Benno raised his hand, silently demanding recognition. "Michael Renfrew wasn't a criminal," he said. "I always knew that."

"So did I," Anna whispered. "He was our friend. We were sure he was framed, then frightened away to make him seem guilty."

"Just the way they tried to frighten me," Paula said slowly. She looked at Lukas, appealed to him with her eyes. "Was I supposed to go away like my father so you could say I must have been guilty of those thefts? You planted that note near me on Queen's Day to make Christophe suspicious. Then you had me paged. Lukas, you sent that man after me. He—"

Sandi left the couch swiftly and came to stand over Paula. "Lukas had nothing to do with that," she said. "*I* slipped the note when we fell. I knew we'd meet Christophe because Peter told me. Peter wanted us all to be friends again, so he told Christophe where to find us. And

I arranged the telephone call when I went to the bathroom on the way into the hotel. It was also to please me that Lukas told Christophe about your father. It seemed like a good smoke screen."

"I should never had told Lukas what happened to Michael," Benno said quietly.

Sandi didn't seem to hear. "Those threats to you were nothing Lukas or I could do anything about," she said. "They—"

"We'll come back to that," Christophe interrupted. "As soon as I knew enough about diamond finishing to be certain Paula couldn't have made those copies, I stopped considering her, although—" he glanced at Paula, his expression softening "—you people didn't give up trying to convince me. But at that point, I knew she couldn't reproduce the missing gems. Victor, on the other hand—"

"Okay, okay. You know how we did it." Lukas was on his feet. "We'll sort our our own problems from here on. We want you out of our business."

"I don't know how you did it," Benno interjected softly. "Go on, please, Christophe."

"Father—"

"Quiet," Benno snapped, and Lukas retreated to stare out the window.

"Benno," Christophe said. "There's something I don't know yet, something I hope Lukas will explain. I'm sure he didn't intend to hurt anyone. He hoped to get through this mess before needing to implicate anyone. You went along with the idea of keeping the thefts to yourselves and applied for a loan from us. I'm sure neither of you expected that loan to be questioned, and if we hadn't, perhaps Lukas's plan would have worked. Unfortunately we didn't think all was well with you, and we were right. My concern now is that we get at the final truth—the *why* in all this. Until we find that out, I believe there's still danger somewhere in this situation."

A rustle preceded Benno's passage to the drinks cart where he poured a hefty brandy. "What were you going to say about Victor?" he asked.

"Paula led me to the answer," Christophe replied. "Each entry in the log where the inventory is kept is initialed by the finisher. I was excited about that until I discovered the thirteen missing stones had been worked on by different people—according to the book. Then Paula remembered that last stone, the presale, and told me Victor had dealt with it. Jacob's initials, not Victor's, were entered for the job. When I compared the other entries closely, I decided the initials were probably forged in several places. Victor worked on all those stones."

"You can't know that for sure," Lukas murmured dispiritedly.

"He admits it," Christophe retorted. "I confronted him. All I had to do was tell him I knew his history and start praying. It worked. He spilled everything. How he was part of the theft Michael Renfrew was supposed to have committed. You suspected he was and blackmailed him into making the copies. The only payment he got for doing what you wanted was your silence.

"It was Victor who told Michael the police were on to him and he'd better get out of the country even if he was innocent. *You* led Victor to believe Paula was here to find out the truth about her father. That added to Victor's stress and led to the efforts to make her go home. Victor's old fellow-apprentice, Leo Erkel, was an accomplice in the original theft and he felt equally threatened by Lukas's blackmail. Erkel helped Victor get the inferior gems to make the duplicates with. Thanks to you, Lukas, Erkel set out to get rid of Paula any way he could. By the way,

Paula, Erkel borrowed Willem's car that morning you were hurt.''

"Stop!" Sandi breathed heavily. "Lukas had nothing to do with the threats to Paula. Neither did I. It was all that man Erkel's idea. I found out afterward..." She hesitated. "We heard from...from Victor...about the car and the thing with the knife in the alley and how Paula was locked in the elevator—"

"What elevator?" Lukas asked, turning around.

Sandi stared at him, her lips parted. "I probably forgot to tell you. They locked you in the elevator at Kohl's didn't they, Paula?" She knelt, her fingers working together once more. "I'm sorry, Paula. We never expected them to try to hurt you."

Exhaustion overwhelmed Paula, and intense sadness. "I remember his eyes now," she said, tracing patterns on the Oriental rug. "At De Pilsener Club he watched me, and I felt strange. I saw his eyes before, through a ski mask."

"And I knew him when he came out of the club," Christophe added. He moved without Paula hearing him and gently helped her up. "He followed the night we went on the canal cruise after having dinner here. He had a knife then, too, and expected to use it.

"Victor made sure I knew you'd been at the club with Frank and the people from Metter's. What he didn't expect was to run into Leo Erkel outside and have the man's name linked to his. That must have killed him. As soon as I heard it, I remembered the personnel records from all those years ago when your father and Victor and Leo worked for Benno's father."

"I want to leave," Paula said.

Christophe put an arm around her shoulders. "We aren't finished here."

"It's up to them now." She looked from Lukas to Sandi, who still sat on the floor. "They must decide what happens next."

"The way they tried to decide last night? We were supposed to be dead now, Paula, don't forget that."

"Dead? What do you mean, *dead*?" Anna rose and walked around to grasp the back of her chair. "Tell me what you mean."

Paula rested her cheek against Christophe's shoulder. "I don't want to do this," she murmured.

"I can't believe you would try to kill us, Lukas, but there doesn't seem to be any other explanation." Christophe put Paula gently from him. "Wasn't it you who tried to drown us on a barge in Brouwersgracht last night?"

Benno's glass bounced when it hit the rug.

"Oh, my God," Lukas said. "What are you saying?" He helped his father to the couch.

"Brouwersgracht?" Sandi said incredulously. "Isn't that where you're buying a barge, Christophe?"

Paula swung toward Christophe and caught his blank expression. "I'm not buying a barge. A house. Not a barge and not on Brouwersgracht," he said distractedly.

"You never mentioned buying a house here," Paula murmured.

"Someone tried to kill you," Benno said quietly, almost to himself. His eyes were unfocused. "I don't understand."

Christophe went to the old man's side. "Last night someone tricked Paula and me aboard an old barge on Brouwersgracht. We were trapped inside and the thing was deliberately sunk. Thanks to Paula's quick thinking, we didn't go down with it." His words came rapidly. He was trying to soften this for Benno, Paula thought, feeling afresh her love for Christophe St-Giles.

"But you think my son did this?" The veined hand Benno held up trembled.

Christophe took the man's fingers between his own hands. "I *don't* think that. But I believe whoever did could tell us why Lukas stole what would eventually be his when I know he's never wanted for anything."

"You speak as if I weren't here," Lukas said. "We will attend to our own problems. Everything will work out—you'll see. We'll start with the pear-shaped—"

"Don't!" Sandi interrupted harshly. "Don't let this man bully you into anything. Make him go away."

"Allow me this," Benno said, removing his hand from Christophe's. "I know there may be charges to be brought for what this man Erkel did. Victor I will deal with. But please, allow me time with my son to find out why he did such a terrible thing to us—and to decide what the future must hold. We'll make everything right with you, I promise."

"I'm not worried about that," Christophe said softly. "Take the time you need, Benno. I pray to God we can save Kohl's."

Paula and Christophe didn't speak until they were in his Saab. "You didn't want to go back to your place, did you?" Christophe asked. "I need you with me."

"I couldn't be anywhere without you today, Christophe. I don't want to think about what's happened."

"We can't wait long to sort out what it is Lukas isn't telling us. But I think we need time to catch our breath first."

They drove in silence for several minutes.

Christophe maneuvered the car through streets teeming with late-afternoon traffic to another canal and turned south. "They let my secret out," he said finally. "I did something impulsive, which is not supposed to be my style.''

Paula immediately knew what he meant. ''Buying a house? Surprising, but not so out of character.'' She rolled down the window and closed her eyes against the strong breeze. ''Perhaps you're more impulsive than you like to admit. Some people would have said you were out of character when you did as Benno asked and left them alone. *I* know you would never have done anything else.''

''Thank you for that.'' He touched her cheek and she turned her head toward him. Christophe glanced at her mouth, then concentrated on the road. ''Buying a house after seeing it once is different, though, don't you think? Would you like to see it?''

''I'd love to.'' And, Paula thought, she'd love to know why he'd bought it, and if he intended to live there permanently. Some questions couldn't be asked because the asking gave away too much.

''Do you like this canal?'' Christophe asked, parking close to the water. ''This area?''

''Prinsengracht? It's lovely.''

She got out while he was switching off the engine. All the narrow adjoining buildings were seventeenth century, but each was unique.

''Okay,'' Christophe said with a sigh. ''This is it.''

''The sandstone one?''

''Yes.''

The hesitancy in his voice caught her attention. ''What's wrong? You sound funny. It's a beautiful house. Must have cost a for—'' She clapped a hand over her mouth and felt herself blush.

Christophe laughed. ''A fortune, yes. It did. But if I'm going to open a branch here for St-Giles, I have to live somewhere and if a barge didn't seem quite right before, after last night I *know* it's out of the question."

Her heart did strange things. "You're going to live and work here?"

"Yes," he said easily and guided her up a flight of worn steps. "The decorators have already started work, but I don't feel too secure about what they're doing. Someone Peter recommended is arranging everything, but . . . well, I want you to tell me what you think. There's still some beautiful old furniture in the place. It's in bad shape but I think it should be refinished. I'll show you the living room first." He let them in and shut the door. "The place was divided into apartments before it came up for sale. There's a lot to be done, but . . ." His face flushed slightly. "Tell me what you think of the color in here."

Double doors led into a long room. Exposed oak beams, old and slightly crooked, spanned the width of a high ceiling. A few shrouded pieces of furniture stood in a central clump: a table, two straight-backed chairs and a desk. The wooden floors were bare. A ladder, paint supplies and tools littered the space by a far wall.

Paula managed not to gasp when she looked at a partly painted area.

"You don't like the color," Christophe said flatly.

Paula glanced from his disappointed face back to the peacock-blue walls. "It's fine." She hated to hurt him.

"It's not fine." He frowned. "You hate it. *I* hate it." He threw his windbreaker on the covered table. "I should have waited for your opinion before they started."

"The house is wonderful," she hedged, moving to the window. "You'll be able to look out on one of your beloved canals whenever you feel like it." And he would be here, in the same city as Paula, indefinitely. Her heart soared.

"I wanted you to like it."

"What?" She stared at him blankly.

"The—my house." His tone exuded dejection, and she quelled the urge to run and hold him.

"I do like it, Christophe," she said hastily. "I already said so. It's marvelous."

He grimaced, forming deep grooves in his cheeks. "All of it?"

"Oh, you!" Paula stuck her right forefinger into a painter's tray. "This is a lovely color, one of my favorites. It's too dark in a small space, that's all." She dabbed playfully at the end of his nose, leaving a smear. "So what? If you don't like it, either, have it redone with something pale. White, even. To make the room feel larger."

"I knew it." He paced, hands behind his back. "When the decorator suggested this I almost said I wanted your opinion. But I didn't have the right, did I?"

"I'd have been glad to help." Was he simply overreacting, or suffering from the same intense sensual awareness as she? "Why does it matter what I think?" She knew what she wanted him to say—and that he'd know she was fishing.

Christophe stopped in front of Paula. He rubbed at his nose, then studied his paint-stained fingers. Apparently deeply absorbed, he made a careful line from the point of her chin, down to the low V at the neck of her blouse, between her breasts. "Now we match," he said.

Paula tried to hide a shudder. "You didn't say why you care if I like this room—the house." His rapt attention on her mouth made it hard to think. "The paint looks silly. On your nose, I mean. Here, let me wipe it off." She wetted a decorator's rag with water from a jar containing a lonely lilac bloom.

Christophe stood patiently still during her ministrations. Finally he caught his bottom lip with his teeth and Paula realized his eyes were closed. She paused to watch his quiet face and felt his hands come to rest on her shoulders, lightly, yet burning her flesh.

He turned his head abruptly, clasped her hand and kissed the palm. "Finished?" he asked. His stillness had been plainly forced, a supreme effort.

"Christophe," Paula whispered, touching his sharp jaw, feeling the slight roughness of his beard. "We aren't finished. I think we just began." She trailed the backs of her fingers down his neck.

"Meaning?" His voice was equally soft. He wouldn't push, yet they both knew he'd planned this time alone. "Paula," he persisted when she didn't immediately respond. "What are you telling me? What do you...we want?"

She turned away, walked slowly to the lone table, then faced him, edging backward until she sat, feet swinging. "You want to make love to me, Christophe—and I want it. We've waited long enough—far too long."

"Ah, *chérie*, my lady. Always direct. You destroy any control I have—and I'm glad. I can't see anything but you anymore and I don't want to. But..." He made a sweeping gesture. "Not here."

"Aren't you going to do something about this?" She lowered her head and undid the top button of her blouse to reveal the faint trail of paint between the shaded cleavage. "Fair exchange—do you know that saying?" Her smile was softly questioning and deliberately provocative.

Christophe stared at her, light from the bowed window casting a burnished glow about his windblown hair. With evident preoccupation, he began to take off his shirt. "Fair exchange—yes. I think I remember that." The shirt was pulled free of his pants, slid from broad shoulders, until his torso was naked—beautifully, muscularly naked, dark hair spreading wide across his tanned chest and narrowing to a slender line at his navel before it disappeared beneath his belt. He dipped a shirttail in the same water Paula had used.

Paula couldn't breathe. He was so incredibly sexy, so dear—familiar, yet mysterious—intoxicating.

"Come close to me, Christophe." The little, distant voice didn't sound like her own. "Touch me."

He came, trailing the shirt. At her knees he stopped, resting fingertips lightly beneath the hem of her skirt. He slid his palms upward over smooth skin until he grasped both thighs. "As you say, sweet, I want to make love to you." He leaned to place a fleeting kiss at the corner of her mouth. "But I want to sleep with you afterward—to feel you in my arms when I wake up and then make love to you all over again. I want...." He faltered, then seemed startled to remember the shirt he still held. In a single sweep, he wiped her tingling skin, stopping at the shadowy dip beneath her blouse. He rested two tentative fingers on the spot, then replaced them with his lips.

As he raised his head, Paula kissed him, holding his face between her hands and leaning urgently against him. He opened her mouth wide with his and Paula moaned.

At the involuntary parting of her knees, he moved nearer to her body and she slid her fingers down to his tensed ribs, smoothed the hard muscle at his sides, reached to surround his waist. His subtle, clean scent made her throat constrict.

"Paula," he muttered, "Paula." His swift, hard little kisses covered her face, nuzzled her jaw high to make way for his lips to explore her neck.

His hands tangled in the hair at her temples. The sudden moisture of his tongue on her ear sent a thrill into her coiled nerves, brought aching heat to her breasts.

He shifted slightly. For a moment, he continued to kiss her while he unfastened her blouse, then he raised his head to watch his own hands at work, the gradual parting of the silk as far as her waist. Paula saw him swallow convulsively when he dropped the garment behind her on the table, never taking his eyes from the peach satin camisole, held in place only by tiny rolled straps and a wide band of lace clinging to the top of her breasts.

She didn't move. Every cell in her body gave him her unmistakable message and he must have felt it, known it.

"Paula." His voice broke. "I'm only a man. I don't think I can stop this now."

"We aren't going to stop." She shook her hair back, tilting her chin and lifting her breasts. Wanton? Perhaps, but it couldn't be wrong—not with Christophe, not feeling as she did with him.

His teeth, carefully closing on first one, then the other nipple, through dampened satin, were an erotic stimulant. Paula heard a small noise from her own throat—the answering intake of Christophe's breath. The camisole straps slid away. Each throbbing breast was surrounded and lifted in his warm hands. He pushed together fractionally, trailing his tongue over soft flesh, before his mouth opened wider. Paula buried her fingers in his hair, pressing him close.

After a moment, Christophe stood, his breathing labored, chords raised in his strong throat. He pulled the camisole over her head. "Lady," he said. "I can't think straight anymore."

She spread her hands wide on his chest. "I don't want to think at all," she said in a husky voice she didn't recognize. His skin was heated. Slowly, holding back, savoring each moment, each sensation, she massaged him, punctuated every touch with a tiny kiss until his grip on her shoulders hurt.

Her nails fumbled at his belt. Christophe's features darkened. She dropped her lashes, cupped his straining zipper, closed her eyes at the immediate stricture in her belly. He was aroused beyond endurance.

"Wait, Paula." His words were barely audible. "Wait a minute, my love."

Love. Her mind was already darkening as he moved away. He lifted first one, then her other foot, letting her sandals fall to the floor before he knelt. So slowly that Paula had to make fists to stop herself reaching for him, Christophe kissed a trail from one instep to her knee, then inched up her skirt until he found her groin.

"Please..." She couldn't finish the thought. "Please— no. No—" And the fire he breathed into her center cut off anything else she might have said.

Paula's elbows locked, her weight supported on the table with the heels of her hand, while Christophe undid her waistband. He slipped the linen beneath her, taking skimpy satin bikinis with it, before he gazed up at her once more. "You're beautiful," he said hoarsely. "Perfect. Beautiful breasts." He covered them, making small circles over her nipples with his palms. "Smooth skin." The caresses moved across her shoulders, down her spine to her ribs, waist, the flare of her hips.

He put both hands behind her bottom while he pressed his mouth into her navel, and below—down, until she cried out. But she'd never remember her words. Her mind became a white-hot blur, joined to every seared nerve ending by a voluptuous chord of ecstasy.

When her brain cleared and she gripped his biceps, urging him to his feet, Christophe stood over Paula instantly, and she saw the jagged rise and fall of his chest. Her kisses covered every unclothed inch of him until she sucked at taut flesh over his belly and eased low, beneath the waist of his pants. She undid the belt, and the zipper, but he stilled her hands and swiftly removed the rest of his clothes.

Paula gazed into his dark eyes for one endless moment of total understanding, before clamping her legs around his waist, unleashed desire making her strong.

"Sweet, sweet lady." He entered her with a single thrust, jarring a moan from her throat.

His thighs were iron on the backs of her calves, his need fiery steel within her. Their passion mounted, became one, faster—reaching. Nerves, open and raw, surged along the path to Paula's womb. She gritted her teeth and could only hold on, riding the tide of sensation.

With their climax, Christophe lifted Paula, wrapped her tightly against his final, explosive drive. A force burst deep inside her, and she clenched her jaw to stifle a cry.

She felt him sway slightly, grab the edge of the table. The rustle of their clothing, tossed to the floor, came a second before he knelt, still holding her close. Gently he unwrapped her legs from his waist without breaking contact and lay down, stretching Paula on top of him and nestling her face into her neck.

"You are... I want you to marry me," he said. "Don't say anything until you think, *chérie.*"

The pulse in Christophe's throat beat fiercely and Paula pressed her lips against its rapid rhythm. Moisture she tasted there was salty—her own hot tears? "I don't have to think, darling. Can you be happy with someone like me?" She squeezed her eyelids together. Falling in love with this man had been inevitable. A minuscule shred of caution made her rest her mouth on his sweat-slick shoulder and wait for his answer.

"Like you, Paula? I couldn't be happy with anyone *but* you. That's why I persuaded my family we must open a branch here—where you can carry on your apprenticeship. That's why I bought this house—for you. When we got here I felt like a fool knowing you might not . . . you might not . . ." His teeth came together.

"I want to marry you," she said simply. "Thank you."

He held the back of her head, and his laugh rumbled against her face. "How like you to say it that way. Rest, my love. For a little while. The closest thing I have to a bed is a futon upstairs. But I'll need more energy that I have now to get us there."

Paula arched away from him, resting her elbows on his chest. "We can wait . . . a little while." She reveled in being joined with him.

He stroked her back, made long sweeps from her neck to her bottom and pulled her down on his chest again. "A very little while," he murmured against her ear, and she felt his renewed quickening within her. "I love you, Paula."

Chapter Seventeen

Paula stirred when a current of cool air slithered beneath the bedroom door and across the futon. She pulled the down quilt over their naked bodies and snuggled back against Christophe. He muttered in his sleep and wrapped an arm tightly around her.

She should be able to sleep, too, Paula thought. She should be too blissfully exhausted to do anything but drowse in this wonderful man's embrace.

Her eyes refused to close.

Beyond the high window, the sky had darkened and a few stars sparkled like distant pinpricks in a black velvet cradle. This night was peace and security, a magical dream time. Why couldn't she turn off her brain?

Sandi. Paula wriggled until she sat up. "Sandi!" she exclaimed. "Christophe, wake up. I know what it is. I know!"

She was out of bed, scrambling into her clothes, before Christophe reacted. He switched on a lamp standing on the bare floor beside the futon. "What are you doing, Paula?" he asked, rubbing both hands over his face. "It isn't morning, sweet, come back to bed."

"Get up," she urged. "We have to go to Lukas's and Sandi's. Sandi knew, Christophe. Please hurry."

"Sandi knew what?" Christophe asked, slowly pushing aside the quilt. He got to his feet and stood with his arms crossed, shivering.

Paula grabbed his clothes and tossed them to him. "She knew about me being locked in the elevator at Kohl's and Lukas didn't. He'd obviously heard about the other things that man did to me—why not the elevator? And someone told her you were buying a barge on Brouwersgracht. Who would do that and why? I think Sandi's got our missing link. She was told that about the barge to lay the groundwork for what would be said after we were found dead." Paula shivered now. "You'd have been showing me the barge you intended to buy when we accidentally got locked in. The hole in the side would have been slowly letting in water and sinking the thing for days, and by the time they pulled us out, any other damage to the barge would be put down to the beating it took under water."

"Okay, okay." Christophe's eyes were finally wide open. He hopped from foot to foot, pulling on his pants. "That all sounds logical—except I don't see why she didn't tell Lukas about the elevator. You didn't tell me, by the way." His shirt buttoned, he shoved the tails into his pants before buckling his belt.

"At first I was afraid to tell you. I wasn't sure what you believed about me. Then so much happened, I forgot."

"Why do we have to rush to Lukas and Sandi's right now?" Christophe had put on his socks and shoes and began raking his fingers through his hair. A day's growth of beard shaded his jaw.

Paula found a comb in her purse. "You missed it. So did I until a few minutes ago." She combed her hair rapidly. "Lukas started to say something about a pear-shaped diamond. He was going to tell us they still had it, but Sandi stopped him. She intends to get rid of that stone and quickly. I feel it in my bones. It'll be tonight. We have to stop her and make her tell us the truth."

"My God," Christophe said. "There was a pear-shape among the stolen diamonds. It was the most valuable stone. I thought that presale must be all they had, but they held out on the big one. I hope we're not too late."

The clock in the Saab read eleven-thirty when Christophe parked in front of Lukas and Sandi's house. Paula, Christophe close at her heels, leaped out and ran to buzz the intercom. Instantly, without inquiry through the speaker, the door swung open.

Paula clutched Christophe's sleeve. "They always ask who's here," she whispered.

"Maybe—" Christophe stopped. Light from the hall flooded a pale yellow pool over the steps, and Lukas stood in the doorway, his hair wild, a faint sheen of sweat coating his tense face.

"Are you all right, man?" Christophe grasped Lukas's shoulders and backed him inside. "You look ill."

Paula followed, closing the door behind her. Lukas only stared, his gray eyes oddly hollow.

"Lukas." Christophe shook him. "Say something. Where's Sandi?"

"Gone," Lukas muttered and twisted away. He stumbled into his apartment and dropped onto a leather ottoman. "She's gone out." Paula saw him rally, felt his struggle to regroup.

"Where did she go?" Christophe glanced at Paula and she nodded encouragement. "Lukas," he continued. "We *have* to know where Sandi is."

"I don't know. Give me time. Let me think."

The room's angular contemporary furnishings seemed cold to Paula. While she watched Lukas wrestle with his own turmoil, the expensively converted apartment with its ivory walls, its careful arrangement of leather and chrome pieces, took on a brittle quality. The man on the ottoman seemed to shrink and his sterile surroundings to expand.

"There is no more time," Christophe said quietly. "There was another diamond, wasn't there? The pear-shape. And she's taken it to someone."

Misery contorted Lukas's features. "He called. She knew he would. She had to go. It was for her brother, not for her, not for us. Sandi wanted to get her brother back."

"Sandi's been giving the diamonds to her brother?" Christophe said slowly, his expression blank.

"No, no." Lukas jumped to his feet. He shook his head, beating closed fists together. "This other man—the one we don't know—picks up the stones. He contacted us and said he could get Hans back if we gave him enough diamonds."

"Wait," Christophe said. "Tell us everything, but calm down. We have to work together, my friend. Start at the beginning. Hans is Sandi's brother, yes?"

"Hans, yes—Sandi's older brother." Lukas took two cigarettes from a silver box. Distractedly he gave one to Christophe and pulled a lighter from his pocket. "She had two brothers. The three of them were in foster homes while they grew up. She never speaks of her parents. The oldest brother left care as soon as he could and went his own way. Sandi doesn't know what happened to him. She and Hans were very close. When he was old enough he made a home for them here in Amsterdam. He worked his way through college and ended up teaching physics in some Berlin university."

"Sit down, Lukas," Paula said, touching his arm lightly. "We'll all sit—"

"We can't waste time," Christophe interrupted. He drew deeply on his cigarette.

Paula stared hard at him. "Lukas is worn out. Can't you see that? This will go faster if we don't panic."

"Right, as usual." Christophe inclined his head to her, smiling faintly. "Go on, Lukas."

They all sat. Paula's heart beat rapidly. Her own sense of urgency clawed at her nerves, but she knew rushing Lukas would achieve nothing.

"Six years ago, Hans disappeared. He'd been involved in some underground work, helping people escape from East to West Berlin. The night it happened, he was driving a vehicle into the East. His objective was to create a diversion while two men got out. He never returned. Sandi waited in Berlin, alone, for almost a year. She made inquiries among Hans's friends. They were as much in the dark as she was. Eventually she had to give up and come back here. She'd been a model in a small way, and by then she needed money badly. She . . . she's lovely . . ." He covered his face and Paula heard the faint choking noise he made. She looked at Christophe. He'd involuntarily reached a hand toward Lukas. He closed his fingers and returned them to his lap.

"She is lovely," Paula said softly. "And she became very successful. What happened next, Lukas?"

He kept a flattened hand against his brow, shielding his eyes. "She started to live again—emotionally, I mean. We met and married and were very happy—we are happy, or could be. Then this man contacted her, always by phone or note. He said Hans was alive and being kept prisoner by the Soviets. He told her about a network of people who, much like Hans had done, were finding ways to get people out. But their operation was expensive, he said, and some—like us—could afford to help more than others. He wanted diamonds because they're easily transported and highly negotiable. We were helping to pay for those who could not pay and eventually Hans would be returned."

"Only he never has been, and the demands for diamonds have gone on." Christophe bowed his head. "This was extortion, Lukas. I don't know if Sandi's brother is alive or not, but whoever's been doing this had no intention of returning him as long as he kept making you pay. Now I understand where the money is—nowhere I'm likely to find it. Why didn't you tell me? I would have helped. We could have avoided coming to this."

"Sandi was afraid," Lukas said. "She wouldn't hear of risking the chance to get Hans back. She became almost possessed. When you showed up she came close to breaking. We'd already stopped collecting stones, but she was afraid we might need more and knew we probably couldn't get any while you were all over us."

"Why did she believe this man's claims?"

Lukas got shakily to his feet. "Because he knew all the facts. He repeated every detail about Hans on that last night, including the names of some others involved. I believed him, too—then."

"You don't now?" Paula said.

"I don't know what to believe anymore. Sandi's taken that stone and gone to meet him. She thinks the value of the diamond, and her revelation that there can be no more, will convince the man to bring Hans to her. She even hopes it will be tonight. My God, Christophe, she wouldn't let me go with her, and I'm scared to death."

Christophe rose and hugged Lukas quickly. "So would I be if it was Paula."

Lukas didn't notice the comment but Paula glowed. They had to sort out Lukas and Sandi's terrible trouble, then it would be time to get on with their own future—together.

"Now." Christophe clamped a hand on Lukas's shoulder as if to transmit his own strength into his friend's sagging body. "She took the diamond where?"

"I don't know." Lukas's voice cracked.

"Oh, hell…wait…" Christophe said, stubbing out his cigarette. "She thought Hans might be brought to her this evening. Was a place for making the transfer of her brother ever discussed?"

Lukas squeezed his eyes shut. "The Blue Angel—the new World Trade Center."

Paula started for the door. "We can try it. How long ago did Sandi leave?"

"Just before you arrived." A limp shrug raised Lukas's stooped shoulders. "I thought you might be her—that she'd changed her mind about going." Desperation darkened his eyes. "Would he kill her, Christophe? I couldn't live without—"

Christophe took Lukas's arm and shoved him ahead. "She's not going to die. Let's get there and hope it's the right place. I'd roust Peter for reinforcements, but we can't afford the delay. It'll take us half an hour to make it. I'll drive—you direct."

The powerful little car sped south through Amsterdam's central district until buildings became sparser and more industrial in appearance. At Lukas's instruction, Christophe turned onto Beethoven Straat, and minutes later the glass towers of the Trade Center loomed against the sky. Blue by day, its mirrored panels were black at night, festooned with glittering reflections of nearby lights.

"Leave the car in the loading dock," Lukas said. He opened the door before the Saab had completely stopped.

A guard slouched at a revolving door. Christophe threaded a hand through Paula's elbow and sauntered past.

"Evening," he said pleasantly. "We want to see the city from my office. Multicorp—fifth floor."

The guard grunted, straightened a fraction, then resumed his original position. Paula felt Lukas at her shoulder and prayed he would do nothing to give them away. "Multicorp?" she muttered to Christophe once they were inside.

"Why not?" He gave a short laugh. "Every building should have one."

Their footsteps echoed through the huge, office-lined lobby. Paula smelled lilacs, too sweet, too heavy, as she passed an alcove. Christophe pulled the three of them to a stop and silence seemed to swell and suffocate.

"She's not here," Lukas said loudly.

"Please, Lukas," Christophe said gently. "She could be anywhere. Be patient."

"There she is." Paula urged Christophe to a railing where they looked down into a lower level scattered with round tables and wrought-iron chairs. "There," Paula whispered, pointing to a table half-hidden by a potted tree.

"Oh, thank God." Lukas ran past them to a still escalator and started down. "Sandi!" he called.

"Damn," Christophe said, dashing for the steps. "The fool couldn't wait."

Sandi had jerked around and looked up. By the time Lukas, then Christophe, leaped from the bottom of the escalator, she was wrenching open a door beside a closed coffee bar. She glanced over her shoulder once before slamming the door. Christophe and Lukas followed, bumping each other in their haste.

Sharp clattering of heels, echoing shouts ricocheting along concrete walls met Paula when she wrestled the heavy door open. Dim lights illuminated an underground garage. She saw one running figure—Lukas—then Christophe heading in the opposite direction. They called Sandi's name repeatedly and darted from pillar to pillar. Only two cars were in sight.

Paula edged along the wall, her palms flattened behind her. Carefully she watched for any move, any glimpse of the magenta sweater Sandi wore. At a corner, Paula peered around and drew back. There was no sign of Sandi. "Christophe!" she shouted, "Lukas! Check the cars!"

She heard a door open, saw the bright flash of Sandi's sweater and swore under her breath. Why had she shouted instead of going quietly to each car herself?

Sandi headed back into the building. Her long hair had come loose and flapped about her shoulders.

Paula was first through the door after Sandi. Inside she stopped, breathing heavily. Christophe and Lukas skidded to a halt beside her. "I can't see her," she gasped. "She must ... Oh, no, look. Up there."

Two figures faced each other at the top of the escalator. Sandi's auburn hair glimmered as she pushed it back. The tall man facing her gestured, leaning close, then grabbed and shook her. Lukas and Christophe ran, but Paula was quicker. She took the steps of the other paralyzed escalator two at a time and reached the top in time to see Sandi being shoved through the revolving door. Paula opened her mouth but no sound came. The man wore a ski mask. They should have had Leo Erkel arrested.

"Where's the hell's the guard?" Christophe yelled, heading for the exit. They almost fell over the man's body on the top step.

Paula had started to bend over him when he moaned and sat up, rubbing his head. She rushed on, scouring the darkness, trying to listen for noises other than the ones she made. She heard Christophe ask the guard if he was all right and tell the man to call the police.

"Wait, Paula," he called. "Stay here." Christophe caught up with her and gripped her arm.

A scream sounded, somewhere to her left.

"Sandi," Lukas groaned, breaking into a run but in the wrong direction.

The distant rumble of a train grew slightly, blurring Paula's concentration, before it faded.

Christophe's fingers dug into her elbow. He looked in every direction, his face tense and watchful. "You go back to the building," he said.

Another scream severed the silence. Paula jumped and spun away from Christophe. "Split up!" she yelled, wrenching free. "I'll take the left."

"Paula, no!"

She ignored the plea in Christophe's voice and ran out of the forecourt to a sidewalk. Across a wide street she saw light bouncing off a glass-enclosed bus stop and headed for it. When she was almost there, scuffling, to the right now, stopped her and she advanced more slowly. All that mattered was saving Sandi from that creep. When he'd followed Paula he still hoped to save himself. That would have been enough to stop him from killing her. Tonight was different. Tonight he knew they'd found out about him. He would do whatever was necessary to escape with the diamond.

Paula wanted to call out. Instead she pressed her lips together and tried to make no noise. She crept forward, crouching low, past the bus stop, away from the street— away from help. Sandi mustn't panic. Between them, they could do something as long as they kept their heads.

She didn't notice the drop-off until she fell, slipping and banging, several feet down a bank.

"Stay where you are," a man's voice hissed. "Don't move or you'll both die."

From the ground, Paula stared up at the man and clapped a hand over her own mouth to stifle a scream. His left arm and hand were clamped around Sandi. In his right hand he held a gun pointed at Sandi's temple.

"What do you want us to do?" Paula heard her own small voice. It was steady but seemed far away.

"Over there. Move."

He waved the gun, and in that instant, Paula lunged with both feet, smashing into his ankles.

"You bitch!"

He stumbled back a step, flailing and losing his hold on Sandi.

"Sandi, run!" Paula yelled and flung herself at the man's legs. Bone cracked. She yanked harder and he cursed as he fell, Paula's arms still wrapped around his knees.

Something sharp came down repeatedly on her shoulder and Paula ducked her head, praying for help. He was hitting her with the gun. How long before he pulled the trigger?

His next words were Dutch. He wrestled Paula to her back and worked to capture both her hands on one of his. The gun's dark barrel glistened.

He was going to shoot her.

Paula writhed violently. The gun was slowly lowered to her eye level.

"No, no." Sandi's moan surprised them both. Paula had thought the other woman gone. The man above her started and lost his grip on her wrists.

"Get off me," Paula cried and kneed him in the crotch. Grunting, he doubled up on top of her and Paula grabbed for the gun.

The single shot, close to her ear, echoed on and on. She smelled acrid powder, felt the body above her jerk, then slump over her, heavy and flaccid.

Paula closed her eyes and turned her head away. Something moist and warm splattered her neck. Blood. She was going to be sick.

"Sandi, Sandi." Lukas's voice murmured close by.

Paula felt consciousness slip before the weight rolled away from her and strong arms gathered her up. "Where are you hurt, Paula?" Christophe whispered against her lips. "Say something, *chérie*. You're bleeding."

She shook her head, gulping air, her mind clearing. "Not my blood," she croaked. "His."

Christophe helped her up but kept an arm around her. "Lukas," he said. "We'd better take a look at this bastard. The police should find us pretty quickly but he needs help now."

"He's dead," Paula announced flatly. She'd killed a man.

"Not necessarily," Christophe said, dropping to his knees. "But maybe we'd all be better off if he was."

Lukas joined Christophe and Paula knelt on the other side of the man. "I killed him," she said. Sweat had turned cold on her skin.

"Stop it," Christophe barked abruptly. "The gun's in his hand."

"I made him fire it," she commented dully. "I shot him."

Christophe sighed, reaching beneath the ski mask to feel for a pulse in the man's neck. "Wrong. He shot himself. He would have killed you if he could. And he's still alive."

"Thank God." Tears sprang into Paula's eyes.

Sandi sank down beside Paula and took her hand. "He was going to shoot us both, Paula. He said so. This is all my fault."

A siren wailed closer and closer, and whirling light revolved above them. Men's voices calling to one another jarred Paula as much as the slamming of vehicle doors.

"He needs air," Christophe said, carefully peeling off the mask.

A policemen arrived, his flashlight homing in on the man's face.

Bright frothy blood oozed from the corners of the wide mouth. Blue eyes found Paula's and he tried to smile. Immediately a cough racked him and he lifted his clenched left fist to his lips.

Paula caught Sandi as she fell sideways.

"Do you know this man?" The policeman asked. Other uniformed men scrambled down.

"Yes," Christophe said and buried both hands in his hair.

Lukas found a kleenex and dabbed ineffectually at the man's blood.

"This is Peter Van Wersch," he said and began to cry.

Friday of the Fourth Week:

"There's nothing we can do," the doctor said. Tired eyes, too old for his years, swept over each of them. "He wants to see you all. It won't be easy."

Peter lay on a bed in a small observation room, tubes and wires linking him to a battery of monitors above his head. His skin blended with white sheets and walls. Only his eyes, flickering open as Paula and the others entered, showed a trace of lingering life.

"Hello, Peter," Christophe said, going directly to his side. "This is tough, old friend."

A nurse sat watching the monitors. "He must be quiet," she said without turning. "Perhaps you can persuade him to open his left hand. We'd like to clean it."

The dead must be clean, Paula thought bitterly. She stayed a little apart from the others.

Lukas and Sandi stood at the bottom of the bed. "May we have some time alone?" Lukas asked.

The nurse began to protest until she caught the expression in Lukas's eyes and nodded, understanding, silently admitting what she'd been taught never to admit: a hundred nurses, watching a hundred monitors, couldn't save Peter Van Wersch's life. She slipped from the room.

Peter motioned to Lukas and, when he moved close, slowly opened his left hand. In the palm, smeared red with his blood, lay the huge pear-shaped diamond. "Take it," he whispered. "The rest are in my apartment—the freezer—ice cubes. I didn't want them." He coughed, and a trace of blood appeared.

"Don't talk." Lukas wiped the blood away. "You need to save your strength."

"I'm going to die," Peter said and tried to smile.

Sandi held his hand. "Why, Peter? I thought you were our friend. That's why I confided everything to you after Paula told us what had happened to her. You used the information I gave you, just like you used the story I told you about Hans. I never guessed, but you were the only one Lukas and I ever told and you used it against us."

"You had everything." Peter looked at Lukas. "You and Christophe. Golden boys who had it all. Christophe left. If he'd stayed away, we might not be here. But for him it was the same—everything he wanted, he got. But he didn't matter, Lukas. It was you who mattered."

Paula glanced around the stricken faces circling the bed. Peter had raised his hand to Lukas who slowly took the diamond.

"You told me about the man trapping Paula in the alley with the knife." Sandi's voice cracked and she cleared her throat. "We loved you, Peter, but you pulled our strings as if we were your puppets. Because of you, the way you suggested that man's threats to Paula might not be so bad for Kohl's if they made her leave Amsterdam, I trapped her in the elevator to try to make sure she was frightened away. Then I didn't dare tell Lukas. I wanted her to leave and take the suspicion with her like her father had." She began to cry. "It was me telling you about Christophe walking through a gem sale that made you try to kill him and Paula, wasn't it? You said Christophe was trying to buy a barge on Brouwersgracht so I'd help out with the appropriate excuse for them being there when they were discovered. I did all this. It's my fault."

Paula's hand closed around the remnants of the tulip in her pocket. She pulled them out and stared, her vision blurring. "I figured someone had used the old door from the alley to slip me the note yesterday morning. Christophe had mentioned Lukas and Peter lived in the backhouse once, and that they came and went by that door. One of my pots of tulips is in front of it now. Yesterday afternoon I noticed it was pushed away and the tulips smashed. I thought Lukas must still have a key and that he'd left the note, but it was you, Peter. You used your old key to get in and leave the note. You tried to kill us. Why? You could just have stopped what you were doing before it was too late."

"I only wanted him to stay my friend," Peter whispered, indicating Lukas. "I started this to show him his wife didn't care as much for him as I did, that she'd put

him, and his family, in jeopardy for her brother's sake. But
he still preferred her. She'd betrayed him for a man who's
probably dead, but he still wanted her most. I gave him his
chances. Why didn't you come to me, Lukas, like you
would have done before? You never confided in me. I
would have stopped if you had. I wanted you to give her
up and be my friend again. But it was only her. You forgot me."

Lukas bowed his head. "I never forgot you, Peter. I
trusted you."

"I tried to kill them for us," Peter said, his voice growing fainter. "If…if they had died, it would have been only
you and me… Don't you understand yet? Lukas, I love
you. I've always loved you." His eyes closed, and a steady
buzzing came from one of the monitors. Paula looked up
and felt the others do the same. The lead on the cardio-
gram monitor had gone flat. Peter's lips parted and a
breath slipped softly out.

"He's dead," Paula said.

A doctor and two nurses arrived simultaneously, one
pushing a cart. The doctor was already reaching for pad-
dles.

In the waiting area, Lukas turned to the others. "They
never give up—even when it's all over." He ran a hand
over his face and bolted from the building.

Christophe hesitated before following him.

"I called Benno just after we got here," Sandi said
without inflection. "I didn't know we'd be getting the
diamonds back. He'll be relieved, though I can't expect
him to forgive me."

"He will," Paula consoled, peering through the glass
doors Lukas and Christophe had used. "So will Anna.
They love you."

"Erkel's skipped Holland," Sandi said. "Philip Metter contacted Benno about it." She laughed mirthlessly. "Something good may come out of this, after all. Kohl's and Metter's could be on speaking terms again."

Paula blinked rapidly, feeling the other woman's misery. "I'm sorry about your brother, Sandi. You must have adored him."

"I did. But we all have to learn to let go. I almost had and I will again, as long as I still have Lukas."

"You do, and you always will," Paula reassured. "I think it's time we went home."

"Paula," Sandi said, looking away. "Peter used you. He used me, too, but that was different. He had a reason to punish me. He meant what he said about being in love with Lukas, and I should have guessed that somehow."

"Sandi," Paula began, "please—"

"No. I have to get this out. The things Leo Erkel did to you, then what I did, only helped Peter. They were an unexpected bonus to his plan to get back at Lukas for not being... I hate this... Peter must have longed for Lukas to become his lover and when he married me the love turned to hate."

Paula reached for Sandi's hand. "You couldn't know all this would happen. You were only trying to get Hans back, and no one will blame you for that."

"I blame myself for being selfish. Can you forgive what I've done? I'm not sure I could."

"I can forgive, Sandi. And I know Christophe will, too. Please, let's get out of here."

Outside the swinging doors, Paula and Sandi stopped, silently reaching for each other's hands.

Lukas, crying quietly, rested his face on Christophe's shoulder. Christophe held him. As the doors swished shut he glanced up. Tears glistened in his eyes.

"WILL LUKAS AND SANDI BE OKAY?" Paula asked Christophe.

He stood behind her at the edge of the canal. "I think so," he said. "I pray so."

A tourist barge slid past, cutting the water's surface, leaving a fanning V of ripples in its wake.

Paula turned toward Christophe and stood on tiptoe to kiss his jaw. He immediately found her mouth with his own. Seconds later he raised his head. "We both need sleep," he said. "Our futon awaits."

They had spent the morning with the Kohls, and going to Prinsengracht and the sandstone house had seemed natural afterward. Together, they crossed to the steps and Christophe unlocked the door.

In the bedroom they began shedding their clothes, watching each other, tired, Paula knew, but not too tired to be aroused.

When Christophe lay, his arm beckoning her to his side, Paula knelt on the edge of the futon, savoring the sight of him. "You're going to let everything drop, aren't you?" she said.

"Yes. As Benno says, not only were the stones Lukas's to take—stretching it a bit since they'd been sold—but the losses were covered, and now the diamonds are all back in the vault. I think Benno and Lukas will draw closer together, and I want that. Did you realize Peter was left-handed?"

"No."

"If he'd held the gun in his left hand instead of protecting the diamond, you might be—"

"Don't," Paula said. "We're both alive and well. I can't help being sad about Victor having to take early retirement, though. Poor Victor."

Christophe lunged unexpectedly and pulled her over him. He gazed up into her eyes. "You wonderful softie. I love you. Tomorrow morning we buy rings—Benno insists on helping there. On Monday we'll attend to formalities. I want you to be Paula Renfrew St-Giles by the end of next week."

She grimaced. "That's quite a name... Oh, Christophe, I can't stop worrying about Lukas and Sandi."

"They'll be fine. I'm sure they will."

"Why didn't I guess about Peter? Something should have clicked before it did." Paula sank her teeth into her bottom lip. Christophe's hand on her breast made concentration difficult.

"You didn't guess because Peter was too clever. As a man, I can't believe I never suspected what he was. He fooled me for years. But we all tend to believe the obvious. Seems to me a lot of things around here have turned out to be other than they appeared. Except you, *chérie*."

"Christophe..."

"Shh," he whispered, rolling her to the futon. "We need to catch up on our... *sleep*."

They laughed.

HARLEQUIN HISTORICAL

Explore love with Harlequin in the Middle Ages, the Renaissance, in the Regency, the Victorian and other eras.

Relive within these books the endless ages of romance, set against authentic historical backgrounds. Two new historical love stories published each month.

HIST–A–IR

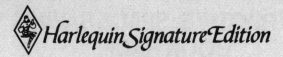

Harlequin Signature Edition

Violet Winspear

THE HONEYMOON

Blackmailed into marriage, a reluctant bride
discovers intoxicating passion and heartbreaking
doubt.

Is it Jorja or her resemblance to her sister that
stirs Renzo Talmonte's desire?

A turbulent love story unfolds in the glorious
tradition of Violet Winspear, *la grande dame* of
romance fiction.

ATTRACTIVE, SPACE SAVING BOOK RACK

Display your most prized novels on this handsome and sturdy book rack. The hand-rubbed walnut finish will blend into your library decor with quiet elegance, providing a practical organizer for your favorite hard-or soft-covered books.

Only $9.95

Approximately 16" x 8" when assembled

Assembles in seconds!

To order, rush your name, address and zip code, along with a check or money order for $10.70 ($9.95 plus 75¢ postage and handling) (New York residents add appropriate sales tax), payable to *Harlequin Reader Service* to:

In the U.S.

Harlequin Reader Service
Book Rack Offer
901 Fuhrmann Blvd.
P.O. Box 1325
Buffalo, NY 14269-1325

Offer not available in Canada.

BKR–1

Take 4 best-selling love stories FREE
Plus get a FREE surprise gift!

**Two exciting genres in one
great promotion!**

Harlequin
Gothic and Regency
Romance Specials!

GOTHICS—
romance and love growing
in the shadow of
impending doom . . .

REGENCIES—
lighthearted romances
set in England's Regency
period (1811-1820)

SEPTEMBER TITLES

Gothic Romance	Regency Romance
CASTLE MALICE Marilyn Ross	THE TORPID DUKE Pauline York
LORD OF HIGH CLIFF MANOR Irene M. Pascoe	THE IMPERILED HEIRESS Janice Kay Johnson
THE DEVEREAUX LEGACY Carolyn G. Hart	THE GRAND STYLE Leslie Reid

Be sure not to miss
these new and intriguing stories
. . . 224 pages of wonderful reading!

---

1. How do you rate _____
   (Please print book TITLE)

   1.6 ☐ excellent   .4 ☐ good   .2 ☐ not so good
   .5 ☐ very good   .3 ☐ fair   .1 ☐ poor

2. How likely are you to purchase another book:
   in this *series*?   by this *author*?

   2.1 ☐ definitely would purchase   3.1 ☐ definitely would purchase
   .2 ☐ probably would puchase   .2 ☐ probably would puchase
   .3 ☐ probably would not purchase   .3 ☐ probably would not purchase
   .4 ☐ definitely would not purchase   .4 ☐ definitely would not purchase

3. How does this book compare with similar books you usually read?

   4.1 ☐ far better than others   .2 ☐ better than others   .3 ☐ about the
   .4 ☐ not as good   .5 ☐ definitely not as good   same

4. Please check the statements you feel best describe this book.

   5. ☐ Easy to read   6. ☐ Too much violence/anger
   7. ☐ Realistic conflict   8. ☐ Wholesome/not too sexy
   9. ☐ Too sexy   10. ☐ Interesting characters
   11. ☐ Original plot   12. ☐ Especially romantic
   13. ☐ Not enough humor   14. ☐ Difficult to read
   15. ☐ Didn't like the subject   16. ☐ Good humor in story
   17. ☐ Too predictable   18. ☐ Not enough description of setting
   19. ☐ Believable characters   20. ☐ Fast paced
   21. ☐ Couldn't put the book down   22. ☐ Heroine too juvenile/weak/silly
   23. ☐ Made me feel good   24. ☐ Too many foreign/unfamiliar words
   25. ☐ Hero too dominating   26. ☐ Too wholesome/not sexy enough
   27. ☐ Not enough romance   28. ☐ Liked the setting
   29. ☐ Ideal hero   30. ☐ Heroine too independent
   31. ☐ Slow moving   32. ☐ Unrealistic conflict
   33. ☐ Not enough suspense   34. ☐ Sensuous/not too sexy
   35. ☐ Liked the subject   36. ☐ Too much description of setting

5. What *most* prompted you to buy this book?

   37. ☐ Read others in series   38. ☐ Title   39. ☐ Cover art
   40. ☐ Friend's recommendation   41. ☐ Author   42. ☐ In-store display
   43. ☐ TV, radio or magazine ad   44. ☐ Price   45. ☐ Story outline
   46. ☐ Ad inside other books   47. ☐ Other _____ (please specify)

6. Please indicate how many romance paperbacks you read in a month.

   48.1 ☐ 1 to 4   .2 ☐ 5 to 10   .3 ☐ 11 to 15   .4 ☐ more than 15

7. Please indicate your sex and age group.

   49.1 ☐ Male   50.1 ☐ under 15   .3 ☐ 25-34   .5 ☐ 50-64
   .2 ☐ Female   .2 ☐ 15-24   .4 ☐ 35-49   .6 ☐ 65 or older

8. Have you any additional comments about this book?

   _____ (51)
   _____ (53)

Thank you for completing and returning this questionnaire.

NAME _____
(Please Print)

ADDRESS _____

CITY _____

ZIP CODE _____

BUSINESS REPLY MAIL

FIRST CLASS   PERMIT NO. 717   BUFFALO, NY

POSTAGE WILL BE PAID BY ADDRESSEE

NATIONAL READER SURVEYS

901 Fuhrmann Blvd.
P.O. Box 1395
Buffalo, N.Y. 14240-9961